Praise

"*Letters in Time* is like a wonderful meal with a delicious balance of engaging characters (both sweet and bitter), a fascinating peek at history, a captivating community, and a slow-burning romance for dessert."

— Donna Weaver, *USA Today* Best-Selling Author

"Susan Reiss captures the magic, mystery and charm of that quintessential Eastern Shore town – St. Michaels. Secrets lay hidden for generations among the stunningly beautiful estates along the Miles River. Can't wait for her next book."

— Kathy Harig, Proprietor, *Mystery Loves Company* Bookshop

"I really enjoyed this and the book before it as well. Weaving the history along with the present gave added depth to the story."

— Goodreads Review

Delightfully different! This book was different than the mysteries I tend to usually read. It very cleverly blends a current day story with a historical paranormal twist that was quite touching."

— Amazon Review

"A wonderful tale of life filled with struggles, tragedy, love, memories and everything in between. The author does a great job at conveying it in both books I've read. Emma, both of them, are strong women. Both struggling to lead their lives their own way in their own lives. There is no sex, smut, or anything to ruin a delightful tale."

"Each story grabs you by the heartstrings and doesn't let go - it is so intriguing, it kept me turning the pages to the end."

"Readers will encounter twin sisters, legends of buried treasure, mourning jewelry, christening gowns, old diaries, silk fabrics, bridal gowns, red-bottom shoes, loves lost, bullets dodged, wedding ceremonies, and spouses gained. This was another engaging novel by a lovely author I've come to admire!"

"The details are intricately interwoven to provide the reader with a gripping story full of surprising twists and turns. Both excellent character development and beautifully presented descriptive prose describing the area keep the reader captivated."

Praise for the St. Michaels Silver Mysteries

"*Tarnished Silver* is a fabulous debut novel! Abby Strickland is someone I can relate to, my kind of heroine. I admire the way she rises to the challenges thrown in her path. She's a brave and loyal person whom I would love to call a friend (if she were real, of course). Susan Reiss is a great storyteller."

— Kassandra Lamb, Author of the Kate Huntington Mystery Series

"Greatly enjoyed Susan's first three books. Love character Abby Strickland's sterling silver tidbits as well as her curiosities in solving mysteries. Keep 'em coming!"

— Amazon Reader Review

"This is a series that captures the local flavor of our area – St. Michaels, the food and the quirky characters who live here and visit. The descriptions of all the real places make me feel like I'm there. The mystery kept me turning the page. This is a series I recommend to my library patrons... and to you."

— Shauna Beulah, St. Michaels Branch Manager, Talbot County Free Library

"Loved *Tarnished Silver*. Can't wait to see what happens to the characters next as the author made me care about them."

— Goodreads Review

"A mystery which could be a made-for-TV movie."

— InD'tale Magazine

—

Also by Susan Reiss

Portraits in Time

Susan Reiss

Ink & Imagination

INK & IMAGINATION PRESS
An imprint of Blue Lily Publishers

This is a work of fiction.
Any resemblance to a person, living or dead, is unintentional and accidental.

Cover Design by Rachael Ritchey, RR Publishing

Website: www.SusanReiss.com
Bookbub: Susan Reiss
Goodreads: Susan Reiss
Facebook: Susan Reiss

For Bobby and Marie
who held the light at the end of the tunnel
when I needed it.

And to the rest of that part of our family:
Chris and Jackie, Allison,
Logan and Mackenzie

Chapter One

"If you can see a world within a portrait, I would be happy with that."

— *Danny Fox, British Painter*

Ah, what a spring morning! The sun was bright. The sky was blue. The birdsong was loud enough to wake me from a peaceful sleep. Dressed for a comfortable day at home, I was humming as I made my way down the stairs for my first cup of coffee when the shock of loud banging on my front door almost made me lose my footing. It was insistent and growing louder.

My first reaction was to be afraid. *Don't be ridiculous*, I told myself, and marched to the door, digging in my heels with every step. A quick peek out the window confirmed TJ's truck was outside. Relieved, I unlocked the deadbolt, twisted the knob, and opened the door. The tall man burst into the Cottage.

"At last!" he proclaimed and stomped down the hallway to

my kitchen, slapping a newspaper against his thigh with every step.

"And good morning to you," I mumbled as I closed the door and followed him. Something must be terribly wrong for him to act like this. His handsome face always had a healthy glow from his time outside working on the farm, but now, it was red from anger.

In the kitchen, he was a caged animal. Mumbling, he paced back and forth, then exploded. "Can you believe it?"

As he turned to smack the newspaper down on the table, I cried, "Wait!" and scooped up the gift-wrapping paper and ribbon littering the kitchen table and the open box holding my birthday gift from TJ: a luxurious silk scarf of bright flowers in red, white, yellow, and fuchsia, all from last night's perfect dinner celebration. It was easy to understand a person needed to blow off steam from time to time, though nothing should be damaged in the process. When my things were safely on the dining room table, I tucked myself into a corner of the kitchen, hoping to learn what had offended this normally mild-mannered man and whispered, "Now!"

"What's the use?" he grumbled, the newspaper clutched in his hand at his side, shoulders slumped. Then, without warning, he reared up and raised the newspaper up toward the ceiling. "They won't get away with this." And he smacked the paper down on the table.

It was hard to imagine what could have upset him to this point. The outburst drained away some of his anger.

"Is there nothing going on in the world, so they have to dredge up old news? I don't understand," he complained. "Can't they keep their nose out of other people's business? I'm entitled to privacy."

He continued to complain and protest, only I had no idea

what he was railing against. I stepped toward the table to steal a look at the paper he'd been carrying. His words stopped me.

"Don't touch that," he barked, pointing to the newspaper. "I don't want you to soil your hands."

The offending pages of the crumpled paper had unfolded so I could at least see the masthead. It was the local paper, known for being thin, because not a lot of news happened here. There was the random crime, coverage of ribbon-cuttings and awards, and some national news. What could light his fuse like this?

He groaned in disgust when I grabbed the paper and scanned the front page. Nothing jumped out at me, but there was an intriguing headline:

Unsolved Mysteries

I was about to turn the page when TJ's rigid index finger stabbed that headline.

Unsolved Mysteries!" He proclaimed. That woman might as well have tacked on the phrase, At Waterwood!"

My face scrunched up in confusion. What was he talking about? I pulled the paper closer and started reading. A useless effort because TJ took up his loud rant again.

"Why can't she leave it alone? It's an old story," he declared. "Buried treasure. Ha! Everyone loves stories about buried treasure. That doesn't make them true."

When I could finally get a word in, I asked, "Is this about—"

"...the treasure Benjamin allegedly buried before he took supplies to the Confederacy? Yes!" He waved his arms around. "I know what you're going to say. Daniel wrote about the treasure in one of his letters to you..." He closed his eyes and gave his head a quick shake. "Not you. The other Emma. His Emma. The plantation Emma." He moaned. "You know what I mean."

And I did. I clearly remembered the correspondence I'd had with a ghost named Daniel beginning on my first day in the Cottage. More than 160 years ago, the plantation owner, Benjamin Ross, one of TJ's ancestors, felt conflicted about his loyalties. He tried to keep his head down and quietly tend to his vast plantation he'd christened Waterwood. But the angry tempers of those on the Maryland Eastern Shore wouldn't allow it. True, the state remained in the Union, but his plantation's economics and way of life closely mirrored those of the South. He felt compelled to help in some small way, so he decided to deliver some supplies to the Confederacy. After gathering what could be spared during wartime, he headed south with the son of his trusted plantation manager, Daniel. The young man was devoted to Waterwood and Benjamin's daughter, Emma. Before they left on their journey, Benjamin gathered the money, valuables, and silver pieces of Waterwood in a chest. In those unsettled times, neighbors couldn't be trusted, and neither could the banks. With Daniel's help, they buried the chest somewhere on the plantation to keep it safe. Sadly, Benjamin returned to Waterwood alone. Daniel had been killed during an assault by Union troops on the Southern position where they had travelled to deliver the goods. Or at least that is what was believed at the time. Daniel was only able to clarify what happened in his letter that appeared on the antique desk...that Joshua who later became Emma's husband fired the shot that ended his life. It was the continuing story of that chest that was still causing trouble now.

TJ had barely taken a breath. "It's going to start all over again. Every treasure hunter within a hundred miles... FIVE hundred miles, is going to descend on Waterwood with those wacky metal detectors. I swear, they all look like space aliens with their big headphones and wires running all around their bodies. They're going to crawl all over my land acting as if they have a right to be here. It's so wrong." He stabbed the headline again with his finger. "And this woman has unleashed the hounds to make my life, our lives, miserable AGAIN!"

I wanted, needed, to help TJ calm down. So, as casually as I could, I said, "There's one way to keep strangers away."

"I know, I know," he said as he paced around my tiny kitchen. "Make a big announcement. There Is No Treasure!" He threw himself into a chair. "Nobody would believe it... even though it is probably true."

"Why do you say that?"

"Look, you did some research when Daniel wrote about the location of the chest." He flung his arm in the direction of the huge centuries-old oak tree dominating the land on the opposite side of the creek. "Remember when Stefani and her band of hoodlums dug up all the ground around the Lone Oak. Frankly," TJ continued with a worried frown on his face. "I've been watching the tree carefully, alert to any signs of distress. Those kids were ruthless. They didn't care if their shovels damaged its roots."

"So, that's why the tree company was working there." I should have known TJ would do whatever was necessary to save and nurture a living icon of Waterwood.

"They were careful to fill in the holes and feed it, even trimmed some of the branches." TJ shook his head. "Yeah, it's possibly the most attention it has gotten in decades." He sat back and sighed. "At least, it's okay... so far. It doesn't need people crawling all over it again. Those people have to stay off my land... and yours!"

"You're right." I didn't want to remember or relive the harrowing moments when Stephani had taken me hostage and thrust me into a battle for my life. "Okay, there is a way to keep strangers away."

"And what would that be?" TJ said with a little whiff of snark as he folded his arms across his chest. "Get all of my gun-toting friends to stand guard along the road?"

The image of a string of men amped up on testosterone holding guns sent a shiver through me. Trying not to show my horrified reaction, I tried to sound casual. "No, we just have to find the treasure first!"

I thought he would scoff at the idea, but he didn't. Instead, his eyes wandered to the ceiling as he mulled over the idea. That's when I knew I was in trouble.

In only a moment, his eyes drifted downward and landed on my face. "You're right, Emma! You can do it. Look at all the secrets of my family you've unearthed. If anyone can make it happen, you can."

I was a little shocked at what my casual comment had caused. He was absolutely convinced I could find the treasure and keep the crazies at bay.

TJ put his hands on the table and pushed himself up from the chair. "I'll leave you alone so you can get to work," TJ said as he headed to the door.

"What are you going to do?" I asked.

"Isn't it obvious? I'm going to go to Easton, to that news-room, and straighten out this reporter." He looked at the by-line of the article. "This Robin Hunter," he said with contempt. Probably some newbie right out of school. Probably still using a crayon."

"TJ!" I huffed. "That isn't fair. You don't know her, do you?"

He turned and looked a little sheepish. "No..."

"Remember, she's only trying to do her job."

He went back on the offensive. "Well, she can do her job

without messing with my life. If she needs me to school her, I'll be happy to do it. To work, Emma!"

He stomped out of the Cottage. As the sound of TJ's truck driving away faded, I put my head in my hands.

He will calm down by the time he gets to Easton. Yes, of course he will. Won't he?

Chapter Two

"The portrait is one of the most curious art forms. It demands special qualities in the artist, and an almost total kinship with the model."

— — *Henri Matisse, French Painter*

I thought I was going to have a calm day to myself to do some research for my book, maybe draft a new scene. But no, I had to open my big mouth and my plan evaporated: *We just have to find the treasure first!*

Eight little words that landed me in a whole lot of trouble. Now, I was supposed to find a treasure buried more than 160 years ago. Others had tried. One young man lost his life trying to get rich. There might have been others. There was no map, no real instructions on the location of the treasure, if it even existed.

I just had to find the treasure so the world will leave Waterwood alone. I dropped my hands and shook my head. "Easier said than done, TJ."

8

But first, I wanted to do something down at the cabin: write a letter to Emma. It was only important to me, but that alone made it something I needed to do. The treasure hunt could wait a few minutes more.

Along the path, two gray squirrels chased each other in daring aerial maneuvers. Across the creek, the bare branches of the Lone Oak were swelling with buds of new leaves. Soon, a veil of spring green would appear draped over its limbs. Even the cloud-filled sky couldn't dampen my spirits for it held the promise of life-giving rain. All was full of hope. What could possibly go wrong on such a morning?

Inside the cabin, I sat down at the antique plantation desk, and opened my fountain pen to write.

The Cottage

Dear Emma,

It is early spring here and Waterwood is slowly coming alive. I too feel I am waking up from a long winter's nap.

During dinner one night, TJ and I talked about the many portraits hanging on the walls of Waterwood House. I once studied with an art history professor who focused on biographical details of a person's life presented in a portrait rather than the artist's brush strokes and technique. I suggested to TJ there might be historical representations in the Waterwood portraits that would give us more insight into the past. He agreed and I have permission to research the paintings there.

I hope I am correct in assuming the portrait of your father Benjamin captures his handsome features and his stature. I am looking forward to investigating the representations of Waterwood life painted in the background.

*I must add, I love your portrait. Do you have a story
about how it came to be? I would enjoy learning about it.*

*I seem to be transmitting my excitement about spring
and new projects to this page, babbling on and on. Thank
you for your forbearance in letting me share my newfound
delight in life.*

With warmest spring wishes,
Emma

With the joy that comes from sharing, I covered my pen,
squared up the letter in the center of the writing surface, and
headed back to the Cottage.

Now, all I had to do was figure out how to find a treasure
chest buried somewhere on a plantation of acres and acres
more than a century ago. I'd first heard of the buried chest in a
letter dated 1862 from Daniel that had mysteriously appeared
on Uncle Jack's plantation desk. Yes, the desk was haunted. At
the time, Daniel thought he was writing to his long-lost love
Emma, not a 21st century woman with the same name. He had
opened his heart and recalled events only the two of them had
shared. Would a query from me upset him? Would he resent
my interference in their personal matters though it had brought
about their reunion. The last thing I needed was an angry
ghost. That confusion and my decision to correspond with him
led to some amazing adventures. Would those two be willing to
help now?

I cleared off the dining room table, opened my laptop, and
found a copy of Daniel's letter to Emma about the treasure:

*Emma, your father was very nervous about his deposits
at the bank and paced all night, trying to puzzle out the
best thing to do. The next day, he went into town and*

converted all his money deposits to gold and silver and brought them home. He had me bring down a strongbox from the attic. Then he filled it with the precious metals and other valuables he collected from around your house.

Interesting. Benjamin, Emma's father, had truly amassed what would be considered a fortune today. Paper money of that period was probably worthless today, even if it survived being underground for all those years. But he was smart to convert his deposits to precious metals. The value of gold today was high. When I saw the results of an online search, I sat back in my chair to catch my breath. In 1862, a troy ounce was valued at about $31.00. Today, its value was around $2,000! And it didn't take into account any historical value.

Now, the possibilities of what such a cash infusion could do became real. It could move TJ's plans forward to renovate Waterwood House or grow his custom farming business. This wasn't a frivolous exercise. This search could have significant implications...*if* the treasure was still buried somewhere on Waterwood land.

I reached for the pad to take notes as I read the next section of Daniel's letter:

Late in the night, we went out to the Lone Oak. By lantern light, your father carefully walked off a complicated pattern. After we buried the chest and covered it over with dirt, grasses, and leaves, he swore me to secrecy and gave me a sacred charge. If anything happened to him, I was to make sure you had access to the valuables for your use.

Remember, your father put the strongbox there for you.

Those instructions were straightforward. One only had to

figure out his complicated pattern and dig *if* the treasure was still there. Evidently, one descendant of Benjamin and Emma believed the stories of treasure. Stefani wanted to find it and set herself up as a makeup artist in New York. The search she started led to murder. I'd never know if an unseen hand— Daniel's hand—had played a part in protecting me. I tamped down the trembling sparked by the memory of that harrowing experience. This line of thinking was getting me nowhere. I went back to Daniel's letter with its complex instructions.

> *If you have need of it and I am not near at hand, take someone you trust and a shovel to the spot below the limb where we loved to sit and dream. Look to the dawn and walk, counting out the day of your birth. Turn toward the place you loved to play in the mud across the water.*
>
> *Walk again, counting out the month and pray as we did as children before bed.*
>
> *I am sorry to be so opaque, but one never knows into whose hands this letter may fall. You and I share a history that began when we were small children.*
>
> *Knowledge of these places is part of us and can never be forgotten. They are ours alone. No one else can interpret these direct actions and steal what is rightfully yours.*

Daniel had encrypted important information in a very basic, but effective way. I had seen the month and day of Emma's birth at the family cemetery. I understood the first direction was to the east, but from where? He referenced a limb of the Lone Oak, but which one? What if the storm had knocked a limb to the ground? Where was Emma's favorite spot to play in the mud? And how did they pray as children? Those words conjured up an old lithograph of a child praying by her bed, on her knees. What was Daniel suggesting? Instead of guiding me, my mind was getting muddled.

In a quiet moment, I realized there were more curious events connected with Waterwood Plantation and its 19th century family than the location of a treasure chest. There were questions needing answers, secrets deserving resolution. What had happened to her baby daughter? Her husband had lied to Emma that the baby had been born dead. My research had uncovered an additional connection to Philadelphia and a woman named Annabelle. Could she have been involved in the sale of Emma's youngest child? I had things to investigate. My novel would have to wait. If I ended up with a lot of material, I might write a whole series of books.

As I closed my computer and put my notes aside, I had to shake my head. Daniel had written those words so no one else but Emma could interpret those clues. He had done a good job, but I wasn't ready to give up yet.

While I was working, the sun had broken through the morning clouds which heralded a bright spring day. I didn't want to stay inside. I was drawn to the open air. The winter had been mild. The time spent in front of the fireplace in the living room had been cozy. I'd made progress through part of my stack of 'books to read' which felt like an accomplishment. Of course, I'd gained a few pounds while sitting there, nibbling. Maria, my housekeeper, created savory meals, including creamy soups made from seasonal vegetables like squash and carrot. They also contributed to the weight gain. I wanted, no, needed to get outside, walk around, and do a chore. So, I grabbed a sweater, furniture polish with a rag, and headed out the front door.

Chapter Three

"I have never seen a beautiful painting of a beautiful woman. But you can take an ugly woman and make a beautiful painting of her. It is the painting itself that should be beautiful."

— — *Max Ernst, German-French Painter and Sculptor*

I set out on the path to the cabin and realized yet again how different the Shore's environment was from my part of the world in Philadelphia. Here, Mother Nature had planted a patch of wildflowers—some tiny, some showy—in white, red, yellow, and one in blue. These early blooms had clusters of small petals. They could be part of the spring collection for a tiny parasol shop visited by the local magical population, if one existed here. My students would love to hear stories about them.

Here, birdsong filled the air beginning in the moments before sunrise. It was a natural alarm clock sorely missed in the gray hours of winter and now, welcomed. A symphony barely heard in the city.

Would I miss these differences if I moved back to the city? Would coming down here a few weekends a month be enough for me?

Living on the Shore was a little like being in a country with a different language. It was funny how words meant different things, not only around the world, but just across the Chesapeake Bay. Growing up in a suburb of Philadelphia, my friends and I would put on our boots and go to a creek to collect salamanders, bugs, and all kinds of plants. Here, the creek ambled by the Cottage at its own natural pace, carving its way deep into the land, but one step off the bank could land you in five feet or more of water. Here, you might have to swim about 300 feet to get to the other side of the creek where the Lone Oak still stood guard at Waterwood. So many differences. The more I learned, the richer, more complete I felt.

Inside the cabin, I dusted off the pervasive yellow pine pollen that had collected on the desk. I was tempted to write to Emma again asking for some answers to the clues in Daniel's letter. Even though she had always answered quickly in the past, I was hesitant to contact her now about something so personal. What if there was a limit on the number of letters allowed to pass through this portal that was a desk? And how would I phrase my request for information?

Hey, Emma! Where is the treasure buried? Did you dig it up during your lifetime?

Using the straightforward approach of the 21st century with a woman with 19th century sensitivities would likely be considered rude. No, I needed to learn more. I would wait before I reached out to her for answers again.

I locked the cabin and set off down the path, thinking. TJ believed I could find the treasure and protect Waterwood from trespassers. It was a compliment and a burden. What should my next step be? I sifted through several ideas of ways to move forward and rejected one after the other. I shivered a little. Had the sunlight been blocked by a cloud making it too cool for just a sweater or was it my lack of confidence making me chilly? Then I stopped in mid-step, wanting to slap my head for being an idiot. My adventures into the past had taken me to Waterwood House. That was where I'd found Emma's portrait and the miniature she'd painted of Daniel. That was where I'd found her diaries. That was where I'd opened her secret room in the attic.

The attic!

That was where I needed to go. Thankfully, my relationship with TJ had grown so I did not have to ask his permission before going into Waterwood House where he lived. He trusted me not to paw through his personal belongings.

At the Cottage, I exchanged my sweater for a coat and headed up the drive to what was once the main house of Waterwood Plantation. To prepare myself for another look into the past, I took a few minutes to walk around to the front of the house facing the water. In the early 19th century when it was built, the preferred method of travel was by boat. Roads and pathways were often bumpy and rutted, even washed out, making a trip by carriage or wagon bone-rattling and sometimes perilous. The house was designed to face the water to welcome visitors and family alike.

The original house was in the center, marked by two-story columns painted bright white. It was flanked by several additions on either side designed to blend well with it. I could visualize our friend Cookie as a lovely bride taking TJ's arm, walking out the front door, and down the lawn to meet her groom at the floral archway by the water.

With a smile and a sigh, I went to open the heavy front door with its cast iron ring door knocker and slipped inside. The police had told TJ to lock the house, but, like many of the locals, there was an aversion to city-ways like locking their homes and even their cars.

Inside, I gazed at Emma's portrait hanging on the foyer wall. Seeing her sweet face filled with contentment always made me smile. Her life wasn't always easy. During her marriage to Joshua, she'd lived with disappointments and betrayals, even the suspicion he was a murderer. The strains she endured took a toll. TJ had found a portrait of her family, including some of her children. In it, Emma looked drawn and pale, as if the footsteps of time had left a beaten track on her face. I'd always thought a portrait artist did his best to make the subjects of a painting look their very best. If that was the most flattering representation of Emma, I shuddered to think what she truly looked like. TJ kept the painting hidden away in a dark corner of the attic.

There were other portraits hanging on the walls here. I wondered what clues and curious tidbits might be waiting for my inspection. Another thought crossed my mind about how times had changed. Today, many pictures are taken as selfies or closeups. When faces fill the screen, there is little to remind someone where or under what conditions the picture was taken.

In Emma's time, it took days and weeks for an artist to capture a person's face and presence in oil paint for future generations to see. Those pictures captured in oil paint long ago required hours of conversation followed by sitting for the artist so he could capture the subject on canvas. The word portrait grew out of the word portrayal. The family paying for the painting expected the person to be presented in the best possible light. Was it vanity or arrogance that led someone to commission a portrait? At that time, it was one of the only ways to capture someone's personal appearance. I was thankful the people in TJ's family had made that choice. Now, I didn't have to tax my imagination to envision what they looked like. I didn't have to guess what impression they made on others. I could look at the portrayal of the people who were at the heart of Waterwood Plantation from the beginning of its existence. Their portraits now lined the walls of the foyer and the main staircase, welcoming visitors to the home they had built. They were present in oil on canvas to remind the current residents, their descendants, of what and who had come before. A few landscapes interspersed among the portraits also told what was at the heart of all their efforts, tears, and trials: Waterwood.

I had come to look for any clues to the treasure hiding in these paintings. In college, I was required to take an elective called Art History 101. For example, the portrait of a woman could feature her beauty, elegance, and feminine wiles, all draped with costly satin and delicate lace. The portrait of a man could present a type of biography. He was usually a man of substance, since commissioning a portrait required a financial investment. A talented artist would take the time to learn about his subject's accomplishments and acquisitions, elements he would use to impress others since the painting would hang in a prominent place.

Some specific things included in a portrait might provide significant information about the subject. A medal might be a reminder of his military service. A clear blue sky might project optimism during a troubled time. A miniature worn around a lady's neck, as in Emma's portrait, might recall a lost love.

Ready with a little notebook, I stepped back to Emma's portrait. Then stopped. I had studied the painting many times.

I was always impressed by her loveliness and kind demeanor. The only item to draw my attention had been the painted miniature hanging from a satin ribbon around her neck. I'd later learned she had painted the face of her beloved Daniel on the pendant. Emma wasn't a brilliant artistic talent, but I was grateful to have a face to represent the person who had begun our ghostly correspondence and deepened my connection to Waterwood. Other than the miniature painting, I didn't believe there was any other aspect in her portrait to shed light on my treasure hunt.

There was a portrait in a heavy gold gilt frame of Emma's father, Benjamin, hanging about halfway up the staircase. Balanced on the steps, I had to crane my neck a little to take in his full-length pose. He was standing on one side of the painting in front of a velvet drape. On the other side was a landscape vista of what I suspected was Waterwood. I sat down on the step beneath the portrait. Leaning against the wooden balusters supporting the wide handrail, I could set my notebook on my knee to take notes.

I began with the man himself. He stood erect, looking almost heroic. He appeared to be tall, but according to a search on my phone, the average height of a man in the 1850s was 5'8". He was not smiling, which I remembered was normal for a portrait done in the 19th century. Men wanted to look serious and thoughtful. The drape behind him was the color of red wine which brought out the healthy glow of his face. It was the face of a man who spent time riding over his plantation, supervising and directing activities, benefiting from the open air. His black suit was well-tailored and appeared to be of fine quality. A black tie was held in place with a stick pin, but it was difficult to see the design. A watch chain was draped across Benjamin's vest. There should have been a pocket watch at one end and maybe an interesting fob at the other. I'd have to ask

TJ if he had any other pieces of jewelry stashed away somewhere.

At Benjamin's feet was a black Labrador retriever with a white patch on his chest that, in some places, would be considered a flaw, but it was valued on the Shore. To Benjamin's left was a grand view of what I thought was Waterwood with vast green fields of crops. Waterwood House was represented. I looked closer. Something was wrong. Then it hit me. The house was missing two additions. Benjamin or another member of the family must have built them later. I noticed what I called my Sea of Christmas Ferns I walked into when I was searching for the Confederate Secret Line for passing messages during the Civil War. It gave me an idea of the width and breadth of the plantation in Emma's time, and it was impressive.

Then something caught my eye. A small blotch of deep yellow surrounded by a green field of big, leafy plants. I struggled to my feet, careful not to tumble down the stairs, and peered closer. It seemed the artist had meticulously painted the elongated petals atop tall green stalks with their face to the source of light.

"Sunflowers..." I mumbled.

Chapter Four

"The sunflower is a symbol of life, happiness, light, and love."

— — Folklore

"In Benjamin's portrait?"

I almost lost my balance when I heard TJ's voice. A quick grab for the handrail saved me from tumbling down the steps. When I looked, TJ was standing at the bottom of the staircase with his arms outstretched, ready to catch me.

"I'm sorry," he said. "I didn't mean to startle you. I thought you heard me come in,"

Behind TJ, Ghost strutted into the foyer, his head high with a sense of ownership. Seeing me, he sprinted up the stairs, his nails clicking on the hardwood floor. He gave me a light lick in greeting. TJ's big white Lab had accepted me into his pack.

"Mind if I ask a question?" TJ continued.

"Oh, I'm sorry." I started to move down the steps.

"No, you don't have to leave. You can be here on your

own." He shook his head. "That isn't what has me curious. Are you boycotting chairs?"

I looked around and realized how odd I must look, draped over the steps, writing in a notebook. "No, I was trying to analyze Benjamin's portrait, looking for clues. According to my art history introduction class..."

"...in a prominent, rich man's portrait, the artist often embedded clues about his character, his holdings, and his accomplishments. I know, I was listening to you."

A little wave of warmth drifted through me. "I thought I might find something helpful in his painting," I said quickly. "Photography really changed things, speeded up the pace of capturing people's faces, places, events. We lost the time to reflect on the little things that might have meant something to the people in the photos."

"Like the sunflowers." TJ added.

"Yes." A lilt of surprise was in my voice. "Why would Benjamin grow sunflowers? Wasn't the climate too cool for them to thrive? What value would they add to Waterwood?"

"Waterwood Plantation was Benjamin's pride and joy after his wife and daughter." TJ held out his hand to me. "Come on, there's something I've been meaning to show you. They're in the library."

"They?"

"You'll see. Come on."

I followed TJ through the main parlor and into the library. The treasures I had found in this room while researching the secrets Joshua tried to keep hidden had been helpful in exposing a spy ring. But it was more than that. I felt at home here. The library was often my favorite room in the house. Sunlight streamed through the library's tall windows where long golden velvet drapes framed Waterwood's rolling lawns and a wall of evergreens outside. Inside, shelves of books—most leather-bound—covered the library walls. Over the fireplace was a landscape oil painting of Waterwood itself with fields of corn and inlets of water.

TJ sat down at the massive honey-colored oak desk and pulled open one of the deep drawers on the side. He lifted out first one large book with a rough black cover of an old-fashioned ledger then another and another.

"What...?" I started to say.

He flashed a sparkling smile. "It's all your fault."

"Me? What...?" I repeated.

"I've always respected the history of my family and its connection to Waterwood but from a distance. You've shown me it's a living history and there is a lot to learn here. One night I couldn't sleep. Too many thoughts about the upcoming spring planting. I started wondering about another farmer, my ancestor Benjamin, Emma's father. I know he planted much of the acreage in tobacco, a high-value cash crop. It seemed everyone smoked or chewed back then. I deal with the damage it did to the soil every day. Tobacco sucked out the nutrients and depleted the quality of it. But it got me wondering what else was planted."

"Did they keep records?" I asked.

TJ laid an open palm on the three ledgers. "Yes, they did. That night, I figured if I found anything at all, they would have been kept by the plantation manager, in this case Daniel's father."

My breath quickened. Another find. Another window into the past.

"I followed your lead." He shrugged as if it was the most logical thing for him to do.

"What lead was that?"

"I went up to the attic armed with my industrial-sized flashlight and looked around." He raised his eyebrows. "There's a lot of stuff up there, Emma."

"I know," I responded with a chuckle, but tell me about these?"

"They were stacked on top of a tall dresser. They're heavy so I looked at the dates and only brought down these three. They gave me a sampling of what was happening over different periods of time." He reached over and pulled one volume from the stack. "I think this is where I found the first reference to the sunflowers."

I moved to where he sat at the desk and peered over his shoulder as he leafed through the pages.

"Oh," I said. "Daniel's father had beautiful handwriting."

"I forgot to tell you. These aren't the plantation manager's records. Benjamin kept his own set of historical notes about Waterwood." He ran his finger slowly down a page of words written by his ancestor. It was a masculine hand written in cursive with a little slant to the left. TJ had always felt a connection to Waterwood through the land, but since we had forged links to some of the people in his family, he had developed a growing awareness of them and who they were. He seemed to be caught up in the words written by Benjamin.

"About the sunflowers," I said to break the spell.

TJ started a little as he snapped out of his revelry. "Sunflowers. Yes." He turned the pages. "Let me see if I can find the first mention Benjamin wrote. You see, he planted a small field of a few acres in an area protected from prevailing winds but in direct sunlight." He stopped and ran his finger down a page. "Yes, here it is." And he read aloud:

"We finished planting the field of sunflowers today. I'm glad I didn't have to send to England for the seeds. This flower is native to the Americas. Though Elizabeth is a city girl, I am glad

she has taken an interest in the crops we grow here at Waterwood.

Thankfully, she does not monitor our everyday activities. I do not want to endanger the surprise she will have when the plants grow tall and burst into bloom. For this field is for Elizabeth.

Since coming to Waterwood as my wife, she has discovered the joy of feeling the warmth of the sun on her face. Her practice of leaving her bonnet in the house almost every time she walks on our land causes her dear mama to fret about the state of her complexion in almost every letter she writes. To me, the blush of pink given her cheeks by the sun only endears me more to her beautiful visage. I look forward to the day I see her walk among the sunflowers surrounding her with brightness and love."

Salty tears prickled my eyelids. "That is..." My voice cracked into pieces. I started again. "That is beautiful."

"Yes, he really had a way of expressing himself and he took the time to put down the right words. It must have been unusual, because men were constantly bombarded with bills, orders, negotiations for purchase, and sale of crops. Those responsibilities must have eaten up a lot of time. I have trouble keeping up even with email and texting."

"They didn't have television to suck up their evening hours. They didn't scroll through sites on the internet. I've seen it in Emma's diaries, too. Writing must have been an event. Just the sheer effort of dipping the pen in the inkwell time and time again made them *slow down*." That was how I felt when I first began my correspondence with Daniel. To honor the connection and somehow draw us closer, I always wrote my letters to Emma at the desk using my fine fountain pen, a gift from Uncle Jack.

"What a beautiful story," I said. "Is the sunflower field still there?"

"No." The corners of his mouth turned down in regret. "I've never seen a sunflower at Waterwood." He gave a heavy sigh. "It's been a long time. Unless the plant reseeds itself or the farmer plants more, they probably died out a long time ago."

"So, the only other record of the field is in his portrait," I said.

"And in these ledgers, journals, whatever you call them," he said as he closed the book. "I've only scratched the surface, as they say. Benjamin kept a record of the plantings each year, weather and its effects on the land, crops, and waterways. There are short mentions of the financial health of the plantation here and there. The more detailed record of sale prices and costs must be in the plantation manager's records. Haven't found those yet."

TJ lifted the large books one at a time and returned them to the desk drawer. "These are more valuable to me. He preserved his innermost thoughts on these pages. He wrote about his pride in building an ongoing enterprise to take care of and protect his family and the other people of Waterwood. Not every plantation owner was a success. Just like today, not every farm turns a profit. Though a farmer works hard, he can't always provide for his family. Benjamin wrote about his fears, misgivings, his uncertainties as he looked over his land." TJ closed the drawer. "The same thoughts shared by every farmer today. It's as if more than 160 years haven't passed and we're standing together looking over the fields."

TJ stood up and gave me a triumphant smile. "Finally! Finally, I was able to answer one of your questions about the history of Waterwood. Man, it feels good!"

"I bow to you." And I did. "As a matter of fact, kind sir, would you consider going up to the attic with me for a few minutes?"

"For what purpose?" He knitted his eyebrows together, suspecting a trap.

I held up my hands in surrender. "Fear not, I know we've talked about doing some organizing and cleaning..."

TJ leaned away from me, wary now.

I continued quickly. "But this isn't that time. There are some paintings up there. I need some help moving them so I can see them."

"That's it?" As I nodded, his shoulders relaxed. "I can spend a little time doing that—"

I finished his sentence. "Then you have to get back to taking care of modern-day Waterwood."

He smiled. "Let's go."

I followed him up the main staircase. As we passed Benjamin's portrait, I asked, "Can you show me where you found Benjamin's ledgers?

He paused on the second landing.

"Or not," I said quickly, hoping I hadn't crossed a line. Maybe he wanted to keep the ledgers to himself, at least until he'd read them. I could understand his feelings. I'd felt a special connection when I had found Emma's diaries. "The number one priority is the paintings."

A quick glance showed the strain was leaving his face. I would respect his right to the ledgers.

"I'll race you up the steps!" An audacious challenge considering I'd been on crutches less than a year ago. The sound of our pounding footsteps thundered through the house. A little out of breath, I reached the door to the attic first, though I suspected he'd let me win.

After he opened the door and grabbed a big flashlight, he asked, "Do you have a plan of attack?"

I slipped past him and entered the massive space, covering the whole footprint of the main house as it was originally built.

Talk about a treasure, the things relegated to the attic by the family over the years were valued even though they had outlived their usefulness. Sure, there were one or two broken or worn-out items, but most were in good condition, nothing that a good dusting and a little polish couldn't fix. When the family members spent most of their time at Waterwood, seeing the same things every day, it probably got boring after a while. There were all kinds of furnishings, appropriate for a house with a number of public rooms on the first floor and so many bedrooms upstairs I'd lost count. There were trunks and armoires filled with fine clothing and fabrics. The mistress of the house never knew when something would come back in fashion. I loved the hats, both for men and ladies, and shoes, though the tiniest of feet were required.

Off to the side were paintings stacked against the walls and sturdier pieces of furniture and that was where we headed.

Chapter Five

"The earth paints a portrait of the sun at dawn with sunflowers in bloom. Unhappy with the portrait, she erases it and paints it again and again."

— Rabindranath Tagore, Bengali poet, writer, and painter

There were heavy carved wooden frames and simpler ones, stacked in piles, all facing the wall, as if the person overseeing the storage of the portraits couldn't handle the disapproving looks of being relegated to the attic. I reached out to move a framed painting on the top, but its weight was too much for me.

I turned to TJ. "Now you know why I'm glad you're here. Please put those muscles of yours to work so we can see what there is to see here."

Instead of reaching for the heavy frame, he waved the dust away from his face, dust my small movement of the painting had kicked up. "You were right. We need to get someone up here to take down the dust."

"The dust of more than a century." I glanced around. "Who knows what it's hiding?"

TJ coughed as he pulled his phone out of his back pocket and frowned. "That reporter is ignoring me. She must have gotten the message I left at the newsroom. You'd think she would have the decency to acknowledge it, at least by text." He reached out to the stack of paintings. "Let's find out what we've got here." He put his large hands on either side of the carved wooden frame, squatted a little, and lifted it several inches off the floor. He rotated and gently lowered a landscape to the floor. Stepping back, he said, "Not what you were looking for, is it?"

I moved closer to look at a familiar scene, rendered in brush strokes that lacked confidence. "This wasn't done by a professional artist. The work looks tentative."

"Not everyone could be a John Constable, the famous English landscape artist," TJ said, reaching for the next painting.

"Oh, look. It's the view out the front door of Waterwood House."

TJ stepped back to consider the scene. "Not much has changed about the water view. The trees are taller, the foliage is thicker, but the scene is the same."

"You're right! Look!" I pointed to the far shore off to the side. "There is even a Great Blue Heron!"

"An ancestor of the one you're always seeing there?" TJ chuckled.

"Let me see." I knelt down by the right corner of the painting. "Shine the light here, please." When he did, I gently brushed away some of the accumulated dust. I had to lean closer. "Yes! The scene captured by an ancestor of yours. It's signed in tight script, E. E. R. C. I think it was painted by your several greats-grandmother, our Emma. Emma Elizabeth Ross Collins."

TJ knelt beside me. "Do you think so? Why did she only use her initials?"

"Remember the time she lived. She would not want anyone to think she was getting above herself or trying to compete with men, such things being unacceptable at that time." I rose and stepped back again to take in the whole scene. "Her mother, Elizabeth was raised in the city from a well-to-do family, right?" TJ nodded. "She would have been trained in the feminine arts, like lacemaking, playing the pianoforte, singing, and painting. She might have taught her daughter as best she could, but out here on the Shore, they didn't have easy access to a painting master or music teacher. On her own, Emma probably didn't have the time to develop her skills, what with her responsibilities as mistress of the plantation after the death of her mother."

TJ lifted the painting and lugged it closer to the attic door. "I'm going to see if I can get this painting cleaned. Then decide if it should be hanging downstairs." After he put it down, he stretched his back. "I thought a canvas was supposed to be light so the artist could move it around easily."

"It's the frame," I said, following along behind him. "Must be solid oak or something. It offers the canvas some protection as well as making it esthetically pleasing."

"I'm impressed, Emma. You must have paid attention in your art history class."

I punched his arm lightly in response to his teasing.

"Hey! No abusing the help." He walked back to the pile. "Shall we see what else we have here?" He lifted the next painting and turned it around. It was the full-length portrait of a man. At first glance, he cut an imposing figure, standing tall in a fine formal coat, wearing a sword at his waist.

"Do you think it's Benjamin?" TJ asked, squinting at the face to see if there was a family resemblance.

"I don't think so. He would have been too young for the War of 1812 and too old for the Civil War and he didn't—" I gasped, my hand flying to cover my mouth.

"What? What is it?" TJ looked at me then at the painting then back at me.

My words came out on a hushed breath. "It's---it's Joshua."

"Emma's husband? That's him?" TJ said in disbelief and a bit of disgust.

I had to look away. It unnerved me to gaze on the face of the man who had caused Emma so much pain and heartache. The man who betrayed not only his wife, but his country. And a murderer.

TJ crossed his arms and continued to stare at the man captured in oils. "Pompous, wasn't he? Wearing a sword as if he had served in the military. The artist probably softened Joshua's features, so he'd get paid, but I think the man looks like the weasel he was."

I felt a stab of guilt. My impression of Emma's husband had soured TJ's opinion of one of his ancestors. "Now, TJ, he—"

TJ held up his hand. "Don't bother. You can't persuade me to feel compassion or pride in this man. A person is known for his deeds and how he treats others. To me, he has no redeeming qualities. In fact, ..." TJ stepped forward and, with a strong intake of breath, dragged the portrait to a corner and turned it to the wall. He walked away, brushing the dust from his hands. Then he stopped.

"Emma, bring the flashlight over here. There is one painting off to the side. Let's see what it is."

He didn't have to turn this painting around. When I shone the light on it, we both gasped... at its beauty, softness, and intimacy. We both just stared.

It was the portrait of a man, sitting in a chair, and a woman standing next to him, a typical composition for a couple of the period. But there was nothing typical about them. The man, wearing a dark suit and a white shirt, was not looking at the artist. His head with thick black hair was tilted slightly, looking at the woman. She was wearing a pale gown shimmering with the mother-of-pearl colors. Her flaxen hair was swept up in a cascade of curls that hung down her back. She too ignored the artist and focused her attention on the man, the center of her world. In return, his face radiated love. He held her delicate right hand in both of his as if it was a fragile flower on the way to his lips to be kissed.

At first, I could only speculate who they were, but when I shifted my gaze to take in the rest of the painting, to the window painted in the background and the landmark centered there, I knew. It was Waterwood House. The man was Benjamin Ross and his beloved wife Elizabeth. They were so secure in their love, they dared to ask the portrait painter to capture their feelings on canvas though it was not in keeping with the attitudes of the day.

When I could finally drag my eyes away, I noticed there was a large wood chair facing the painting and several candle-sticks smothered by wax. Had someone come here to view it? If it was so special, why wasn't it hanging in the main part of the house, instead of being hidden away in the attic? I looked back at the chair and saw a scrap of white cloth on the floor, swept aside.

I picked up the ragged handkerchief with the initials BR and showed it to TJ. "I think Benjamin used to come up here, sit in that chair, and gaze at the painting...after Elizabeth died." I bit my lips, upset with myself for blurting out such a romantic and unfounded idea.

He went to stand in front of the chair and look toward the

painting. I had the wildest idea why he didn't sit down. He didn't want to impose on Benjamin's grief for his lost love.

"Why didn't he hang it downstairs where he could see it all the time?" he murmured.

"Elizabeth died young, right?" TJ nodded. "He probably couldn't bear to be reminded of his loss all day, every day. He had to live in the present, to take care of their daughter and Waterwood. He could only be reminded of her absence when he could handle it, here, in the solitude of the attic, alone."

TJ sighed. "You may be right. Remember the story about how they met at the glittering ball?"

I was grateful TJ was trying to lighten the grief weighing on both of us. When he had first told me the story, I teased him about using the word *glittering*, but this wasn't the time to do that again. "Tell me the story again."

He leaned against a roof support and began. "Benjamin was living out here on the Shore, trying to make Waterwood Plantation a successful operation. Some of its acreage was originally owned by his father. Benjamin's parents decided it was time for their son to wed, but he wasn't showing much interest in anything other than soil issues, crops, and the price of tobacco. Somehow, they persuaded him to join them in Philadelphia for a series of important social events and a *glittering* ball, *the* social event of the year. That's where he first saw Elizabeth and they soon married." TJ turned back to the other paintings.

"No, no! You have to tell the story the way your mother always did. I want every detail, the way you first told me."

He gave me a sly look for a moment then smiled. "I'm beginning to think you are a hopeless romantic."

"We can debate the point later. Now, tell me the story," I insisted. "The right way."

He cleared his throat. "It was the social event of the season.

There were people there from all over the East Coast, even New York, and that was a big deal back then. When Benjamin walked into the glittering ballroom, where all the ladies were dressed in lavish gowns of satin and silk, heads turned to consider the new man in town. Young ladies—and their mothers—took notice. All, except one. She was on the far side of the dance floor, surrounded by several young men who were paying their compliments to her."

TJ held up his index finger and said, "Remember, I've heard my mother tell this story so often that I can repeat her version word for word." He cleared his throat and continued. "Elizabeth had hair of spun gold. Her complexion had the translucent quality of the finest pearl. She wore a silk gown the color of the pink glow of a sunrise. For Benjamin, the rest of the world faded away. He saw only Elizabeth. He had to quickly find someone to make a proper introduction because that was the way it was done. He wanted to be with her, so she wouldn't become distracted and monopolized by the young officers in uniform and sophisticated gentlemen fluttering around her."

TJ sighed. "I guess he didn't have to worry. When Elizabeth turned and saw him, it was clear she too was mesmerized. There was no one else in the room for her, but Benjamin. The next morning, my great-great-grandparents were shocked to discover that Benjamin had proposed to Elizabeth the night before. I guess it just *wasn't done* back then. He should have gone through the formal process of courtship, then asking her father for permission, then presenting his proposal."

TJ glanced at the empty chair across from their portrait. "Benjamin couldn't wait. He had met the love of his life and he wanted to spend every minute with her. This created quite a problem for my great-great-grandparents. He had violated social conventions and he was only twenty-two years old. True, he came from a well-to-do family, but men at that time established themselves before they proposed marriage. Benjamin knew he wanted to spend his days at Waterwood, and he wanted Elizabeth by his side.

"According to the family story, Benjamin made a case to his father. He wanted to pour his life and energy into Waterwood land, raise his family at Waterwood, and to be buried at Waterwood so his body could nurture the land. He did not want to travel to Europe like other young men his age. He wanted to stay at Waterwood with the woman he hoped would be his bride." TJ looked at the tattered handkerchief in my hands. "And you know the rest of the story."

We stood there in silence, together, looking at the two lovers captured on canvas. As if by unspoken agreement, we left the painting where Benjamin had put it so long ago. TJ took the flashlight and returned it to its place by the door. I laid the white handkerchief on the arm of the chair and followed TJ out of the attic.

Chapter Six

"Hanging on to resentment is letting someone you despise live rent-free in your head."

— Ann Landers, pen name of the syndicated advice columnist

We walked down the stairs, each lost in our own thoughts. I kept seeing the portrait of Benjamin and Elizabeth in my mind's eye. To live a true love... Who would have thought to see evidence of their love captured in a painting, existing under a layer of dust, in an unheated attic, in a house on the Maryland Eastern Shore. What a remarkable experience.

Another thought crossed my mind that made me stumble on the steps. TJ was there, grabbing my arm with his strong hand before I could fall.

"Emma! Easy, girl." When he saw I was stable, he released my arm reluctantly. "You were lost in thought. Better wait until you're downstairs."

I forced a laugh to put him at ease and continued down the steps. I wondered what he would say if I told him he was the cause of my stumble. Seeing the portrait of the two lovers affected me more than I would have thought. I was sure there were disagreements, maybe even harsh words over the course of the time Benjamin and Elizabeth had together, but I couldn't imagine anyone, not even great actors, conjuring up the look on their faces. Their emotion came from the heart, not the head.

It was the emotion everyone wanted to experience. The emotion I'd always wanted to share. I thought I'd found it with my high school sweetheart/husband who turned out to be a slimy, manipulative cad. Oh, how I had once relished calling him names. As I turned down the last flight of steps to the main floor, I realized my delight in hating him had turned to ashes. The hurt remained, but I no longer enjoyed attacking him.

A wave of warmth ran over my skin. It wasn't harmful or burning. It felt like I was waking up from a cold nightmare. I'd felt like this before, when I awoke in the hospital and realized I was alive. It was the moment before the pain and fear and drugs slammed into my brain. It was the moment when I knew I would survive.

That was physical. This time, it was about my loving heart. Had I somehow moved on and left him behind? When I thought of him now, there was no anger or sadness. There was nothing. It was time for me to move on, but to what?

"Coffee?" TJ offered as he headed to the kitchen.

"Yes," I replied automatically.

I peered out the little windows on the side of the main door to the scene Elizabeth had tried to capture in her painting. There was almost no sign that time had passed. Little had changed. I began to understand another aspect of why Waterwood was so important to Emma. Yes, it was where she was born and lived with her parents, where she had found true love with Daniel, and a living hell with Joshua, but there was something else. Waterwood was Emma's anchor. This is where she found what I believed everyone wanted: Home.

This realization almost took my breath away. I was facing decisions to guide the course of the rest of my life. I was avoiding them. I had no clear path. I felt adrift, needing an anchor. I was in a beautiful place with a caring, wonderful man in my life. TJ...

"Your coffee is getting cold," he called out.

"Coming."

As he handed me a mug of steaming coffee, I acted quickly to steer the conversation away from what we had found in the attic and the sea of emotions. "So, you didn't find the reporter who wrote the story about unsolved mysteries?" I looked into my mug. "When you do, I hope you don't hurt her."

"No chance of that." He tossed out the words a little too lightly and quickly.

I decided not to second guess him right now. "Oh, good." I smiled. "I guess the drive siphoned off some of your anger."

He shook his head. "Not really. I was still mad. I went to the newspaper, and she wasn't there. They said she was out working on a story."

"What did you do?"

"It wouldn't help to blow up at the receptionist, so I tried a little of my charm." He gave me a wicked grin and winked.

I closed my eyes, going along with his quirky joke. "And...?"

"The receptionist was kind to take a message asking her to call me, rather than dumping me into voicemail. I figure I'm more likely to get a call back that way."

"That's good. You—"

"Then Nelson appeared." TJ looked a little sheepish. "I guess a little of my anger leaked into my voice when I was talking to the receptionist..." He shrugged. "He overheard me and came out to check if everything was okay."

I was confused. "Nelson? Who is he?"

"He's the owner and editor-in-chief of the paper." And he groaned. "And my neighbor."

"Oh?" I was surprised. "Have I heard you mention him before?"

"Probably not. We're not the best of friends." He glanced out the kitchen windows. "Nelson invited me into his office. I tried to explain to him what kind of problems his reporter created for a hard-working farmer when she wrote stories like the one on the front page today."

"Did he say anything constructive?"

"No, not really. He said it was news, but said he would talk to her, ask her to keep in mind what I'd said when they did any other articles. He also said they would add a note that Waterwood is private property. He walked me out and said he'd have his reporter contact me. "I want this to go away..." TJ sighed as he turned away from the sweeping view of some of his fields. "because I have bigger problems."

I put my mug down. "What's wrong?"

He dropped into a chair at the table and his forehead creased with worry lines. "It's all this talk about climate change. I can't save the world, but I can do things to make a contribution and protect my farming operation here at Waterwood. Some of my clients are willing to change how we do things." He shrugged. "It might not be much, but at least it will be something."

"That all sounds good to me," I said tentatively. "Do I hear a *but* coming?"

"It is good." He sighed. "The only problem is getting the right information and coordinating with other farmers..." He paused. "And local government, which means politicians."

Oh, dear. The one thing TJ despised more than trespassers were politicians. This was going to be a problem. I couldn't do anything, but I could listen. I leaned back in my chair. It was better for him to rant to me in the privacy of Waterwood than at a council or commissioners meeting. "Tell me."

"After I left the newsroom, I went over to the state extension service to get some more information. That's when I learned the County Council Commission is debating the provisions of new codes. Here in Maryland, decisions regarding climate change will be in the hands of local officials." He cocked his head, thinking aloud. "I don't hold a whole lot of hope it will work out well."

He drew in a deep breath. "Anyway, that's where I ran into Nelson... again. He was talking with the head of the commission. I haven't seen him in months. Now, twice in one day. As he was leaving, I mentioned it to him as a joke, and he got all defensive. Said..." TJ puffed up his chest and pitched his voice to a deep bass. "I'm just doing my job."

TJ relaxed. "He has gotten a little too pompous for the Shore, I think. Always writing in his editorials about how his paper will give you the facts you can rely on. He is acting like a godfather." TJ stopped and wet his lips, unsure.

"What, what is it?"

"I know this is unfair, but the man has a lisp that drives me crazy. Sometimes, I have to guess what he's saying. When he says certain words, his speech gets so wet, I'm afraid he is going to spit on me."

"Oh, that's unfortunate. I thought—"

"...people did something about a lisp? You're right. Speech therapists can often work wonders, but Nelson has been in denial for years. Guess it started with his parents. They couldn't know he would develop a lisp. Every time he says his name, it comes out as *Nel-thin.*

"Oh, that's sad, but—"

"It was too late to change it. Besides, it's a family name. I think he is Nelson the Third or the Fourth. It must have been easier to just ignore the problem. When he started school, he couldn't even say his own name correctly. The bullies were ruthless. His nickname was Nellie. You can imagine how bad it got. It stayed with him all the way up to high school.

"He went away to college and worked somewhere in New York. When he came here and bought the paper, people were in awe of his money and position. They were afraid to say anything."

"How awful for him."

"Yeah, but now, we live with it... and his arrogance he uses as a shield." TJ glanced out the window again. "But that doesn't have anything to do with climate change. From the farming perspective, there are things we can do, have been doing here on the Shore for a long time. The basic idea is to use plants to get the carbon out of the atmosphere."

"Like plant a tree? A lot of organizations are doing that," I said, trying to be helpful.

"It's more than that. It's all about soil management."

"Soil? But I thought..."

TJ leaned forward, the way he always did when he was excited about some aspect of farming. "If the soil is fertile, plants are stimulated to grow. Corn, soybeans, wheat. It's not just trees. Plants then absorb more carbon dioxide out of the air which in turn nurtures the soil."

"And better-quality soil helps the plants grow," I added. "The cycle begins all over again."

"That's basically it," he said with a smile as he leaned back. "Of course, it means we will have to do some things a little differently. People don't like to change, but..." He leaned forward again, energized. "When I was at the Easton farm office, I talked with one of my contacts there. He showed me a video online that had us both laughing and nodding our respect for the rancher featured in it."

"Okay," I said. "You have to tell me."

"The man raises cattle that feed on grassland out West," he began.

"Mmmm, you're making my mouth water."

He nodded. "Yeah, it might be time for us to go out for some good steaks again. Anyway, here's the interesting part, he raises chickens right alongside the cattle."

"Oh, smart guy. Covers both the beef and the chicken markets." I was proud of myself for putting together a little agricultural logic.

TJ burst my bubble. "Ah, no. That's not why he has a flock of chickens. He uses them to cultivate the grassland to feed the cattle."

I couldn't see a logical way out of this. "How does that work?"

"It's kind of a funny story. Imagine this: The cattle are out grazing on an area of grassland. The rancher has a mobile chicken house ... not a small coop, but a line of coops on wheels, like a train. He takes the contraption out to the grassland, and he parks it close to the cattle and opens the doors. The chickens jump down and follow the cattle. They like to scratch through the... well, there's no reason to get graphic. Let's just call them pies."

"Some people call them meadow muffins."

"You have the right idea. With all their scratching around, the manure gets spread over the field. He doesn't need to run a tractor breaking up the soil. Saves time, saves gas for the tractor, and creates less air pollution. The chickens do the work for him. Then when he moves the cattle to another field, he moves the chickens, too, and they do it all again. Meanwhile, the soil is

43

fertilized which makes the grass grow back lush and healthy for the next time the cattle come to feed in the rotation. We get great steaks, and he improves the fertility of the soil by pulling more carbon out of the air and storing it for use by plants."

"That's incredible. Does this mean you're going to bring in a herd of cattle?" I asked.

"Ah, no. It's just one example of farming ingenuity. There are things we can do, we have to do, or we'll be in trouble. People are already losing their crops to drought. With the heat getting worse, it is getting harder and harder for people to work in the fields. Not everything can be done from an air-conditioned tractor cab. And in this area, we have to be ready for sea level rise."

Now, it was my turn to sit up straight, concerned. "Should I be worried about the Cottage?"

"I hadn't thought about it, but maybe. They're doing things in St. Michaels—getting grants and raising streets and houses. There are some forward-thinking people there. I'll talk to someone." Then he sprang out of his chair like he'd been launched into the air. "But there are other people..." He began to pace around the large kitchen that had fed generations of his family. "You wouldn't believe some of the things I heard when I was up in Easton. With all the evidence of changes in our weather, there are still people who don't believe anything bad is happening. And the real damage is, some of those people are in positions to block decisions meant to move us forward. Politicians." He spat out the word like it was vile.

He emptied his mug into the sink. "There's not much I can do about them right now."

I was glad to hear. He'd been riled up by two of his least favorite people today: reporters and politicians. I hoped I wouldn't have to bail him out of jail for disturbing the peace, or worse.

He straightened his hat on his head of light brown hair kissed by the sun and turned to me. "Look, I need to calm down and the best thing is for me to do something. I need to look at a few acres down on the Point. I'm thinking about cultivating them, but I have to test the soil first. See you later?"

"Sure, I'll just go back..." My words hung in the air. He rummaged around in a big closet and was out the door, ready to tackle one of the endless problems and challenges connected with farming. He left me with the questions about the treasure and what we'd discovered in the attic.

Chapter Seven

"It seems dangerous to be a portrait artist who does commissions for clients because everyone wants to be flattered, so they pose in such a way that there's nothing left of truth."

— *Henri Cartier-Bresson, French Photographer*

I walked back to the Cottage, my head spinning with the things I had already learned from the paintings we had found and the message in Benjamin's ledger. Passing the cornfield along the road, I was amazed at the messiness of the acres there. The straight, even rows had disappeared after harvesting. TJ had explained one night in front of a fire how he had rolled the field to reduce the stubble of the dried-out stalks and planted radishes. Acres and acres of radishes! Was he now in the vegetable business? No, he'd explained. He was growing them to nurture the soil, part of the no-till approach to farming here on the Shore. He'd promised to explain more about it, but right now, it just looked raggedy.

I shifted my thoughts to something I could understand.

Portraits in Time

Even though I knew it was too soon to expect an answer from Emma, I soon found myself on the path to the cabin again. I hustled my steps. At least receiving a letter from her was something I could understand, sort of.

Rushing into the cabin, I was gratified to see several sheets of paper sitting in place of my letter. Emma had answered.

Beyond Waterwood

> *My Dearest Emma,*
>
> *Your letter brought me such joy. My face aches a little from the huge smile your news has brought. Patience? Forbearance at reading of your excitement at experiencing spring? Posh! It was always my favorite time of the year. I remember the delight I would feel surging inside me. Of course, we never spoke of the feeling in those terms. Decorum and restraint were always the order of the day, but now, I can be honest with you. How liberating! How wonderful it is to discover something else we share!*
>
> *Please keep writing. I would love to hear about the springtime happenings and events at my dear Waterwood.*
>
> *Your question about how my portrait came to be made caused me to laugh aloud. I loved the final outcome on canvas, but it was so painful to make it a reality.*
>
> *My father said my mother was a gifted painter. I always loved looking at her works. Somehow, they made me feel close to her. When I was young, my mother's parents arranged for an art instructor to come to Waterwood several times to give me lessons and supply books for me to study.*
>
> *As political tensions grew, it became perilous for him to travel to the Shore. After Momma died, I continued to practice and study on my own, but I didn't feel I had the*

understanding or confidence to do a large work. I was content to paint for my own enjoyment.

A letter from a friend spoke of the imminent arrival of a portraitist at a nearby plantation. My husband declared our generation should be represented on the walls of Waterwood House along with the paintings of my ancestors.

I was included in only one painting, a family portrait. I wept when I saw how the artist portrayed me. Tired, worn, unhappy. He apologized, but I knew he had painted only what he saw.

At last free of the man I had married to protect Waterwood, I felt I deserved to be immortalized in oils without the strain he created. I believed as the daughter and mistress of Waterwood, my portrait should join the others.

The air and sun of my favorite place on earth had rejuvenated my spirit... and it showed. I wanted to be remembered as the woman I was then, not the unhappy woman in that family painting. I made the proper contacts and a visit by a well-known artist was arranged.

The gifted man was quite taken with Waterwood House. He wanted me to sit by one of the large library windows overlooking the fields and water or in the main parlor in front of the marble fireplace. That would have been impossible. Besides, I wanted to stand, proud and free.

Yes, I loved Waterwood House, but it was my father's house. My heart was with the land. I wanted my forever portrait painted outside. The artist finally agreed to work in my favorite spot by the creek across from Lone Oak. Do you know it?

After spending hours standing in one position, I real-

ized I had not given proper consideration to the process. Posing for a portrait is hard work. Good posture is required. I had to stand still for hours. The artist was constantly reminding me in polite ways to stand tall. I kept telling him I wouldn't get any taller than I was when I woke up that morning. My little joke always made us laugh. People think it is the artist who does the hard work. I can tell you; it is not easy being the subject.

> *Be thoughtful if you should be tempted to do it.*
> *Fondly,*
> *Emma*

Heavy knocking on the front door of the Cottage shattered the quiet. I sprinted over and opened the door to see TJ, hunched over, gulping air. His face was ashen.

I reached over to pull him inside. "What's wrong?"

He took a couple more deep breaths and was finally able to say in a shaky voice, "I-I think I found a grave."

"A grave? Were you working in your family's graveyard?" I answered my own question as I walked him to the sofa in the living room and sat him down. "No, that's not right. You said you were on the Point, right?"

He leaned back and settled into the thick cushions. "Right. There's some land by the creek that hasn't been cultivated for years, if ever." His eyes were haunted as he stared at nothing but might have been seeing something disturbing.

"I'm going to get you a glass of water," I said as I made a move toward the kitchen.

But he caught my hand. "No, please don't leave."

I put my other hand on his shoulder. "It's okay, I'm right here." A cold chill ran through me. I had never seen TJ so upset. He was always cool and in control, even when a delusional monster threatened to murder us both. But now...

As we sat together in the quiet, I could hear Ghost barking madly outside. "Did you leave Ghost in the truck?"

He squeezed his eyes shut. "I guess so."

"I'm going to bring him in, okay? He sounds very upset."

Under normal circumstances, TJ would never have abandoned his dog. He looked away, not able to meet my eyes and gave a quick nod of his head.

I patted his arm. "I'll be right back."

As I left the room, TJ continued to stare at nothing.

As I approached the truck, Ghost started pawing madly as if he could get his hundred pounds of Labrador retriever muscle through the window. When I opened the door, he launched himself into the air and shot up the front steps, pawed the screen door open and disappeared into the Cottage. When I made it back to the living room with a glass of water in hand, TJ had his arms around the dog with his face buried in his fur. I put the glass on the end table and sat down to wait.

In a few minutes, TJ sat up, his spirit renewed by the love of his dog. He downed the water and sat back with a sigh, though he kept a hand on Ghost's neck.

"I'm sorry," he began.

"Don't be silly. Do you think we should call the police?"

He grabbed my hand. "No, not yet." He realized he was squeezing my hand too tightly and released his hold. "Sorry. I don't want to bother anybody, bring them out on a wild goose chase until I'm sure I saw what I think I saw."

A strange expression came over his face. Confusion? Self-doubt? "Why don't you tell me what happened, then we can decide what to do."

He looked down and swallowed. Sheepishly, he said, "It's pretty stupid."

"That's okay. Tell me."

"I was over at the land parcel I call the Point. I—"

"Wait. Isn't that the place where the –"

"—witch supposedly lived? Yes, but this has nothing to do with that story. This is a patch of ground on the water that hasn't been planted since I've been here. The ground is just sitting there. I've been thinking it's time to put those acres to use. A line of big old trees once separated the Point from the field next to it. Those trees blocked the sun for part of the day. It's hard to grow corn or soybeans in shadow. But those old trees have finally died from the stress of age and weather. Several came down over the winter. The rest aren't going to make it. It's time to cultivate that land."

"But..."

"Don't worry, Emma. I'll plant more trees in another area of Waterwood. Gotta protect the *wood* part of the Waterwood name."

"You always do. So, what happened out there?"

"Well, my first chore is to check the soil. It doesn't pay to put even one seed in the ground if the dirt is no good. I need to know if it's in great condition, or in need of a little help, or if it is contaminated by the salt in the river water from the Bay. That would make it useless for growing. I had to find out. I was using my test kit. I had—"

I interrupted him. "TJ, this lesson in farming is good, but I want to hear about what you found."

"I found..." he corrected. "or think I found..." He was stuck.

"Come on."

He sighed and leaned back. "It would be so much easier to ignore it," TJ grumbled. "I don't need that piece of land. It's not very big anyway. And taking out all those dead trees would be a lot of work." He moved to get to his feet. "Tell you what, we'll forget all about this, okay?"

"No, not okay. I saw how shaken you were when you arrived. Tell me the rest of the story. You were testing the soil and..."

He sat back, drummed his fingers on his knee, then stopped. "I was testing the soil. I was getting some immediate results using the tubes and chemicals. It was looking good..."

"TJ." I cringed a little when I realized I had spoken his name the same way my mother did when I was in trouble. "Get to it. Tell me what happened."

He sighed again. He was doing that a lot. "Okay. I had to take samples all over the piece of land. The results were consistent until..." He got a faraway look in his eye. Blood was draining from his face again. He was reliving the moment. "The results got wacky at this one spot. I kept testing. The results were only at that one spot. I brushed the soil aside thinking... I dug down deeper. My hand hit something hard. Maybe I'd found the treasure chest, I thought. I put the kit aside and used both hands to find out what was buried there."

He exhaled and hunched his shoulders. "It wasn't a treasure chest. It was white and hard and..."

"You found a bone. It could have been an old bone buried there by some animal or—"

He spoke in a small voice. "It was bone. The forehead of a skull."

I shuddered. "A skull?" I tried to laugh a little. "TJ, you probably found the skull of an animal. You call this area nature's playground. There are lots of small animals out here."

He looked down as his fingers moved as if holding something. A skull. "I brushed away the dirt. It was a human skull." He moaned. "The eyes, they—"

"Eyes? You said—"

He stared at his empty hand. "The holes, were the eyes

should have been, were looking at me. I was holding what was a person... once."

"What did you do? Is it in the truck?"

He grabbed my arm as I stood up. "NO!" He continued as I slowly sat down. "I-I covered it with dirt again."

"Okay, okay." It was clear, I had to take charge. "We need to go out there and figure this out. Then we can call the police and—"

TJ stood, shaking his head, and moved around the room, like a caged rabbit ready to flee.

I stood up, too. "Look, it may be nothing." I stepped in front of him, so he had to stop and face me. "Until we find out what it is, it's going to bother you. Let's just deal with it, get it out of the way, and move on."

When he looked at me, the lines on his forehead relaxed. But then his eyes moved to the side and down to the rug. Something told me he was going to make one last try to avoid this situation, pretend it never happened.

He straightened up and put his hands on his hips. "Look, this is only going to delay what I have to do. You know I hate interruptions to my normal routine, going off on tangents for no real reason."

I laughed and gave him a sideways look. "Come on, TJ. You know there is no such thing as a normal routine for a farmer unless you think planting seeds, taking care of seedlings, keeping your fingers crossed while you watch the sky and the weather maps, and making plans to harvest a good crop is normal. You're constantly solving problems, figuring out strategies, adjusting what you have to do—"

"Okay, okay, I get it." He put his hands in the pockets of his jeans. "I guess you're going to make me check this out?"

"Yes, I think it is the right thing to do. And I want you to show me what you found. It might be nothing at all."

"Okay." He headed to the door and stopped. "You'd better put on your boots. Where we're going, you're going to need them."

After I dug my boots out of the closet and put them on, we went out to the truck. Ghost followed in TJ's footsteps.

Chapter Eight

"The past, like the future, is indefinite and exists only as a spectrum of possibilities."

— Stephen Hawking, English theoretical physicist

TJ drove the truck down the driveway, out to the main road, then back on another Waterwood road then... I was lost and so glad I wouldn't have to remember all the turns to get back to the Cottage. One dirt road jostled us so much I almost hit my head on the window. I guessed it would have been a smoother ride in his big tractor with the heavy-tread tires. Finally, TJ made a turn and we headed into a field. He drove us over to the far edge and stopped by the line of toppled trees he'd described. I love trees and I'm always sad when I see them broken.

He stopped. "We walk from here."

Thankful for the boots, I followed TJ toward the dead tree line. Splinted stumps and broken limbs littered the ground. Suddenly, noise erupted from what were once upright guardians of the Point. The noise wasn't a symphony of bird-song. It was a cacophony of black birds, starlings maybe, in a huge flock. They cackled and chattered at us. A mad sound meant to harass predators or warn away trespassers. The closer we got, the louder they shrieked. Some birds flapped their wings. Were they warning us away?

Unnerved by the birds' aggressive calls, my steps slowed. They had done their job to frighten me, deter me from crossing onto the Witch's Point. Sharp, strident bird noises had always unsettled me. I wanted to leave. TJ pushed forward. He was unsettled about what he thought he had found. He had come to me for comfort and guidance. I couldn't abandon him now. My resolve to help him was stronger than the fright the birds had sparked. I squeeze my lips together and followed him.

When we walked through the line of broken trees, the flock took off, their wings making a rattling sound. I started to throw my arms over my head and crouch to protect myself. TJ came to me and put a hand under my elbow to help me up. His calm attitude gave me strength and relieved my fear. He lived and worked in nature all the time. He was used to the reactions of creatures and knew when it was safe. I stood up and walked with him out to the piece of land known as the Point.

The land was flat, covered with weeds and wildflowers basking in the sunlight. More than a millennium ago, this region was scraped flat as a massive ice formation receded at the end of the ice age. The rock had been chewed up into fertile soil for crops and tobacco.

Looking around, I started jabbering. Was it to cover the sense of unease this place was giving me? "Maybe you stumbled on an old cemetery, TJ. That would make sense, wouldn't it? That would explain..."

TJ crouched down and motioned me to do the same. "Look at the level of the land," he said as he motioned across the ground. "What do you see?"

"It's flat and pretty smooth."

"That's right," he said. "Decades, even centuries ago, when people were buried in wooden coffins, the dirt would sink a little where each grave was located, a telltale signature of a graveyard. Because this parcel is basically even, I don't think we're looking at one."

As we stood up, I focused on the place where the ground had been disturbed. Rich, black soil was mounded around a hole. "Is that where..." I asked with hesitation.

"Yes."

"Why did you dig right there? What made you think..."

He threw his arms wide to embrace the Point. "Like I said, I'm thinking of planting this acreage after I get the old trees cleared out. But I need to know if it's worth the time and money. For example, corn and soybeans don't do well in acidic soil." He leaned over and picked up a handful of dirt. "I need to know about the soil before I go any farther in my planning."

"Okay, I get it. But what made you dig in that one spot?"

"I was testing all over the place with my soil probe. It's the fastest way. It pulls out a sample of about six to eight inches. Then I do a quickie test and get the answers I need. You can see my equipment over there by the hole."

When I turned to him, I had to shade my eyes from the sun in order to see his face. "Then what happened?"

From his expression, I got the feeling he didn't want to think about it again. Then a surge of resolve changed his features. His jaw tightened, his eyes narrowed, and he spoke in a deep, resonant voice. "I'd taken a number of tests. There were no surprises. The results were more or less what I expected, what I wanted. Since I'd be planting close to the water, I had to test over there. That's where the numbers went crazy."

TJ put his hands in the back pockets of his jeans and kicked his boot at a clump of soil at his feet. "I know different things can cause changes in the soil. For example, phosphorus is important in growing crops. Too much can damage or kill the plants which means wasted money and time. When the levels spiked all of a sudden, I needed to investigate."

"You figured something was down there to cause the drastic changes." He nodded. "And you dug down to find out what it was. Makes sense."

"Come on, let me show you." He set off across the open land toward his implements, testing kit, and the hole.

My very first reaction was to turn around and head back to the Cottage. I didn't want to see someone's skull if that was what TJ had found. Yes, I had seen the bodies of recently deceased people, but the key was *recently*. Their skin tone might have been pale or ashy. If I ignored the evidence of blood, they looked like people. This was different. Thinking about what happened long after dying was horrid and repulsive. But I had resolved to help TJ, so I kept walking with him, even though my pace was a little slower than his.

I was a little afraid of how I would react to seeing an old skull. It wouldn't be the first skull I'd ever seen, but it wouldn't be cleaned like the ones in museums. What if I got woozy or my stomach flipped?

Now, you're being overly dramatic. Get over there and stand with TJ, I ordered myself.

When I reached the hole and saw white bone as TJ brushed away the dirt, my nervousness turned to curiosity. If this was a human skull, how had it ended up out here in a farm field? Was it a woman or a man? Why was this person buried out here, far away from Waterwood House and the concentration of people who lived and worked on the plantation? It was hard for me to believe this was the body of a slave. Emma's father had set aside land for a cemetery around the church he'd built for his slaves.

I reached out and put my hand on TJ's arm. "Whatever happened here probably took place a long time ago, but I think we need to find out..." I didn't want to put into words all the possibilities piling up in my mind. "I don't think you can cover this spot and plant around it."

"No, it wouldn't be right," he agreed.

"And I don't think you can take the skull and..." I shivered a little. "Dig down to see if there is more..."

"No, that would be wrong, too."

"I know you don't want people tromping all over your land, but I think we need to report what you found to the authorities. Maybe call Craig..." He was a homicide detective and a good friend. "He would know what to do."

"I think you're right."

While TJ pulled out his phone and walked around until he got a signal to make the call, I wandered down to the water's edge. Below the surface, I caught sight of a little movement in the mud. A claw appeared. Could it be a Blue crab? The life cycle of the Chesapeake Bay waters was beginning again. I looked back at the hole. But one person's life had ended here.

"Emma," TJ called out as he walked toward me. "I caught Craig in a free moment. He is coming out now." TJ started walking toward the truck. "He'll never find his way to this spot, so I need to meet him on the drive and lead him in. We should probably go now."

I paused. "TJ, you're coming back, right?"

"I'll be back as soon as Craig gets here."

"I'd like to stay, walk around a little," I said, surprising myself.

TJ's eyebrows came together in concern. "Are you sure? It will probably be twenty, thirty minutes. Maybe a little more."

"That's okay. I can use the time to soak up the setting, the surroundings, for my book. I'll be fine."

"Okay, if you're sure..." He obviously wasn't sure. "Do you want me to leave Ghost with you?"

"No, after the upset you two had earlier, I think he'd want to be with you. Don't worry. I'm fine. Go, go."

As I watched him drive out of the field, the city girl in me felt the anxieties of being left alone in the middle of nowhere. Then the beauty of the place began to soothe away my unsettled feeling. But there was something about this patch of land. I couldn't exactly put my finger on it but, there was something, almost a sense of menace, in the air.

I shook my head to dismiss the idea. TJ's impression of the area was more important. When he looked at this land, he saw possible new acreage for his farm.

Long ago, in the late 1600s, an old woman might have had a different perception of this place. Abandoned and alone, reviled by the townspeople, accused of being a witch, this might have meant sanctuary to her.

I could only imagine how she would have felt, coming to this place for the first time. The line of trees offered shelter from the people she wanted to leave behind. The town of Oxford was not far away, just across the river on the opposite shore. Civilization, but for her, it was a hotbed of taunts and rejection. Being here, she had chosen to stand against the storms of nature rather than suffer the assault of people's intolerance and prejudice.

Water from a tidal river linked to the Chesapeake Bay lapped on three sides of the Point. More protection. In her time, people preferred to travel by boat due to the poor condition of the roads. She would have been exposed to prying eyes as people moved on the water. At the edge, I'd seen the water was shallow. The land formed a shelf made of mud that could suck down a person's foot or lock the keel of a shallow craft if someone wanted to pry. Here, curiosity could maim or drown. The water was both dangerous and a defense.

But this was also a place where the woman could create her own world. The shallow water would allow her to capture an unsuspecting crab or fish for supper. Fallen tree limbs would provide wood for a fire and materials to build a crude shelter. The strong line of trees offered protection from prevailing winds and storms. As the sun sank to the horizon, shadows would have lengthened over the hard, weedy ground. The trees would appear as a dark wall against those who would pursue her, ridicule her as a witch, threatening her very life.

As the light faded and a full moon rose high in the sky, it could have given silvery comfort to the woman alone. Here was a place she could make a home, where she could find relief, solace, and safety. Perhaps one day, the noise of chaos would recede, and she could listen to the water lapping against the shore. Hear the geese honking in an ancient formation overhead. Taste the salt in the air from the waters of the Chesapeake. In this place, she could live free.

But first, she had to face the charge of witchcraft.

The records in the library's Maryland Room showed Virtue Violl was accused by the townswomen of causing one of their own to lose her voice through the *practice of dark magick*. At that time, the only courts with jurisdiction over the Eastern Shore met in the City of Annapolis, north and west of this spot and on the other side of the Chesapeake Bay.

The sheriff, responsible for delivering the accused for trial, believed the travel presented a serious risk. When he was a child, his mother and grandmother had told him a witch could exert enormous power on water as well as land. She could sink a boat and walk away on the water itself. The poor man tried to face his fears but soon realized he couldn't make the trip alone. He asked, begged, but no one would volunteer to travel with him and the witch since all believed it would lead to certain death.

With no other option, he set out early one morning in a wagon pulled by a good horse with the witch sitting with her hands tied. He thought the woman couldn't cast a spell without the use of her hands. Residents of the town turned out to see him off, waving white handkerchiefs, sure they would soon be using them to dry their tears when word arrived he would not be coming home.

The sheriff guided the wagon up the Eastern Shore of the great bay estuary, northward to a place where the gap between the shores narrowed. There, a ferry crossed the short stretch of water and people could protect him. The journey passed without incident.

In 17th century Annapolis, His Majesty's court took up the case against Virtue Violl. Arguments were heard from both sides. Then the jury declared the woman was wrongfully charged. She was no witch. The next day, the sheriff hired a boat to take them home, no longer frightened of Virtue. After all, the jury of men had declared her innocent... and harmless.

The records reported she settled here, but why had the owners of this land that would later become Waterwood let not one but two women—*witches*—live here undisturbed? Was there a connection? According to the records in the library's Maryland Room, there was none, yet these two women lived on this exact spot seventy-five years apart. When Charles, the reference librarian, said some people believed it was not two different women, but the same one...well, I had to smile. In the rational world, it wasn't possible. Yet...

Chapter Nine

"Never enter the home of another with dust on your shoes
and selfish expectations in your heart."

— *Stewart Stafford, Author and Poet*

A rumble of engines on the other side of the trees drew my
attention. I walked over to see TJ's truck leading Craig's
unmarked sedan and a dark blue SUV of the St. Michaels
Police. After they parked on the far side of the trees, TJ led the
men, including the St. Michaels police chief onto the Point.
Then I noticed another car entering the field, one I didn't
recognize. It was a small, economy car. The driver moved
slowing as if trying to avoid being seen, which was difficult in a
big, open farm field.

"Looks like we have company," I said, but the men hadn't
noticed. Their attention focused on making their way through
the maze of old limbs and dead stumps in the tree line.

Dressed as usual in a coat and tie, Craig was the first to
wave to me. His strong jawline gave him a ruggedly handsome

look. His mouth curved into a slight smile. He didn't smile very often, not because he was unfriendly. He had once told me it was one way the job had changed him, seeing what people could do to other people. But I knew he was a true friend— loyal, caring, and protective.

They made their way to the hole where TJ had found the skull. They stood around, conferring for a few minutes, then Craig came over to me. "Hello. Interesting way to spend your time."

"Not my first choice, but finding *it* rattled TJ, so here I am." I said. "I'm glad he called you."

"I'm here more as a friend and moral support. For once, this isn't my jurisdiction. I contacted the Chief. He will probably oversee the investigation unless there is a role for me. He invited me along as professional courtesy."

"So, you think this is a case for an archeologist?"

"Probably. We'll put in a call to State to send a forensics team to be sure."

I glanced over Craig's shoulder and asked, "Who is your reluctant friend?"

He turned and saw a woman with a glowing head of platinum blonde hair gingerly making her way across clumps of soil and random weeds of the field.

"She should have worn boots," I said, thinking about her heels getting caked with mud.

Craig blinked. "I don't know who she is. Maybe someone the Chief called in?"

"She isn't wearing a uniform," I pointed out, noticing she was wearing a simple, but tailored sapphire blue dress that contrasted with her hair to create a stunning effect.

Craig was staring. "Somebody TJ called in?"

"I doubt it, not the way he feels about having people, even those he knows, deep into Waterwood property."

TJ left the hole and started walking toward the woman.

Craig raised his eyebrows. "Well, we're about to find out."

We both jumped when TJ let out a yell that could have stopped a train.

"HEY!" And he started running toward the woman who was snaking her way around clumps of soil. His shout was an alarm that sent both the Chief and Craig after him. I followed but not at a run.

In moments, the three men encircled the woman, stopping her progress. She took the opportunity to dig her phone out of the big tote over her shoulder. Was she fiddling with it to record the encounter?

As I got closer, I heard TJ firing off questions. "Don't you know you're trespassing? Who are you? What are you doing on my land?"

It looked like she was trying to reply, but TJ wasn't waiting for answers. I worked my way closer as the Chief put his large hand on TJ's arm to calm the situation. "Miss, who are—" He paused. "Wait, aren't you the reporter from the newspaper? Don't you cover the meetings of the St. Michaels Commissioners and Coffee with a Cop?"

A smile of red lipstick spread across her face. There was a spark of satisfaction when she said, "Yes, Chief. I'm Robin Hunter. Good to see you again."

TJ took a step backward. "You're the one who wrote that ridiculous article on the front page of the paper! I drove all the way to Easton ... You never called me... You... " He took a step forward. "I want to talk to you."

Was he going to lunge at her? I wasn't the only one to get that impression.

Craig moved quickly to block his path. "Now, let's all calm down. Ma'am, why don't you tell us what you're doing here?"

"...on private property!" TJ added, his words heavy with

accusation. He turned to the Chief. "You ought to arrest her for trespassing!"

Instead, the Chief took it all down a notch. He put his hands behind his back, stretched his neck, and settled back into a relaxed position. "Why don't we find out why she is here first."

TJ protested. "But..."

A quick glance passed between the Chief and Craig. The detective touched TJ's arm and gestured toward the hole with his head. "Why don't you come with me? I could use your help over there." When TJ didn't move, Craig nudged him and walked away with TJ in tow.

The Chief gave them a few moments to get out of earshot then turned back to the reporter. "He's right, you know. You're trespassing on private property."

"You're the reason I'm here," she purred.

The Chief's brows knitted together in confusion.

"Like any good reporter, I monitor the police frequencies. You were telling the dispatcher where you were going and why."

"Yes, but—"

"I figured a skeleton would make a good story. It's part of my job, Chief. Now, why don't you tell me what's going on. You found a dead body? Who is it? Is it murder? Do you have any suspects? What about—"

I could understand why TJ was so riled up. This pushy woman was a piece of work. In only a few moments, she had irritated me, and I was going to let her know it. I stepped up and cut her off. "Do you ever take a breath? Or do you only spew out questions then make up conclusions when you write a story?"

"EMMA!" The Chief growled. His ebony skin glistened with beads of sweat.

I turned on him. "Did you see her article in the paper this morning? She wrote about *unsolved mysteries...*" I spiced up my words with a little snark. "She might as well have printed an invitation to strangers to come crawl all over TJ's land here at Waterwood! And you may remember, I own property here, too."

Holding up both hands for everyone to calm down, he suggested, "Miss Hunter, why don't you leave now and call me at my office later today. I'll fill you in on what we have—"

She was not to be placated. "Chief, I appreciate it, but my editor will want to know about the murder. He'll worry about the safety of the community if there's a killer running around loose."

Fat chance they'll worry about the community. He'll probably want to increase his run of copies. But I kept the thought to myself.

"That is not the case here, Ms. Hunter, I assure you," the Chief insisted.

"Then why won't you—"

He took a quick breath and spoke slowly and softly in order to snare her attention. "There is no murderer running around the county, looking for his next victim unless..." He paused for effect, and she leaned in. "Unless his name is Methuselah. You see, the grave probably dates back to the 17th or 18th century. This isn't a modern crime scene. It's more of an archeological investigation. We'll be calling in the appropriate forensics team trained to deal with this type of situation. When I have anything more to report, I'll let you know. Now..." He gestured to the treeline and the general direction where she'd parked her car. "If you can be a little patient, you'll get your story, that is, if you're still interested. There is nothing sensational here."

She began to sputter. "But... I want... who..."

The Chief repeated his gesture toward her car. "That's right, Ms. Hunter. That is your cue to leave."

She took in a breath and let it out in a huff. "But---" She stopped when she saw the Chief slowly shaking his head. She looked over to the place where Craig and TJ were standing by the covered hole. "Can I..."

The Chief continued shaking his head.

I thought I heard her utter a curse under her breath. Her eyes shot daggers in my direction as she tried to stomp away on the soft soil all the way back to her car. The Chief and I watched silently as she went. I almost burst out laughing when her foot rolled off a clod of dirt and she cried out in pain. It would serve her right if she twisted her ankle.

"Em-ma," the Chief said softly with a lilt of warning.

He had read my mind and I wasn't surprised. I glanced at him, ready to object but melted. He was right. We didn't need more confrontation.

Pleased that he'd made his point, he started talking as if nothing had happened. "Yes, I think this is a very cold case." When Craig and TJ joined us, he asked Craig what he thought.

"Yes, I agree with you," the homicide detective said.

"We need to bring in the archeological forensics unit," the Chief confirmed.

Craig nodded again. "They can kick it over to an archeological team, maybe at the University of Maryland, if it warrants historical investigation. Somebody might be interested in excavating the site."

"I think we're talking about only one individual, one grave." The Chief glanced back to the hole. "But it's curious. The person wasn't buried in a coffin. I thought I saw some random threads, maybe from a blanket rotting away."

"Or a quilt." I told them what I'd learned at an auction of

Civil War artifacts months earlier. Southern women—mothers and sweethearts—gave their men handmade quilts to remind them of home and to keep them warm when they had to march to the chilly North. If the soldier died in battle or from disease, his body would be wrapped in his quilt and buried. "Do you think the burial could have dated back to the Civil War Era?" I asked.

The chief's lips tightened into a thin line. He stuck his thumbs in his belt loaded with equipment and stared at the horizon. "Might be. It looked old enough to me."

"This was a plantation at that time," I reminded him. "Do you think it could be an unmarked grave of a slave?"

"I'm no expert," the Chief said, "but I think the shape of the skull is wrong. I went to a workshop for law enforcement about how to make a quick identification of a skeleton. We learned the skull of a person of African American descent would be longer from front to back and have a forward slope from forehead to chin that pushed the jaw forward." He turned so I could see how his profile matched his description.

Craig made a different suggestion. "Maybe it's a really old skeleton from the time the Native Americans lived on this land?"

The Chief shook his head. "I don't think so. Their skull is rounder and doesn't have the large bony upper brow I have." He pointed to the area. "This skull is long and narrow. The eye openings are rectangular, looking a bit like aviator sunglasses. The teeth are smaller and set close together in comparison to the other people who lived out here on the Eastern Shore." He nodded to himself. "Yes, I think we'll learn this was a white man or woman, probably of European descent, who was well-fed, perhaps even privileged."

"Why do you say that?" I asked.

"At first glance, all the teeth seemed to be there and in good condition. His or her diet must have been regular and good quality."

"That's a pretty specific analysis." I said with admiration. "You must have been listening carefully in that workshop."

"Law enforcement is about more than catching bad guys. There are a lot of fascinating subjects connected with it. It almost always gets down to observation."

"Okay, from your quick observation, do you think the person died of old age?" Craig asked.

The Chief shook his head. "No, he or she was an adult, but there is a clear sign of the cause of death."

I looked over at the hole. "What caused..."

"My first clue was at the back of the skull. It is bashed in."

My jaw dropped. How had I missed it? But I hadn't gotten close enough to inspect it.

The Chief chuckled. "Don't feel bad. This is probably your first experience seeing a skull in the open air like this, right?" I nodded. "Don't worry about it. It's easy to get distracted by the reality of seeing a human skull in the dirt. And of course, there are the questions: Who was this person? Was it a man or a woman? Why was the person attacked? Why wasn't the body buried by a church or in a graveyard? So many questions."

"We'll get answers when the forensics team comes out and looks at the site," Craig added. He looked up at the sky, beginning to darken over our heads. "We'd better get a tarp over the hole and get back before we have trouble finding our way."

After the men secured a cover, we made our way back to the vehicles parked across the field. They said we would have to wait for answers, but I wasn't willing to wait for the scientific experts. I wanted to go to the one person who might know the story. The former mistress of Waterwood: Emma.

Chapter Ten

"Symbiosis: the living together of two dissimilar organisms, especially when the association is mutually beneficial."

— *Webster's Encyclopedic Unabridged Dictionary of the English Language*

I invited TJ to stay for dinner, thinking a little normal activity would help. He was wound up tight, preferring to pace rather than sit while I heated the dinner my housekeeper Maria had left. A dinner of comfort food. As usual, she had made enough for two people. While the food warmed in the oven—Maria's preference over using the microwave—I took a bottle of TJ's favorite craft beer and a glass of wine for me into the living room. The small fire TJ had built took the chill out of the spring evening air.

I sat down on the sofa and patted the cushion next to me. "Why don't you sit down and tell me about the political problem you discovered on your trip to Easton."

"You want me to talk politics? You really want to upset my stomach before dinner?"

I realized my mistake, but my worry dissolved when he smiled and sat down next to me. He pulled a long drink from the bottle then stared into the dancing flames in the fireplace.

"Do you know there are people who still don't believe the climate is changing?" He was up and pacing again. "There's some guy who was all about protecting our environment when he was running for office and now that the election is over, there are rumors he is torpedoing people's efforts to get grants and such to do something. Talk about lying to his constituents."

"I don't understand. How can a political official affect a grant award?" I asked.

"Sometimes, the grant needs matching funds. That's where the politician comes in. If he works behind the scenes so the matching-funds vote never comes up, the application is dead. I don't know how somebody in power can do that. He doesn't get it." TJ glanced at me. "Not an intriguing subject, is it? I can see your eyes glazing over."

"No," I objected. "I—"

He patted my shoulder. "I didn't mean to be so brusque. It's okay. A lot of people don't want to hear about it, don't want to talk about it, don't even want to think about it."

"It's scary," I said softly.

He nodded. "Very scary. The more I learn about what will probably happen, I want to run for the hills. But I won't." He shrugged one shoulder. "I can't leave Waterwood behind. So, I have to do what I can to take care of my land and what will help the planet in some small way."

"You recycle, right?"

He tried to stifle a burst of laughter. "We've got to do more, Emma. I've been talking with other farmers here on the Shore about something the experts are urging us to do now."

"What's that?" I curled my feet up on the sofa and settled back. This topic of conversation was so much better than treasure hunters and newspaper reporters.

"It's called no-till farming."

"But I thought—"

"Farmers ride around their fields on tractors, dragging along an apparatus to break up the soil before planting, right?" I nodded. "I bet your kindergarten kids drew pictures of the farmer tilling his fields."

"Yes, and the tractor was always red." I frowned a little. "I don't think John Deere would have appreciated it."

He laughed. "You're right. Their corporate color is green, kind of like British racing green." He let out a big laugh. "Imagine the farmer roaring around the fields like the Indianapolis 500 race, back and forth, up and down the rows."

"Instead of around and around and..." I drew circles in the air with my index finger as I pretended to be dizzy and fell off the sofa. My little antic made TJ plop back into the pillows, unable to control his belly-laughs. It was good to see him relax, having fun. Light glinted off his eyes, now a deep shade of green like the leaves of his healthy crops. The strain that had been there since he'd read the newspaper article melted away.

The timer buzzed in the kitchen. I got up. "Dinner's ready."

We had a relaxing meal in the kitchen. Maria had worked her magic, as usual: delicious roast chicken with macaroni and cheese, green beans, and of course, dessert. Her famous brownies. TJ groaned when I put them on a plate and led him back to the living room. He couldn't say no to his favorite. After he stirred the fire back to life, we settled on the sofa. Hearing Ghost sigh as he rolled himself into a ball in front of the hearth made us both smile.

TJ had shed the worries and horrors of the day. The little

lines around his eyes from squinting at the sun had smoothed. His coloring had relaxed to a warm glow. Wanting him to enjoy the rest of the evening, I steered the conversation to one of his favorite topics: farming.

"You were going to tell me about no-tell farming."

He cleared his throat. "That's no-TILL farming."

"Right," I said with a smile. "I guess it's about harvesting your crops then leaving the fields alone. For the next growing season, do you just spread the seed?"

He held up his hand. "Whoa there, lady. Let's back up a minute. It's all about the soil. If the farmer tills it, stirring it up all the time, the quality of the soil is going to degrade."

"And that affects the quality of the crops, too."

"Right. Remember the stories from the Great Depression about the Dust Bowl? The farmers put livestock grazing land under the plow to grow wheat. No longer anchored by natural grasses and loosened by deep plowing, the severe drought allowed the rich topsoil to blow away in huge clouds. Here on the Shore, tilling loosens our topsoil. When it rains, the soil can be carried off to the waterways. If we don't till it, if we allow weeds to grow in the fields, the soil is more likely to stay in place during wind and rainstorms. Extreme heat will have less of an effect. We have to pay attention to the quality of the soil and if there is a problem, we have to find a solution." He looked at me and cocked his head. "What are you smiling at?"

I could feel the huge grin on my face. "I *love* your passion. You're opening my eyes to what it means to be a farmer. And how much you love it!"

He dropped his eyes to the floor and shuffled his feet. "Yes, yes, I do," he said in a voice soft and low. "Like I told you when we first met, I'm here by choice. I'm smart. I have a degree." He shrugged. "I guess there are a lot of things I could do, but I

CHOOSE to be a farmer. And life conspired to bring me to Waterwood, to bring me home."

I felt a pang of envy and I watched him bank the fire. Oh, to know where you belonged, doing what you love. Yes, I was jealous. How I wished I felt as confident as TJ did about where I should be and what I should do with my life now that everything had changed.

TJ looked at his watch. "This has been a great evening but it's getting late. I have to get some things done before the forensic anthropologist arrives. He called to say his team will get here tomorrow. Want me to pick you up?" he asked as he walked to the door with Ghost on his heel.

"Yes, better call first to be sure I'm up and ready. By the way, I think I have an idea of..." My words hung in the air. He had headed out the door, distracted by the endless problems and challenges connected with farming and now, the discovery of a nameless skeleton.

Chapter Eleven

"A portrait, to be a work of art, must not be like the sitter. To paint a human figure, you must not paint it; you must render its surrounding atmosphere."

— *Umberto Boccioni, Italian painter*

The next morning, I was up at sunrise, eager to watch the forensic experts at work and to find out what they discovered. But first, I had a research task of my own to complete, one that would remain a secret from the officials. Dressed in jeans and two sweaters against the spring morning chill, I hustled down the path to the cabin, careful not to spill my first cup of coffee.

As I entered the cabin, I looked around as if I was seeing it for the first time. The word Spartan would describe it well. The walls of wood planks were not painted. Neither was the floor or ceiling which was really the raw underside of the roof. The only pieces of furniture in the one room were two chairs and the magnificent antique plantation desk that dated back to the beginning of Waterwood. Its wood was either walnut or cherry. After feeding its thirst for conditioning oils and wax, the grain became defined, and its depth always drew my attention and appreciation of the beautiful antique. But this wasn't the time for thinking about furniture.

It was time to write a letter. I sat down at the large, flat writing surface, pulled a fresh piece of paper from the stack, and uncapped the writing instrument I used to compose a letter to a special friend. I wrote:

The Cottage

Dear Emma,

Now that spring has brought life back to Waterwood, the farming operation is becoming active. Your descendant TJ treats the Waterwood land with tender-loving care though farming methods have changed since your time. Large machines have taken over the backbreaking tasks demanded in the fields. He employs scientific information to nurture the soil. Under his direction, Waterwood is thriving and expanding.

It was that expansion that led to a surprising discovery this week. There is a parcel of land he calls the Point along the water's edge. It is the place old women once called home. The acreage has not been cultivated in recent memory. A line of trees grew to separate it from a large field. Those trees blocked the sun's rays from reaching any rows planted on the Point therefore wasting seed and work time. The acreage has lain fallow until now.

The life span of those trees has come to an end. TJ wanted to remove their dead and rotting wood and reclaim the soil. As he began, he discovered a small place that raised his curiosity. Upon investigation, he discovered some poor soul had been buried there. Do you have any knowledge of this person, unknown and forgotten?

I do not wish to cause you any distress. Of course, there was no way you could have known about all the happenings, good or bad, at the vast Waterwood Plantation.

I look forward to your reply.

With affection and respect,
Emma

I left the letter in the center of the desktop and hurried back to the Cottage. TJ arrived as I was putting some supplies—muffins and a thermos of coffee—into a basket.

"Ready?" he asked as he grabbed an apple spice muffin. Maria knew it was his favorite.

"Are they here yet?" I scurried around the kitchen collecting last-minute things I thought would be needed.

He tried to stifle a yawn. "They called me before sunup. They left earlier than planned. The weather forecast calls for heavy rains coming in later. The lead guy said they would have trouble preserving the scene so, they wanted to get started right away."

I stopped and shot a piercing stare at him. "You didn't call me!"

"Emma, I was half-asleep. I barely had time to pull on my jeans before they were on the drive. There isn't much to see anyway. The first thing they did was check out the hole I'd dug then they put up yellow crime scene tape. All you can really see is a group of people in white protective suits. They stood around, peering down at the hole and started digging. I can't make heads or tails of what is going on. They won't let us get close enough to see what they're really doing."

His explanation siphoned away my irritation. "I still want to go."

"Okay," he said, grabbing the basket. "Don't blame me if you get bored."

When we got to the field, I saw TJ had cleared an opening in the downed trees so vehicles could get through and drive closer to the scene. The doors of the forensic team's van were open to give them access to their tools and equipment. It also blocked what they were doing. TJ drove his truck through but steered away from the site. He set up a couple of folding canvas chairs he'd brought and put my basket next to me.

Craig walked across the field to our little base camp. His face lit up when he saw the muffin I offered him. Between bites, he gave us a progress report. "They're working away, removing the dirt, brushing it away from the bones. It appears to be an intact skeleton."

"What do they know so far?" TJ wanted to know.

"Preliminary examination shows it is the skeleton of a man, buried probably 100-200 years ago." He gave his head a little shake of impatience. "As always, these experts push back when I ask for more specific information. They want to take everything back to the lab, do their tests, and all. One question has them scratching their heads. It's the way he was buried."

"What do you mean?" I asked.

"There was no coffin," Craig said. "He was just put in the ground. I thought he might have been a slave, but the lead—the forensic anthropologist—says no. He uncovered the torso and said he thinks it is the skeleton of a white male, probably of European descent. Remember, everything is conditional until he writes his final report after doing his lab work."

"So, the Chief was right in his initial observation," I noted.

I gazed over at the site where the experts were working. "It's strange, a white man buried out here away from everything. "

"It is a mystery and I'm glad it's not my case." Craig pulled his car keys from his pocket. "I made sure everyone has my mobile phone number. They'll call if they find any surprises. I'll check back later. Thanks for the muffin, Emma." And he set off toward his car and the rest of his day.

We settled back with our coffee then it hit me. TJ was not running off to do something or another. ""You're going to stay here and watch them work? Nothing else to do?"

"I have an impressive list of things to do, but I'm thinking if I watch them, make them feel uncomfortable about holding up this farmer's plans for this parcel, they might work faster."

I didn't think it would have any effect, but I kept my thoughts to myself. Watching the forensic team work wasn't as exciting as I thought it would be. They had cordoned off the area to keep nosy people like me away. I could understand why they would do it. Bystanders could get in their way. We might even contaminate the scene in some way though I couldn't imagine how after so many years. It was hard to believe it was just yesterday when TJ and I walked back and forth over that spot. Now, we weren't allowed anywhere near it.

Yes, watching from afar was boring, but I had no plans to return to the Cottage, not yet. I wanted to be here, in case. I stole a glance at TJ, quietly holding his coffee, eyes glued on the cluster of men in white suits. I could only imagine how bothered he was to have these strangers on his property, though he was hiding it well. At least, they were professionals, all concentrated in one area. But still...

TJ's silence worried me, so I spoke up. "You know, when they finish their work and move..." What should I call him? "Move the mystery man. Then you'll be able to farm this parcel of land without any problem."

He gave me a sidelong look that said, *Yeah, right!*

I tried to point out the soil might test uniformly after they'd removed the skeleton and the dirt around it, as if I knew what I was talking about.

"Yeah, except there will be yet another mystery attached to this point of land. First, there was the story of the woman charged as a witch, Virtue Violl in the 1600s. Then there was another old woman in the 1700s named Katie Coburn, and now, Mystery Man. The gossips will have a field day, especially when they hear he was a white man dumped in an unmarked grave. People love to talk about the skeletons in a prominent family's closet." He pointed toward the site. "Now, we have a real one. Lord knows, my family who worked this land back then wasn't perfect, but they don't deserve to be maligned and criticized, especially by people who have no clue." Ghost barked. He was relegated to the truck so he wouldn't bother the strangers on his farm. "Okay, boy. I'm coming. We'll take a walk. I need one, too."

TJ released Ghost from his confines and commanded him to *stay close*. Obediently, Ghost sat at TJ's feet and looked up at his human. "Think about it, Emma. Back then, people were jealous of the families that built up big plantations." He held up one hand. "Now, I'm not condoning how they did it. But they did it. People made up rumors that are still flying around today. Think of that first witch. People still talk about her after more than four hundred years. And don't get me started about the treasure chest. I only hope they find out who this guy was and there's no grim story connected to him. Waterwood doesn't need any more myths or rumors."

He put his hand on his hips. "Think of what Emma went through back then. Rivalries between the supporters of the Union and Confederacy were bad enough. She was the mistress of a plantation with a *history* and people didn't want to know the truth. Think of how she must have felt." He shook his head. "It doesn't seem fair. I need a walk to clear my head. Come on, Ghost."

I watched as they set off through the gap in the tree line and out to the field. TJ was right. Emma of Waterwood probably had a rough time with some neighbors. After all, Waterwood Plantation had been the largest in this part of the county. The fact that men, women, and children were held in bondage here still made TJ uncomfortable. He knew his ancestor, Benjamin, tried to maintain humane conditions, but the fact it happened here still bothered him.

There were people in Easton who made their anti-slavery feelings known to local slaveowners. During an earlier visit to the library's Maryland room, I'd read about St. Michaels being a hotbed of abolitionists and they were militant. Yes, Emma might have had a difficult time with all the politics and speculation circulating at that time and no man around to protect her. According to her diary entries, her husband Joshua was often away visiting the big cities. Probably because of her father's reputation for compassion, she seemed to have been able to put up an invisible wall to protect Waterwood and all its people.

People's curiosity was still alive today. Look at how we rubberneck when we pass an accident on the road. How we gobble up tales of misfortune about movie stars and bands. *The more things change, the more people stay the same,* I thought with a sigh.

I leaned back in my little camp chair and sipped cold coffee. I was eager to go back to the cabin to see if Emma had responded, but I tried to persuade myself she had not had ample time to compose another of her long letters filled with explanations and emotional connections. I had to content myself with what was happening right in front of me. But everything had gone cold and boring. I never realized how tiring it was to stand around watching other people work, especially when I really couldn't see what they were doing. As they excavated the grave, they slowly sank below ground level which meant I could see less and less. It would have helped if I could have heard what the technicians were saying, but each was working silently.

I perked up when I saw the Chief coming my way. He looked all around, taking in the surroundings. "This is a nice spot. Lots of openness. Great water view. Good place for a house."

I held my breath, hoping he wouldn't launch into the stories of witches haunting this place. It was a relief when he spoke again.

"I find this work fascinating. I'm glad the town is quiet, and County and State are happy to have me be the on-site presence for law enforcement."

"I wish I could share your enthusiasm. This is about as exciting as watching paint dry. I have no idea what's going on."

"Is this your first?" I nodded. "I remember my first crime scene excavation. It was great. I had a front row seat." Distaste must have shown on my face because he backpedaled quickly. "I mean it wasn't great for the victim. It was just a fascinating experience."

"So, you know what's going on over there?" I asked, perking up at the possibility of learning something.

He drew in a deep breath. "I know just enough to get into trouble."

"Maybe you know how the expert—"

"The forensic anthropologist," he clarified.

"Yes. Craig said he's already determined it is a skeleton of a white male. That means you were right."

He dropped his chin a little. Beneath his solid, imposing appearance, he was a little shy when the conversation turned to him. "I go to workshops and learn things I hope I'll never need in the field." He raised and dropped his shoulders. "This time, the information came in handy. I guess the anthropologist has done his preliminary gross observation."

I cringed. "Looking at a skeleton is kinda gross."

He chuckled. "For some people, it is. For these guys, it's a wondrous opportunity to look into the past."

"So, what is a gross observation?" A lesson in forensics was better than sitting here twiddling my thumbs.

"I don't mean to be funny. It's simply what they can see, without the help of technology. They can draw broad conclusions based on their knowledge and experience. The first question the forensic anthropologist tries to answer is what was the age of the person at the time of death?"

"How?"

"They look at the teeth. An adult will have all his teeth. Of course, some may be missing due to accident or decay. Then there would be an empty space. If there are teeth below what would be the gumline, it would probably be the skull of a child."

"And if there are few or no teeth at all, would it be an old person?"

"You've got it. They can also look at the leg bone and the connection to the knee, but I don't remember the details." The Chief folded his arms across his muscular chest. "Then they can determine the sex of the skeleton by observing the pelvis. It is very different between a man and a woman. A woman's pelvis has an opening large enough to allow the passage of a baby's head during birth." He shifted his gaze to the grave where the experts were working. "So, we've got a white male buried far away from the main house, murdered, and no indication of why. It's a mystery."

A mystery I'd like to solve.

We settled back into the monotony of watching from faraway. I wished I had my phone so I might begin the research the mystery in front of us. I'd left it at the Cottage because cell coverage could be spotty in this area.

When the Chief's phone rang, I hoped he wasn't going to leave. At least he was someone to talk to, someone who could answer questions.

"Okay, I'll be right there," he said and ended the phone call. "Gotta go. See ya." And he headed for his SUV.

Alone, I sat in the big field with the massive sky dome, hoping the few facts we had so far would solve the mystery here.

Chapter Twelve

"A lot of people who behave well at the table do so only when a special guest is around."

— *Michael Bassey Johnson, Author*

Later, when the Chief returned, two men came over to talk to him. They were outside the cordoned off area and TJ was heading over to join them. I didn't want to be left out, so I made my way through the winter weeds and hard soil clumps. As I got closer to the men, my right foot slipped off a hard lump of dirt. With arms flailing and some quick foot action, I kept myself upright, barely.

"EMMA!" TJ shouted and raced to me. Holding my arm to steady me, his face crinkled in concern. "Are you okay? Is your leg...?"

Yes, my leg. The left one, mangled in the car accident. Target of surgeries. Focus of hours of physical therapy. How was it? I was afraid to find out. I raised my eyes to see the Chief and the stranger watching me. I did *not* want anyone's pity.

Biting my lip, I raised my chin, carefully lowered my foot to the ground, and gently put weight on it. Nothing. No Pain. Not even a twinge! I wanted to scream in delight, but it was important to maintain decorum in front of these men.

"Okay?" TJ whispered.

I nodded and he slowly released his grip on my arm, ready to grab hold again if necessary. But it wasn't.

Watching where I was going, I whispered to TJ, "Who are these people?"

TJ sighed. "I wish the man over there all dressed in gray wasn't here. That's Nelson Jennings, the owner and editor-in-chief of the local paper and..." he added with another sigh, "my next-door neighbor." TJ slowed his steps. "He's brought a photographer! Look, the guy with the big bag, a camera bag slung over his shoulder." TJ's jaw clenched. "I thought he was only being a nosey neighbor. He's here to cover the excavation for his paper."

"TJ, take a deep breath. The police are here, which makes it public. They have it taped off as a crime scene, even though whatever happened was a long time ago. If you make a big deal about it, he will, too. If you act unconcerned, he might lose interest."

He leaned in and stared at me. "You don't really believe what you just said, do you?" He relaxed a little when I gave him a weak smile. "Remember, this is the guy who let his reporter resurrect the rumor of buried treasure at Waterwood. If I could—"

"Why don't you introduce me. Maybe..." I gave TJ my sweet, but conspiratorial smile and batted my eyelashes, but only twice. My little act worked and made TJ laugh. "Come on." I took his arm as if we were going on a Sunday stroll and we walked up to the group of men standing on Waterwood land.

The man named Nelson didn't waste a moment. "What were you two talking and laughing about over there?" But he pronounced two words with a lisp: Two and talking.

"You must be the editor. Ever the nose for news." I beamed at him. "TJ has told me a little about you."

Nelson shot a suspicious glance at TJ. This man was obviously partial to gray... gray collared shirt and jacket that accentuated his wavy hair going gray. But it was his eyes that grabbed my attention. They were slate gray and mesmerizing.

"You almost took a tumble over there, young lady," Nelson said.

I forced a smile that felt wooden. The man didn't deserve polite treatment...to comment on my awkwardness! And to call me *young lady?* I thought we were beyond that, but... I kept smiling. "I'm a city girl, born and bred. I'm not used to walking in farm fields."

The editor looked down at my feet. "But you've learned something about Shore life. Those boots will get you through just about anything."

They had, but I wasn't about to share the story about Joshua. He didn't deserve to know about TJ's ancestor, the Confederate spy, his activities, or my search for his drop points along the Confederate Secret Line right here on the Shore. He could find his own stories.

"I'll keep that in mind." I let my eyes trail around the whole group, drawing them in. "I think you're a little late. We're all a little late for the story here, don't you think?"

"Maybe, but news is news." Nelson turned to the Chief and said, "I really appreciate you calling me this morning with the update of what's going on. I don't know where Robin is." He scanned the area looking for his reporter. "She was fired up about this story yesterday." He turned to TJ. "And when she came into the newsroom after her visit here, well... " His eyes grew wide as he sighed. "TJ, let's just say, you weren't her favorite person."

TJ took in a breath that puffed up his chest and raised his shoulders. He was ready to lash out at the newspaper man.

I jumped in. "TJ is a little protective of Waterwood. This land is private." With a little swagger of my head, I went on to say, "I agree with him. My Cottage is located within the old plantation boundaries. The thought of strangers tromping around is unnerving. That article on the front page of your paper yesterday about unsolved mysteries was an open invitation to any and all to come to Waterwood and snoop around. In fact—"

The Chief spoke up to defuse the growing tension. "TJ and I talked about it. We're going to work out something and..." His words trailed off when he too noticed the expression on the editor's face. He wasn't listening to a word the Chief said. He was staring at me.

Finally, the editor broke the silence. "That's curious. Why is your property within the old plantation boundaries?" His eyes narrowed, waiting for my answer.

And with my simple comment meant to support TJ, I had made things worse. A quick glance around our little group put me on alert. The Chief showed natural curiosity. Holding his breath, TJ had tightened his lips and leaned forward as if ready to defend me from attack. My next words needed to redirect this man with a nose for a news story and save TJ from doing something to further enflame the situation.

I took a deep breath, glanced up at the blue sky overhead, and gave a quick shrug. "Oh, you know..." My brain kicked into overdrive. "You know, years and years ago, how a younger son or even a daughter would be given a piece of land to call their own? It was more of a family gesture, but in the case of my property, it was a financial necessity. It was sold off and here I am." I changed my expression to one of concern. "But what about your reporter? You must be worried. Does she often disappear?"

As the man shifted his attention, I glanced at TJ. When our eyes met, we shared the thought we had dodged a bullet. We didn't want treasure hunters poking around the property, but we certainly didn't need someone nosing into the deed for my Cottage and the history of Emma and Joshua in the 19th century.

Nelson looked around and said, "It's not like her to walk away from a story, especially this one. When I last saw her, she was spouting a whole list of questions. The answers will be the basis of her article." He scowled. "Now that I think about it, she didn't even call in this morning. That's why I drove out here myself. Figured I'd cover the activity until she took over again." He shook his head slowly back and forth. "It's just not like her." Then he laughed in a sickly way. "Maybe I should report her missing, Chief?

"That's no laughing matter, sir," the Chief responded, his face a mask.

This group was a powder keg. "I'm sure she'll turn up any minute." I detected a groan coming from TJ and wanted to punch his arm.

The Chief took Nelson and his photographer over to the grave while TJ and I stayed behind, brooding. He barely took his eyes off the forensics team at work. I wondered if he resented every weed they disturbed, every spoonful of soil they bagged for analysis.

Then things changed. TJ's cellphone rang. It was the Chief, looking toward us, waving us over.

"The Chief said the forensic anthropologist has something to show us, all of us. Come on, let's go."

"Inside the yellow tape?" I asked, almost exhuberent.

"As long as we stand where he tells us." TJ drew his eyebrows together. "We're not to touch anything and to follow his instructions. Okay?"

"Deal," I said.

As we approached the open grave, a short man in the white suit climbed out of the hole and wiped his face with a white towel. The protective plastic suit—in this case, to prevent contamination of the site—must have made them feel like they were working in an oven. How exhausting, but when the little man looked at me, I was surprised at the piercing blue eyes, peering through glasses with light brown plastic frames. He wasn't tired. The man was exhilarated.

It all made sense when Chief made the introductions all around. The enthusiastic man was the lead forensic anthropologist, Dr. Felix Bergstrom. After mopping his face, he cleared his throat and prepared himself to address the group. We waited patiently.

When he seemed to have organized his thoughts, Dr. Bergstrom began the summary of what he had found so far. "My preliminary findings ..." He held his right index finger up in the air. "And please remember those findings are drawn from only my gross observations." He paused to let the point sink in. When he spoke, his voice was pitched a little high for a man, but every word was carefully enunciated. "My report will be more detailed and based on scientific findings as well." He cleared his throat again and assumed a professorial attitude. "In this case, we are dealing with the skeletal remains of a white male, perhaps in his late twenties, early thirties. He was well nourished and in good health. On my initial examination, he does not show signs of manual labor. As you can see, his clothing is almost gone from exposure to the elements in the soil. There are some fragments. If you're interested, you might have them analyzed. I suspect you'll find they are good quality.

If I were forced to put forward an opinion, I would say this is the skeleton of a gentleman."

The Chief voiced the question we all had. "Why do you say that?"

Dr. Bergstrom's blue eyes sparkled. "Because of what we found." This forensic anthropologist had a flair for the dramatic, probably because he rarely had a live human audience who could appreciate what he had to say. Most of his time was spent in silence with bones and statistical reports.

"I have gathered some initial evidence. Let me show you."

Chapter Thirteen

"Portraits are most successful when they manage to convey the sitter's personality and spirit."

— —*John Singer Sargent, Artist*

F irst, Dr. Bergstrom held up an evidence bag filled with something black, something I couldn't identify. He must have read the confusion on our faces.

"I'm not certain, but I suspect this is the remains of a gentleman's hat, perhaps a top hat of some design." He set the bag aside. "But this is what I wanted to show you." Dr. Bergstrom held up a plastic evidence bag for us to see. Rather pleased to see our confused expressions, he pulled open the bag and reached inside with his gloved hand. Slowly, he pulled out an elaborate gold chain, link after link, until a circle of gold glinted in the sunshine as it swung gently, free from the dirt of the man's grave. It appeared to be a finely-tooled gold watch.

"As the body decomposed, it fell down through the chest cavity to the bottom of the grave." The watch continued to swing gently as he admired it. "The case is engraved. It has held up well considering where it's been for more than a century. I suspect it is gold of a fine grade. It needs to be cleaned, of course. I would take it to an antique watch expert. Don't try to clean it yourself. And definitely, don't try to force it open. In the hands of an expert, you may learn some interesting background of its manufacture and its owner."

I had to stop myself from reaching out and grabbing it. "Wait, is that an initial on the case, doctor?"

He looked and smiled. "There is a coating of dirt and dust, but I think you've spotted another clue to the standing of this man, Miss Emma. There are two initials intertwined: G and M. There might be more information inside, perhaps an inscription."

TJ reached out his hand for the watch, but the dramatic doctor pulled it back, out of reach. "We have to record and photograph it."

His comment seemed to remind the paper's photographer why he was there. He opened the big camera bag weighing down his left shoulder and took out a complicated SLR camera. He added a long lens and started doing his job.

The Chief agreed with the doctor. "That's procedure, TJ. You'll get it back when they are finished with it since it was found on your land."

"Speaking of being finished, when do you think you will be done?" TJ wanted to know.

"Not until tomorrow," the forensic anthropologist said. "But we'll get the skeleton moved before the rains come."

"Can't you—" TJ began.

"I want to see if there is anything else in the bottom of the grave. We don't want to miss something and lose it forever when the grave is filled in again."

I stepped forward. "I have a question. Can you tell why the man was buried way out here?"

The expert reached down into the grave and raised the man's skull into the sunshine. "I can't tell you exactly the reason he was buried, but I can make an assumption." Dr. Bergstrom held up the skull, no longer half-buried in the dirt, facing me.

I cringed. Most people grow up thinking a skull is a scary thing. Toys of smooth skulls and empty eye sockets are everywhere at Halloween. Seeing a real skull, taken from the earth, was something else entirely. This had once been part of a real human being. It had once housed a man's brain, the place where all his memories were stored. It was the source of all his skills and abilities—from breathing to emotions. We didn't know anything about this man, except he had survived childhood and grown into an adult, probably a privileged man, a gentleman. Still, I hoped his skull wouldn't show up in my dreams.

Then the forensic expert turned the skull around and we all gasped. He waited a moment, then made the pronouncement. "This man was murdered. The back of the man's skull was caved in by a hard object. Note the jagged edges surrounding the hole. This might be your first clue as to why he was buried way out here in an unmarked grave. It was hard to prove a murder had been committed back then without a body."

As we stared, the only sounds were a small flock of geese honking overhead and the rapid click-click-click of the photographer's camera.

Dr. Bergstrom turned to the Chief. "This was a homicide." Then the expert handed the skull to one of his assistants. "You are probably wondering how I know that." He stepped away from the open pit making us wait while he slipped back the white head covering. "Ah, that's better."

I got the idea Dr. Bergstrom was enjoying having a captive live audience waiting with their mouths hanging open.

He slowly turned full circle with his arms held out as if to gather in the surroundings. "Look around you. We're far away from everything, relatively speaking. I assume the road we drove in on led to the main plantation house in some round-about way, correct?"

TJ nodded.

"We are a long way from the center of activity. I surmise the only people who walked this part of the plantation in the 19th century were slaves and overseers. The family wouldn't come out here." He looked down and moved his feet in the soil and weeds. "It would dirty their fine shoes. They wouldn't have an interest in seeing close up how they made their fortune."

I glanced at the water and our lecturer anticipated my question.

"Of course, there were people on the water. But, again, there was no reason for anyone to guide a boat to the shore, to this place, and poke around."

I slid my eyes in TJ's direction, and he gave a tiny shake of his head. He'd had the same thought. We were not going to mention the two women who'd once lived on this point of land.

The forensic anthropologist continued. "This was a perfect place to dig a grave and leave it unmarked. I'm amazed you found it at all." He inclined his head toward TJ in acknowl-edgement. "Then you add the evidence of violence..." He shrugged his shoulders. "and there can only be one conclusion."

"Yes, his skull was cracked open..." I fought down the shudder caused by my own thought. "But it might have been an accident. He could have fallen and hit his head maybe?"

Dr. Bergstrom's lips spread into a slow smile. "If it was, don't you think the person or persons involved would have notified the authorities? Wouldn't they want someone to contact his family? Let them know what happened to him?" He shook his head slowly for dramatic effect. "No, I believe the facts will support my conclusion. This man was murdered. The evidence, even his existence, was covered up literally to hide that fact in an unmarked grave. No one learned the truth. A perfect murder, until now."

"And there is no reason for me to open a criminal investigation," the Chief said staring at the skull. "The murderer is probably dead, and the truth of what happened here died with him."

It was TJ who recovered first from our silent musings. "Like you said, it's all in the past. Nothing we can do about it now. Finish up what you have to do, sir, so I can get back to work. I just want my land back. Thank you." He turned and headed back toward his truck.

After saying good-bye, the Chief and I followed him. Just beyond the police tape, I stopped. "It's not fair."

The Chief stopped and pulled on his left ear. "You've lost me."

"Your anthropologist made a good point." I turned and looked at the open grave in the middle of a field blocked by a line of trees. "Nobody knew there was a man buried on this piece of land." A thought flashed across my mind. Did the old hags, the witches, know the body was here? Did one of them kill the man and discard him in a grave, ignored and forgotten? I didn't want to get into a discussion about witches and folklore with the Chief. Instead, I resolved to set the idea aside until I could raise the question with TJ.

"That's right. Unless he finds some kind of identification, this man will remain nameless, known only to the angels."

"Yes, but..." I insisted. "There must be a way. If this was a modern crime scene, you'd take fingerprints..."

The Chief shook his head. "That's not going to happen here."

"And you would take DNA and hope for a hit in some database, right?"

"Yes, but—"

"Chief, I read an article about scientists finding viable dinosaur DNA that was a million years old. Dr. Bergstrom put the age of the bones in the 19th century. That's what, a hundred, two hundred years ago? Maybe..." I raised my eyes to meet his, deep and chocolate brown, hoping he would guess my idea.

But he didn't. "What are you suggesting, Emma?"

"Could you ask Dr. Bergstrom if there is any viable DNA in those bones and if we could have a sample? That's all we need, just a sample. I'll handle the rest. It's our land, I mean it's TJ's land," I corrected softly. "But what happened here is part of the history of Waterwood. TJ has a right to know why a stranger was buried in the soil he loves so much. Please, Chief. I think the good doctor will listen to you. He is more likely to honor the request if it comes from you."

He searched my face and must have recognized my determination. With a deep sigh, he agreed and turned back to the cordoned off area. I fought to control my excitement and walked normally to the place where TJ was pulling some tools and things from his truck.

"Hi! I—"

"What were you and the Chief talking about?" TJ wanted to know. "Nothing that's going to delay those people from closing up shop, I hope."

He was grumpy. This invasion by strangers had reached his fields, his domain. This was not the time to mention my idea of getting the skeleton's DNA tested. I'd talk to him about it after I'd done some research to learn how it worked.

"Oh, nothing really. The Chief has another question for the forensic anthropologist," I said lightly.

"He does or you do?" His tone made it clear he suspected something was up.

My stomach growled, saving me from answering his question.

"It must be getting close to lunch time," I said, trying to sound casual. "I wonder what time it is?" I would have checked my watch—if I wore one—or looked at my phone—which I'd left on the kitchen table.

In response, TJ looked up at the sun and its position in the sky. Ever the farmer. "Yes, I think you're right." And he focused on the workers in white again. I hung around the truck, petting Ghost and rubbing his ears through the window. I think he was antsy too. TJ didn't dare let him out of the truck in fear that he'd run over to the spot where all the activity was happening. TJ couldn't remember the last time he had used a leash on his dog. So, Ghost and I continued to wait in silence.

Then my stomach betrayed me. It felt like the rumbles rolled over the open fields so everyone in the county knew I was hungry. TJ noticed, took out his keys, and held them out to me. "Here, go back to the Cottage and get yourself something to eat."

I felt a mixture of disbelief and horror. Was he suggesting...?

TJ rubbed his forehead. "Look, I know you don't want to drive but..." He jangled the keys at me. "Come on, Emma. I can't leave. Take the keys. It's not so far to go."

Had my blood frozen in my veins? It must have, because I couldn't move. He came over and put his arms around me, cradling my face against his chest, and whispered. "Come on, it's okay. I believe you can do it. The truck will keep you safe. There will be no traffic. You won't see another vehicle between here and the Cottage.

Sure, but I would still be behind the wheel.

"Everybody who is supposed to be here is here. Look over there." He gestured to the clump of official cars, a truck, and a van. "Nobody's going anywhere, and you won't have to go out on the street."

He pulled away a little, his green hazel eyes boring into me only to make the point. "You can do this." He pressed the keys into my right hand, turned me around in the direction of the driver's door, and gave my body a gentle push. "Go on, now."

My boots kicked up little clouds of dirt as I dragged my feet toward the door. Ever the gentleman, he opened it for me so there was nothing between me and the seat and the steering wheel. With his little nudge, I climbed into the cab and started the engine.

"Don't forget your seatbelt, not that you'll need it," he said with a chuckle. "And if you want to come back with some sandwiches and a thermos of coffee, I would be much obliged." He closed the door and with a double rap on the window, he walked away.

I opened my mouth to yell out something, then thought better of it. I tapped my fingers on the steering wheel.

He could have given me the option of walking home.

Not willing to let go of my irritation, I resolved not to bring back sandwiches and coffee. What was I, a short-order cook and waitress rolled into one? Why did he assume I would do it?

I put my hands around the wheel, my fingers clamped like they were made of steel. Then all my muscles went limp. I felt my shoulders sag. My reaction wasn't TJ's fault. I was afraid. I'd loved to drive since I got my license at sixteen, but now, I was terrified. The accident had scarred me for life in so many ways: my leg hurt every time it rained, the marks from the many surgeries were obvious, and my deep-seated fear it could all happen again rose up without warning. It was a fear that might determine where I lived, even how I would earn a living. It was irrational to let this fear take away my freedom, my independence. It was crazy. I knew it. But still...

Maybe TJ was right. Maybe a short drive on Waterwood land was a good way to start. I made a deal with myself. I'd drive across the field toward the farm road. If I got scared, too scared to continue, I could stop the truck and walk back to TJ or find my way to the Cottage. But that would mean I'd given up. Since the accident, giving up was no longer an option for me.

Feeling sweat trickle down my skin, I put my foot firmly on the brake, started the truck, and reached down to put it in gear. With a deep breath, my foot moved to the right and hovered over the gas pedal. As with all vehicles with automatic transmissions, the truck started to move forward ever so slowly. The movement made me grip the wheel even tighter, but I didn't stab the brake pedal the way I wanted to. The forward momentum continued but the rough ground made it slow going. For me, the snail's pace was fine. There was no one here to laugh or make fun of me. There was only me and I was determined to get to the Cottage.

Suddenly, I laughed aloud. The sound surprised me so much, I almost steered off to the right. I touched the brake and the truck slowed to a stop. I put my forehead on the wheel and started laughing.

After a few minutes, I raised my head and wiped the nervous tears from my cheeks. Why? I was not only driving, but Miss City-Girl was driving a big ole pickup truck. My friends from elementary school all the way up to 12th grade would be awe-struck to see me now. I was always the one with the frilly dresses. Jeans were never my go-to outfit. I always wore my blonde hair styled, from little-girl braids platted with ribbons to match my outfit to long tresses worn down my back in luxurious waves or pinned up in a variety of ways.

A lot of things about me had changed in the past year, starting with my hairstyle. It was shorter now, just above my shoulders with wispy bangs across my forehead. I was learning I didn't have to be in control all the time. I was no longer responsible for everything. I could follow flights of fancy, like exploring the attic at Waterwood House, the shelves of its fine library, or researching the contents of the old trunk that once belonged to its mistress... or corresponding with ghosts.

Yes, I thought as I pulled up to the Cottage and parked the truck, *a lot of things had changed.*

Chapter Fourteen

"It seems dangerous to be a portrait artist who does commissions for clients because everyone wants to be flattered, so they pose in such a way that there's nothing left of truth."

— *Henri Cartier-Bresson, French Photographer*

After I got home and had a bite to eat, I stretched out on the sofa for a quick nap. All the stress of being behind the steering wheel again had sapped my energy. I woke up an hour later, feeling refreshed but unsettled.

Something was bugging me about that point of land TJ wanted to reclaim. It was more than the stories about the two witches. I pulled out all my notes from my visits with Charles, the reference librarian in the Maryland Room. While sifting through the papers, I found something interesting.

There was a story about two brothers who were led by a ghostly apparition to a place on Waterwood land. There, they learned a treasure was buried. In that eerie time between dark and dawn, the brothers returned with shovels and began to dig. They dug deep until a shovel struck something hard. They cleared it by hand and found an old chest. When they forced the lid open, rays of the morning sun glinted off gold pieces and fine silver. As they climbed out of the pit to talk about how to raise the chest, the younger brother went mad with lust for the treasure. He wanted it all for himself. He knew he wouldn't inherit land and was fixed on the dream of living in a big city like New York. The treasure would set him up as a gentleman and give him a ticket into high society. But he would have to share it with his brother who was already in line to inherit the family wealth. Maddened by these thoughts, he picked up his shovel and swung it at his brother. In a shower of blood from the head wound, his brother fell to the ground, dead. The shock of what he'd done caused the young man to drop to his knees and embrace his brother one last time. Then he rolled the body into the pit, filled it in, and made his way home. He never spoke of those events until the last moments on his deathbed when he was an old man. He had stayed on the Eastern Shore and inherited the property after his brother's mysterious disappearance. He had told his parents the older brother dreamed of leaving the Shore and going to New York. The lie was fueled by his own dreams.

The story filled my head as I went out to my patio overlooking the creek to get some air. It probably wasn't the best place to come to think about a search for something of historical interest. The memory of the mild-mannered professor who had lost his life here and the anxiety and sadness his murder caused were still fresh in my mind. I gave myself a mental shake. That situation had been resolved. It was time to deal with the search for the treasure.

Could the story of the two brothers be true? If so, it would be another tragic instance dating back to the Book of Genesis and Cain and Abel in the Bible. If the story of the brothers was true, the chest was still hidden on Waterwood land with a body buried on top of it. Had they found the same chest Benjamin and Daniel buried before they left to deliver supplies to the Confederacy? It was a morbid idea, but there was a body in an unmarked grave. Could it be...?

I rushed back inside and pulled out my notes from Daniel's letter. Then I took down the framed map of Waterwood land from its hook in the living room and carried it back to the dining room and put it on the table. After discovering the reason the Cottage property was once carved out of the Waterwood Plantation in Emma's time, TJ had a copy made and framed it showing the position of the Cottage. Would it reveal yet another secret of Waterwood?

I found my notes detailing Daniel's directions. They began at the Lone Oak then he said to look to the dawn and walk, counting out the day of Emma's birth. Then he said to turn toward the place they loved to play in the mud across the water.

Across the water.

Yes, I think it might be possible Daniel was describing the property now known as the Point. Was the unknown body in an unmarked grave buried atop the chest?

Sharp knocking at the door made me jump. TJ? Perfect timing! I raced to the door and pulled him inside. I led him into the dining room while my words tumbled out.

We were standing over the map and letter laid out on the table when I finished and asked, "What do you think?"

He responded with a slight shake of his head. He was confused, rather than excited.

Maybe I wasn't clear, so I took him through my rationale again. "And now, with the discovery of the body, it just might mean—"

I looked at his face, wanting him to agree. Instead, I saw

dark circles under his eyes. His shoulders were slumped. He was rubbing his temple as if he had a headache. The importance of finding the chest evaporated. The true treasure was standing next to me, and the man was exhausted. "Didn't you sleep last night?"

He answered in a raspy voice. "I haven't really slept since I got those crazy soil readings. All I wanted was to put a few more acres into cultivation. Now, I have this situation with people walking all over my field, cops asking questions, and an unknown man decomposing under my land. It's the stuff of nightmares."

I reached out and touched his arm. "It's going to be alright. You're going to get your acres and..." I put a big smile on my face. "you may have a big influx of money if he's lying on top of that treasure chest. If that's the case, we can leak the story that one of the reporter's mysteries has been solved. You talked to her already, right? It should be easy—"

"I don't want to talk about her," he snapped. "I'm tired of talking about all this."

I felt relieved that his anger at the reporter had cooled. "Okay, but maybe we should go back to the site and tell them not to fill in the hole after they... you know. It will make it easier to see if the chest is—"

"Not today. They were packing up. Working half-day, I guess. Dr. Bergstrom said they'll finish up tomorrow. Can't be soon enough for me."

After he left, I rehung the framed map on the wall. I had to admit I was disappointed. The excitement of possibly finding the treasure was thrilling. Now, I too felt drained.

I flopped into a chair, disheartened. A little voice echoed in my mind. I was being unfair. TJ was coming into his busy season. He had a lot on his mind. He had his own fields to manage along with those of other farmers who relied on him, depended on him. The responsibility put a lot of pressure on him. Plus, he was concerned about climate change and how it was affecting farmers. Not some place on the other side of the world. Right here on the Maryland Eastern Shore. Considering everything, it was no surprise he had little enthusiasm for my pie-in-the-sky idea about a treasure chest.

With that settled, another thought was able to creep into my mind. True, all those considerations and pressures were enough to distract TJ. Or was there something else weighing on his mind?

Don't be ridiculous! He wasn't angry at the reporter anymore. The missing reporter. Was he? Why? What had changed?

I flew out of my chair as if escaping from those terrible thoughts. I needed to do something to support TJ rather than sit, feeling dejected... and suspicious.

I moved over to my computer and began a search for the effects of climate change and sea level rise on farmers. There was an avalanche of material, including things TJ had already pointed out. One thing caught my eye, a report about an upcoming vote in our county commission. If approved, local government could go after grants that required some matching funds. If not, our county was almost on its own. From my days teaching, I knew just enough about the vagaries of funding for specific needs to get myself into trouble. I needed to know more.

The reports and posts laid out positions, pro and con. An editorial written by Nelson, the owner of the newspaper, raised questions about the proposal and called for more study and discussion. His position surprised me because he owned a farm along the shoreline.

I was starting to get a headache. A person could drown in all this political rhetoric and posturing. I think Charles once said Maryland should have been split into two different states, not a big one. The culture and economics of the land west of the Chesapeake Bay were dramatically different from the communities on the Eastern Shore. That difference was obvious today in the 21st century. The First Congressional district of Maryland was bright red politically while the rest of the state was deep blue. Was that why the Eastern Shore came up short time and again when political considerations were addressed? People said the office of the Republican congressman for the Shore tended to ignore constituents who lived in counties considered purple.

My head was pounding. I closed my search and went to find some aspirin.

Fortified with a pain reliever and a chocolate chip cookie, I was eager to know if Emma had responded to my letter about the unknown man-in-the-field. Going to the cabin in the dark wasn't the smartest thing to do—too many things to trip over—but I knew I wouldn't sleep if I waited until morning.

I pulled on a jacket against the evening chill and grabbed Uncle Jack's giant flashlight. It was easier going down the path than I expected. Maybe I was becoming familiar with its turns and half-buried rocks threatening to turn my ankle if I put my foot wrong. Juggling the flashlight, I finally got the door unlocked and opened. In the strong beam of white light aimed at the desk, I saw a sheet of paper with beautiful Copperplate handwriting waiting for me on the desktop. Reaching for it, I was mystified by Emma's response. Not the words themselves, but the length of her letter. It was only a few lines. Never before had one of her letters been so short.

I forced myself to wait until I'd locked the cabin and returned to the Cottage where I could capture it in a photograph before the writing disappeared. After confirming the contents appeared clearly in the electronic record, I sat down to read Emma's words.

Beyond Waterwood

Emma,
I should be gratified to hear Waterwood is expanding
its cultivation, but not at Witch's Point. Disturbing that
poor soul you found would endanger Waterwood and me.
It would be best to leave things as they are, forgotten.

Emma

Rather than answers leading to a pleasant night's sleep, I tossed and turned with questions until dawn. As I watched the sunrise, her short response kept turning over in my mind. She was familiar with The Point, known as Witch's Point to her, which wasn't surprising. She had spent her life on Waterwood Plantation. Had the unknown man threatened Joshua in some way? If Emma had lost her husband, would the social convention allow her to retain ownership of the land? Would she have been allowed to continue to run the plantation? If so, I was sure she would sustain her family. She wanted me to leave the man undisturbed, but I needed to know how he threatened Waterwood and Emma.

I was tempted to run back to the cabin to write another letter, asking her these questions, but I paused. The short length of her response concerned me. Normally, her letters were filled with enthusiasm and information. Not this time. Had I offended her in some way? TJ's warning about upsetting a ghost came to mind and the retaliation and havoc I was tempting by continuing my correspondence with Emma. She had always seemed to welcome my letters and inquiries... until now.

Then I had a thought. Maybe if I changed the subject, we would return to our friendly communication. I could mention the man-in-the-field at another time... I would have to do it now, so I'd be ready for the trip to St. Michaels with TJ.

Chapter Fifteen

*The milkshake was first designed to have a good effect on a person's mood. When the term was first used in print in 1885, it described a "sturdy, healthful eggnog type of drink, with eggs, **whiskey**, etc., served as a tonic as well as a treat.*

I sat at the plantation desk in the cabin, placed a sheet of paper on the writing surface and uncapped my fountain pen.

The Cottage

My Dear Emma,
    I shall take your advice about the Point to heart. Thank you for helping me avoid a mistake.
    May I tell you about an ongoing situation here at Waterwood? It involves the treasure chest your father buried before he traveled South with Daniel to deliver supplies to the Confederacy.
    Over the centuries, the rumor of such a chest has

grown into local folklore. There are continuing conversations and debates about its possible existence, its possible location on Waterwood land, and speculation about its contents.

People have not changed when it comes to fortune-hunting.

Much time has passed since you joined Daniel...

Was that the best way to refer to the fact she was not part of this world anymore? I had never said anything about death or dying or asked questions about her present existence that allowed her to communicate with me. I reread what I had written and decided to continue.

There is truly no way to tell if you ever retrieved the chest, if some energetic treasure hunter found it, or if it still lies buried here at Waterwood.

The subject was raised again by the local newspaper. TJ is afraid strangers will once again swarm over the property, hoping to get rich. It is a continuing concern for the man. His commitment to protect and preserve Waterwood flows in the veins of your family.

Can you offer any guidance? Please know, this man is someone who deserves your trust and admiration. In my humble opinion, Waterwood is in good hands.

Affectionately,
Emma

I left my letter in the center of the desk's writing surface, returned to the Cottage to change, and was ready just as TJ drove up in his truck. We were off to St. Michaels for a few things, nothing urgent. Our trip was more of a distraction from what was happening in the field and the story developing around the missing reporter who had stirred up things about the treasure. Yesterday, when TJ said he had to go to the hardware store for a few things, I was surprised. Wouldn't he want to be at the excavation of the grave, to remind the forensic team to work faster? Maybe the change of scenery would do us both some good, so I invited myself along to pick up a few things for myself.

After we finished our errands, I suggested we stop at the Cove for one of its famous milkshakes. Ice cream always improved my mood. I hoped it would do the same for him.

"It's too early for ice cream," he insisted.

"It's never too early or too late for ice cream. It's a great way to celebrate."

"Celebrate?"

"Yes, the forensic team is getting ready to leave, remember?" I flashed him a smile.

"You're right. It's a big relief. I can get back to what I should have been doing all along."

"Milkshakes it is! Besides, they're a good source of vitamins and calcium." I flashed him an even bigger grin.

He gave me a long look. "I'm not going to win this debate, am I?"

I shook my head. "And if you did, you'd have to deal with a pouty me all the way home."

He looked to the sky. "Saints preserve me. I see the wisdom here for self-preservation." He touched my arm and steered me in the direction of the local drug store.

We worked our way past shelves of pain relievers, cologne, jewelry, novelty gifts, and haircolor until we reached an area at the back of the store. We stepped into that space and right into a 1950-style soda fountain that time forgot. We slipped onto two swivel seats at the worn, but clean counter. The footrest was scuffed by generations of shoes. It was the unofficial heart of St. Michaels. We ordered our milkshakes, vanilla for him, chocolate for me, of course.

Two of TJ's buddies, good ole boys in jeans and tee shirts, came over to where we were sitting at the counter. The one I recognized named Jerry playfully clamped TJ on the back the way guys do. "Hey, Big Guy, are you going to remember your friends when you're famous?"

"Famous? What are you talking about?" TJ's deep frown was back.

His friend laughed heartedly. "Oh, now you're being modest." He peered at TJ and screwed up his face. "It doesn't suit you. I've known you too long."

"No, I'm not kidding. I don't know what you're talking about."

TJ's other friend, shorter and rounder, spoke up. "You mean you didn't see the article in the paper?"

"Oh, that." TJ sagged and took a sip of his milkshake.

"It was quite a write-up and on the front page." Jerry put the palm of his hand on his chest. "I am impressed."

TJ grumbled. "Yeah, well, I'm not."

"Ah, there you go being modest again," Jerry said.

TJ jerked up straight as if he was going to get in the guy's face. "It's not funny, having strangers crawling around my property. They have no respect for privacy or property. It was the police investigation into the murder at Lone Oak that started this whole problem."

TJ's rounder friend said gently. "Hey man, we're just razzing you. People are curious, that's all. Ya add the possibility of treasure, well, everybody wants an easy payday. What did you expect?"

"I didn't expect people to trespass and steal. Things disappeared when the news of the murder broke. With the case back on the front page, people are gonna come out of the woodwork again looking for 'treasure.'" TJ made air quotes around the word. "Do you know that Emma here is locking the Cottage now? She even told me I have to lock the door to Waterwood House. That's hasn't happened since I don't know when. You try having your place invaded. It's a violation. And I have that reporter to thank for stirring it all up again."

His friend took a step back from TJ and put his hands in his pockets. "Well, I don't think you're gonna have to worry about the reporter."

"Why?"

"Haven't you heard?" asked Jerry. "She is missing. Guess your little meeting with her at the paper scared her away. Good job!" The two men laughed.

TJ sat up straight. "I never saw her. And how do you know about this anyway?"

Jerry acted surprised and defensive at TJ's reaction. "Man, everybody knows about it. Mild-mannered, always-in-control TJ losing it in a newsroom.

"You made news ... in a newsroom." The round one added as if it was a big joke. His loud laughter got the attention of the other people in the Cove.

Jerry leaned down and lowered his voice. "TJ, you didn't do something dumb, did you?" He gave TJ a playful punch on the arm. "Naw, you're too smart. Maybe you just scared her away."

Nelson, the newspaper editor, appeared, put his arm around TJ's shoulder, and spoke to the guys. "Come on, TJ wouldn't do anything threatening. He wouldn't harm *my reporter,* right TJ?" He took a step away and waved his hand as if to shoo away the friends. "Enough of this." His pronunciation of the word *this* was very wet causing us all to lean away from him a bit. "You've had your fun. We've all got places to be."

In a chorus of good-byes, Nelson was left standing next to

TJ. "Don't you listen to them. They don't know what they're talking about. I figure I know you better. We've been neighbors for years. I remember when you were so high." He held his hand about three feet above the floor. "Just a boy. You used to come help your uncle with the farm." He chuckled. "Your uncle wasn't sure if you were helping or making more work for him. You sure liked riding on the tractor. Remember how you used to boast you'd drive the tractor one day and be the best tractor driver on the Shore? You used to look at my land next door and say you'd tractor those acres, too. My acres." He laughed, but somehow it didn't sound sincere. "You were a handful, but it was fun watching you grow up. I know you'd never do anything to hurt someone on purpose. You're a good man, TJ." Nelson looked at me. "Sorry to intrude." And he walked away.

The man was slick. There was something about him... TJ asked for our milkshakes to be put in cups to go and he hustled me out of the little restaurant. He wasn't smiling. All the way back to Waterwood, he drummed his fingers on the steering wheel in silence.

When we turned off the road to our driveway, he broke the silence. "I'll drop you off at the Cottage then I have to get out to the Point. I hope those guys are done. I have work to do and it sure would be nice to get back to normal."

I piped up. "Can I go with you? I've been in on this since the beginning. I'd like to see how it ends."

He was quiet but didn't take the turn off for the Cottage.

Relieved, I said, "And you don't have to bring me back. I know the way now and I can walk back to the Cottage."

Still no response as we bounced over the rough farm road to the field. When we emerged from the treeline, it was obvious the investigation team wasn't done. Vehicles—several signature dark blue police cars of St. Michaels and the forensic anthropologist's van were still parked around the excavation site. At least, the crime scene tape was gone.

TJ noticed it, too. "That's got to be a good sign." He stopped, threw the truck into park, and slid out of the driver's seat. He opened the back door with a flourish. "Come on, boy! The tape is down. You can come this time."

Ghost bounded out of the back seat with a giant leap and romped around TJ as they walked toward the gathering of law enforcement and scientific experts. There was a spring in TJ's step, too. This ugly affair was coming to an end.

I hustled out of the truck to join my friend and his dog. It would be the last happy moment I'd have for a while.

Chapter Sixteen

"Anthropology demands the open-mindedness with which one must look and listen, record in astonishment and wonder that which one would not have been able to guess."

— Margaret Mead, American Cultural Anthropologist

We walked toward the excavation where a group had gathered. Everyone was listening while Dr. Bergstrom, the forensic anthropologist, was summarizing his findings again. I inched closer to get a better look at the skeleton of the man who had been hidden away in Waterwood land for a very long time, only to be disappointed. The hole was empty. While we were having milkshakes in St. Michaels, they must have removed the remains to do more tests in their Baltimore lab facilities.

Disappointed, yes, but also a little relieved. These experts with all their education, training, and technical expertise, had my respect. I could never do their jobs. I was much happier surrounded by little people who were eager to try new things in the classroom and concoct complicated games on the playground. I crossed my arms and focused my attention on the good doctor, hoping I'd understand at least some of his comments about the project.

"We've sifted the soil underneath the specimen and the additional time and effort paid off." He turned to TJ. "Mr. Dorset, we found this." Dr. Bergstrom, the short man keenly intent on his subject, stood by the open grave holding up a plastic evidence bag that swung in the light breeze."

"Sorry, Doc," TJ called out. "Can't see what it is from here."

"Based on the little bit of research my assistant did using his phone... you know, you really should see about getting better cell phone reception out here."

"Yes, we know." A little irritation crept into TJ's voice at yet another delay in their forensic team's departure. "What did you find?"

"It appears to be a monogramed cufflink. The intertwined initials *GM* in gold look like they're embedded on lapis lazuli. Expensive. I feel even more confident this man was well-to-do. The initials match those engraved on the pocket watch."

He moved to return the bag to the collection of artifacts taken from the grave when I stopped him. "Would you mind holding up the cufflink so I can take a quick picture?" I whipped out my phone to make it harder for him to say no and took the shot. "Perfect. Thank you so much. Did you find the matching cufflink?"

Dr. Bergstrom frowned. "I'm afraid not. Oh, this excavation has revealed another interesting fact." The doctor grinned. "It seems one of my assistants is an amateur horologist. That is to your advantage."

TJ kicked at the dirt a little, showing his impatience. "Excuse me, sir. I didn't get that. A hor... what?"

"A horologist. A person who is knowledgeable about the construction and manufacture of watches and such. Under supervision last night, he succeeded in opening the man's pocket watch. It was really quite simple. I was surprised he was –"

"Excuse me again, sir. This is important because...?"

The doctor looked puzzled as his eyes flicked from TJ to me and back again. "I thought there was some interest in trying to identify this poor soul."

TJ closed his eyes and sighed. "There is, doctor. What did you find?"

"An inscription. It is still a bit difficult to make out. Cleaning should help make it readable," the doctor said. "The curious part is *if* this is his watch and *if* the inscription was meant for him, his name was Gideon. It seems to have been a gift from Mary."

"Gideon..." I mumbled, thinking how the man now a skeleton was becoming more real to me now that he might have a name. And he had been important to a woman named Mary.

The doctor directed his crew to finish packing up their equipment. Thinking that was all there was to report, our little group broke up. TJ headed toward his truck. I was about to follow when the doctor waved me over to the bin holding evidence bags.

"Oh, there is one more thing." He took out another evidence bag. "We also found this yesterday. I was eager to open it, so I processed it last night." The doctor held out the bag in his fingers gnarled with arthritis probably from all the time spent in nature's elements, digging in the dirt. "I was pleasantly surprised at its condition.

Confused, I looked at the rectangular item about two by three inches in size. "I'm sorry, Doctor. What is it?"

He chuckled. "I am the one who should be sorry. You are so eager for information about these historical finds, I forget you are not a trained historian." He offered me a pair of plastic gloves. "I documented it last night. You can go ahead and take it out of the bag. I want to see your expression when you open it."

I put on the gloves and removed the curious case. I still had no clue what it was.

"When it was new," he described, "the outside was probably covered with burgundy velvet, typical of the mid-19th century. Of course, the fabric didn't survive, but the metal case did. I read about a similar piece found on a Civil War battlefield by an enthusiast with a metal detector. This one is quite interesting and an excellent specimen."

I turned the case over and over, lost in my confusion. "I'm sorry, Doctor. What is this?"

"Oh!" He pointed as he gave me instructions. "Run your finger along the edge."

"There is a little bump here in the center."

"That's right," he said with satisfaction. "Hold on to the case and gently press that bump."

I did and felt the top move slightly as if released. The doctor urged me to open the case carefully. Inside, there was some kind of etching on the right of two people and a woman with a child on the left.

"They are tintypes, I believe. Photographic negatives were printed on tin plates, then varnished, very popular in the 1860s. To our benefit, a tintype is remarkably durable. The lady in this image is wearing an off-the-shoulders gown favored by Southern belles and wealthy women during the Civil War era. That is probably her young son in the other picture with his head on her knee."

"Could the man standing behind her chair be..." I glanced at the open hole where the skeleton had lain for more than a century.

"It's entirely possible." He extended his hand to block the sun from reaching the historic photographs. "Why don't you take the case somewhere out of the light and wind? Then you can begin your investigation."

I gently closed the case and heard the soft click of the lock. I fought the urge to sprint back to the Cottage to closely examine the photographic evidence he'd found. "I will and thank you."

My excitement was met by a deep sigh from Dr. Bergstrom. "I wish we had more time here. This find is fascinating. There are still so many questions. Was this man named Gideon or a thief who took his watch? I feel fairly confident he died during the early days of the Civil War. What was he doing here so far away from the action? Was he related to a family that owned one of the local plantations? He might have been a spy. There is so much we don't know." The doctor pointed at the cufflink encased in a plastic bag. "There are clues to follow, but I don't have time to wander down those corridors into the past." He sighed again. "At least I think we've found all there is to find in his unmarked grave."

I almost smiled at the scientist being ever so careful not to declare something he couldn't prove. I was more of a romantic who was eager to move the investigation forward. "But that cufflink and the watch inscription might help uncover his identity." I said.

He turned his head toward the empty grave and sighed. "We don't do that kind of work, especially when the skeleton is more than 150 years old. We don't have the time or the budget—"

I quickly interrupted. "What if someone else wanted to try

and follow those clues? Someone loosely connected with this land. Someone willing to share the adventure with you?" I tried to make the idea as enticing as I could.

The doctor looked at me, his head cocked to the side, his eyes narrowing. "You are the one who wants the DNA sample." It was a declaration, not a question.

I spoke up quickly. "Yes. I've been researching some of the history of the Waterwood Plantation. Identifying this man might unlock another piece of Waterwood's history. I think it would be worth my time."

The doctor looked back at the empty hole and then turned his eyes on me again. "You realize what you want to do is not easy."

"I figure it requires part science, part patience, and a lot of luck. I'm game to try."

He pressed his lips together, considering, then said, "There is a possibility the bone marrow is viable for a DNA sample." He inspected my face again then his eyebrows relaxed. Having made a decision, he said, "Everyone deserves an identity. If Mr. TJ is agreeable to your investigation, I will do what I can to help."

"Absolutely, he is very supportive of everything as long as it doesn't interfere with his farming operations."

"Good." He dipped his head to acknowledge the possibility. "Then I wish you good luck. Here is my card. Send me your contact information and we'll move forward."

I wanted to respond by yelling YES! but I politely accepted the card, saying. "I will be in touch."

Dr. Bergstrom wasn't done. "There is one more thing." I tensed. "I forgot to bring it up with him."

"I can call him if you'd like."

"Yes, that would be helpful."

I hit speed dial, told TJ the doctor had a question, and

handed the phone over, but not before I turned on the speaker. Sneaky, I knew.

"What else can I do for you, Doctor?" The strain in TJ voice was evident.

"I'm afraid we are leaving you with a rather substantial hole, sir. Do you want—"

"Doctor, I would be more than happy to take care of it. I have the equipment to dig holes and fill 'em in. Do it all the time."

"You're sure it's not—" the doctor began.

"Not a bother at all."

The doctor took a deep breath in relief. "Good, thank you." He handed me the phone.

As the team from Baltimore finished packing up and safe-guarding their equipment and materials, I wanted to skip as I navigated the uneven field toward TJ's truck. He was focused on a large sheet of paper spread over the hood. As I got close, I recognized a drawing of the fields in the vicinity of the Point.

"Back to work?"

"Yes," he said. "I dug out these drawings from the files last night. They're out of date, but it gives me a good overview so I can plan for this new crop area." He moved away from the hood, folded his arms, and spoke softly out of the corner of his mouth. "You know, you've really done it now. What did you promise to do?"

"What?"

"Emma? I know you."

"Okay, I told the doctor I would try to put a name to the man you found. He said he would help. That's all."

"You've set yourself up to do a complicated investigation that will probably be impossible."

"Do you have a problem with me trying?"

"No, I just don't want you to be disappointed."

"I appreciate your concern, but I don't mind. "There are some clues to follow and there might be some DNA evidence. The experience alone might help me in following up the search for Emma's baby.

His mouth dropped open in surprise. "The baby Joshua sold? You're still thinking about her?"

"Emma never forgot."

"Yes, but—"

"It is a big unanswered question hanging over your family. Come on, TJ, wouldn't you like to know if there is someone else walking around with a connection to Waterwood and your family?"

Before he could answer, we were both distracted by the forensic crew's vehicles starting up. I could see the excitement grow on TJ's face as he yelled out, Finally! Things at Waterwood were about to get back to normal. He would be left to his fields and farm work, his true source of happiness. As long as I didn't distract him, he would be content to let me play with the pieces of the puzzle.

Soon, their vehicles bounced over the weedy field, followed by police officers. Nelson, the newspaper editor, stood with his hands on his hips, feet spread apart, taking in deep breaths and loving the view while his photographer caught a few last shots of the empty grave. With satisfaction, TJ watched Nelson head to his car.

"Good! They can go bother somebody else now." He clapped his hands and Ghost sat at his feet. "Okay, Ghost." TJ gave his dog a vigorous rubdown along his back. "Looks like we're back in business." The dog barked as if he understood. Free again to romp around and catch up on all the good sniffs he'd missed left by the strangers while relegated to TJ's truck.

Then the Chief waved as he walked toward us.

"Now what?" TJ muttered.

"TJ," the Chief said, "I know this has been a big inconvenience, disrupting your schedule and all. You've been very patient, and I appreciate it." He pulled out a white handkerchief and wiped some glistening drops of sweat from the top of his head. "I'm so glad this didn't turn into an active crime scene. This heat is getting to me already and it isn't even summer yet."

"I'm afraid it's only going to get worse with climate change. It's making things hotter not only out here in the fields but in my office. There's so much information coming in about what farmers should be doing, I should be in the office more than on the tractor."

"And we've held you up. Again, I'm sorry about all this, but I'm glad you reported it. Now, you don't have to worry about the man-in-the-field." He looked back at the hole where several of his officers were getting a closer look. "And it's been a good opportunity for them to see a real unmarked grave, instead of relying on other departments' pictures and videos." He chuckled. "Though I hope we don't see another one in our neck of the woods for a real long time."

"Next time, if there is a next time, could you leave the media hounds out of it?" TJ said it as a joke, but I knew he meant it.

The Chief sighed. "It wasn't my idea. Nelson said he needed more pictures for an article—"

"No," moaned TJ. "Not more newspaper coverage."

The Chief put his big hand on TJ's shoulder. "It's okay. He said he'd make sure to include a strong statement about everything at the site being moved to the labs in Baltimore, leaving nothing behind to see."

TJ gave him a pleading look. "Are you sure?"

"Yes, but I'll be sure to remind him."

"Please do." He waved over his shoulder as he walked away.

"You must be used to all this," I said to the Chief. "Everything technology can do. All the questions it can answer." My attention wandered back to the still open hole of the unmarked grave. "It's too bad we don't know who the man was, but Dr. Bergstrom said he might be able to get a good sample of the man's DNA."

The Chief's arms hung loose at his sides. "You know, it's not going to tell you why he ended up here in the field."

"I know, but finding out who he was is the first important step." I didn't tell the Chief how I was going to try and make that happen. I had some research to do. I could head back to the Cottage and get started. Ah, the best plans...

Ghost wandered around, filling his nose with the scents past and present. I watched in fascination as he caught a scent around the hole in Waterwood ground and followed it. Dogs could smell so much more than humans. I envied that ability.

"Ghost!" TJ called out for his dog. "Come on, boy. We're going to work."

It was unusual for Ghost to ignore TJ. Instead of running to him, the dog moved to another patch of ground, and sniffed. He sniffed some more. Then he began to scratch at the dirt.

The photographer wandered to Ghost, his enormous camera bag weighed him down so he walked at an angle. "What did you find there, boy?" The man got closer and ruffed up his fur. "Something's got your attention."

Ghost was doing more than scratching now. He was digging.

"Did you find the famous Waterwood treasure? The photographer knelt down and brushed some dirt away. Then he screamed and fell backward.

We all started running toward the man and the dog. When I reached the spot, I stopped abruptly and almost lost my footing.

In the shallow space were Ghost had been digging, a human face looked up at us. Not a skull. A face, partially obscured by clumps of soil.

"No," the photographer breathed as he scrambled back to the face and gently brushed the dirt away. A wail rose from the short young man, his complicated camera and his camera bag forgotten. "NO! Please," he pleaded. He reached out again.

Running up to the spot, the Chief barked, "Don't touch! Don't touch anything."

The photographer pulled his hand back as if he'd touched a hot stove. He moaned and murmured one word that gave the face a name, Robin.

Robin Hunter, the reporter.

Chapter Seventeen

"What's done is done." —*Latin Proverb*

W hat a terrible thing morbid curiosity is. The right thing to do was to turn away from the sight of the young woman's face lodged in the dirt, but I couldn't shift my eyes. I felt disgusted with myself. I first saw that one side of her dirt-streaked face was obscured by strands of striking platinum blonde hair. That should have been more than enough for me after remembering the professor's dead body on my patio and the discovery of the historian's body leaking blood on her living room rug. Those scenes forever stuck in my mind should have satisfied me, but I was still drawn to what was right in front of me. The Chief stood staring at the woman. Somehow their attention to even minute details in the dirt made it alright for me to look, too.

She was young. Life hadn't had time to leave any footprints on her face—no crow's feet at her eyes, no furrows across her forehead, no lines around her mouth. Death had given her smooth, youthful skin an unnatural gray pastiness. Except for the trickle of dried blood from one corner of her mouth, she appeared to be sleeping. Vulnerable. I felt like I was invading her privacy. But, considering she was dead and buried in TJ's field, there was nothing private about Robin Hunter anymore.

The Chief sighed. "Guess we need the doctor to turn around and come back." Then he looked at TJ with narrowed eyes. "You know anything about this?" There was something in the Chief's tone that set off alarms in my mind.

TJ snapped, "Do you think I had something to do with this?"

"I don't know," the Chief said almost casually. "Did you?"

TJ took a quick step back and snapped. "Are you crazy? No." He took off his hat and smoothed down his hair. "I can't believe you'd ask me that." He sounded defensive, which was only natural, to feel betrayed by a friend.

But the Chief would not be put off. "We'll see." He walked away to make the call to bring Dr. Bergstrom and his team back to Waterwood.

In almost no time, the vehicles carrying the forensic specialists came roaring back to the field, but this time, it was different. They had been called back to this natural place of sun, water, and fertile ground to find someone had planted the body of a young woman here recently. After kicking up a cloud of dust, the team parked far away from the place where we had gathered. The people who only an hour before had been quiet, respectful, and deliberate about what they were doing, tumbled out of their vehicles, pulled on protective gear so they wouldn't contaminate the area, and gathered stakes, tape, and kits to work the crime scene.

"Alright," said the Chief. "Everyone, move back so we can mark off the area." He held his arms out at his sides and walked toward us as if he was herding sheep away from the gruesome discovery. "Back farther please."

I noticed Dr. Bergstrom walk over toward the open pit where the skeleton had lain then he turned in a slow circle. After a few moments of consideration, he walked quickly to the area disturbed by Ghost and knelt down. With gloves on, he touched the face. With a sharp nod of his head to show he had made a decision, he stood up and walked straight up to the Chief. I slowed my steps so I could hear what they were saying.

Dr. Bergstrom began. "I believe this is a new addition."

TJ overheard his comment and roared, "Of course, it is. What do you think I'm running here, a cemetery of unmarked graves?" TJ was almost panting. These unsettling events were violations to Waterwood land.

Dr. Bergstrom added, "I believe our presence at the unmarked grave may have masked evidence connected to this new discovery."

"You mean," TJ gulped. "She was here all along?"

"I don't believe so. Since it had been our intent to leave late yesterday, the person responsible might have deposited this body last night, believing it would go unnoticed. With our forensic work done here, there would be no reason to examine this area again. " He turned and pointed. "I believe we should extend the crime scene beyond the normal perimeters."

"Yes, sir. I'll move the people back. My officers are on their way to help," the Chief said.

"Have them park beyond the treeline so their vehicles do not further confuse the scene. My people will set up the tape if it is acceptable to you." But the doctor's tone was clear. His polite comment was only for show. He would preserve what he could. Without waiting for a response, he went to examine the body that awaited his attention. His footsteps were deliberate, showing his resolve to find out why the young woman was dead and who had put her here.

We went back to TJ's truck. Ghost was returned to the interior of the cab. We waited in silence, watching as new crime scene tape cordoned off the area again. But this time was different. The area where TJ found the skeleton had been committed a long time ago. A cold shudder ran through my body. This was now an active crime scene. The beginning of the investigation into the murder of a young woman who just the other day had tried to sneak a look at this place. This discovery was too close to our reality.

Things happened as if in slow motion. Assumptions, emotions, and speculation came with irritating slowness like the drips from a leaky faucet. The victim had probably lost her life in the last 24 to 36 hours. Her absence was noticed when she had failed to report to her job. People here at the site knew her. Nelson Jennings got out of his car and waited by the door, staring up at the sky then off in the direction of the water, like he was avoiding the reality of where the forensic team was working and why. The young photographer stood just outside the newly placed crime tape. His camera forgotten, he stared at the experts working at the place of discovery, tears leaving salt track on his face. I had to look away. His grief was contagious.

The Chief continued to walk us away from the immediate area. His steps were slow, deliberate. He concentrated his attention on the ground, not the people. Was he taking a minute to make sense of this ironic situation? Dealing with a skeleton in an unmarked grave dating back more than a century and a half was one thing. Fascinating. Instructive. With no emotional entanglements. The body of a young woman, alive in this place only hours ago, was something different.

The Chief began with a deep sigh. "As you can see, the forensic team is at work..." He didn't refer to the body or the identity of the woman. "I talked to our homicide detective, and he is on the way."

"Do you mean Craig?" I asked, hoping the man I'd worked with in the past and TJ's old friend would be assigned to the case. He was always dedicated to finding the truth with little drama. I felt confident the whole situation would be resolved quickly. And I realized with a shudder, speed was important to me. The body was found on Waterwood land. The killer must have driven right past the short driveway to my Cottage on the way to this burial place. Had the killer done the deed someplace else and brought the body here? Or had the murder happened here in the field? This crime was too close to home, my home. Again. The reality was unnerving, almost making me want to run away. But the only place I would want to run to was the Cottage.

"So, it is murder?" a man called out from the edge of our group. We all looked to see Nelson rocking from one foot to the other. He swung his attention over to TJ and his gray eyes turned dark. "She is on your land, did something happen between the two of you?"

I gasped. This was the man who had defended TJ to his friends at the Cove. He had known TJ since he was a boy.

"Now, Nelson..." the Chief began.

"I'm sorry. I'm just so..." He took a deep breath. "Forgive me. Robin ..." He stared at the forensic team working meticulously. "Robin is now the story... that's where we need to focus. Chief, we need to grab a few pictures. This is news, real news for our coverage area. If you don't mind..." He called out to the photographer who was getting his emotions under control. "Cam, it's time to go to work."

"Actually, I do mind," said the Chief. "This will be Detective Craig Mason's scene, but until he gets here, I want everyone to move away from the discovery area, but don't even think of leaving. We'll need statements, everything. Got it?"

Standing tall as his photographer approached, Nelson nodded and promised not to get too close. The he instructed, "Use a long lens, Cam.".

While the newspaper people worked, the Chief asked TJ and me to walk with him. "I have to get statements and contact info. My station is too small to accommodate everyone, and Easton is a long haul from here. Would either of you be willing to let us use..."

"The Cottage is too small," TJ said quickly. "This is Waterwood business. We should go to Waterwood House."

"If it is okay with you, we—"

Nelson, the editor, interrupted from behind the Chief. "You won't arrest TJ, will you? After all, it's not his fault. Just because poor Robin's body was found on...buried in his soil, doesn't mean he is responsible. We think we know people but don't take TJ in for questioning. He's a good guy."

What is this man doing? Giving the Chief ideas?!

"If you ask me, I don't think any of us should be detained," Nelson concluded.

He was acting a little fidgety. In fact, we all were. If the Chief gave us the option to leave, we would all run to our vehicles and drive away. Discovery of a skeleton was one thing. Uncovering a body was something else.

The Chief held up his index finger. "I'm *asking* for everyone to stay a little longer. It could be someone saw something yesterday or even this morning that might have a bearing on this new case."

"You sure it is murder?" The photographer choked on the last word while gripping his camera close to his chest.

The Chief reset his feet on the fertile farm soil and stuck his thumbs in his wide black belt. "Well, I can't say for sure, but this situation isn't normal. A young woman dies and is buried on private property. She didn't do this herself. No, this isn't normal at all. It is very possible this is murder, but we have to address a lot of questions before we can say for sure. I'm asking for your help." He held out his arm to direct us toward police vehicles now parked. "Any information, no matter how trivial, would be helpful. We can wait for the detective at Waterwood House." He noticed no one had moved. "We'll try to get you all on your way as quickly as we can. But if you'd all..." He gestured with his arm again.

It felt strange to be free to move around, but I noticed that several of the Chief's officers were standing around us at a short distance. Clever of the Chief to issue a polite invitation in a way we had to accept.

Chapter Eighteen

"I wanted to be a forensic scientist for a long time. It's like putting the pieces of a puzzle together. Solving mysteries seemed like it would be fun, scary and exciting all at the same time."

— Kristin Kreuk, Actress

Our little group drove to Waterwood House with the officers riding along. Did they suspect one of us was the killer ready to make a run for it? I was relieved when I saw the green kitchen door. At least, this was a place I knew, where life felt normal. The officers corralled us into the huge kitchen and made sure to get our contact information and statements about what we'd seen. We were asked to wait until the homicide detective arrived.

TJ took Ghost to a far corner, away from the distraught humans, and crouched down to reassure the dog. I followed TJ's lead and separated myself from the group. There was something comforting about being in Waterwood's kitchen even though it was the scene of a horrendous experience with a gun waving around and an order given to shoot. The high, broad windows let the sun's rays dance around the large room that had once accommodated a substantial kitchen staff made up of slaves supervised by the housekeeper and cook. TJ had refinished a long wooden table now standing in front of the huge brick fireplace where kettles had once bubbled, and bread had once baked in a brick oven. When the modern kitchen stove and microwave were installed, the fireplace only served as a delightful source of heat.

In the center of a heavy mantel shelf hung above the fireplace, a simple clock with a large plain face had reminded the staff of the time as they worked. Medium-sized brown ceramic jugs huddled at one end, now kept there for show and ambiance. A valued china teapot with hand-painted red roses sat safely near the clock, maybe it was a valued possession of a long-departed housekeeper.

A couple of old framed pictures leaned against the brick wall of the chimney. On closer inspection, they looked like they had been cut out of a Godey's magazine popular in Emma's time. I remembered the illustration of the gown she wore for her wedding to Joshua. Looking around the kitchen now occupied by a growing number of people, I wondered if it had ever been the site of a police investigation or worse, a murder. I hadn't come across an entry about a police inquiry in any of Emma's diaries, but some of them were ruined by the roof leak of rain water.

Soon, the Chief walked into the historic kitchen and motioned for us to gather around the heavy oak table. TJ ordered Ghost to stay in his bed and we rejoined the group.

The Chief's eyes were downcast, as if looking at us would make it difficult to manage his emotions. "The body found in the field today is believed to be a homicide victim. Dr.

Bergstrom has done a very preliminary examination. A crime scene team is on its way."

"Can't his team..." I began.

"No, he tells me they are trained to deal with old remains. The people who are on their way know how to do a modern murder investigation and preserve evidence for a trial." The Chief rubbed his forehead, his hand shaking a little. "The body has been unofficially identified as Robin Hunter."

His words caused a low gasp. The information wasn't unexpected but hearing it from the Chief made it all too real. There was no more room for speculation or hope.

"This is my fault," Nelson announced for all to hear. "Robin didn't belong at my newspaper. She should have started at a paper in one of the big markets. I told her when she came for an interview." Pain filled his every word.

Ever alert for information, the Chief stood on the original stone floor worn smooth by decades of feet. "Let me get this straight. She applied for a job, and you called her to come for an interview with no intention of hiring her?"

"Not exactly. She sent me an email saying she would be in the area the next day and asked if she could drop by the paper. I didn't see any harm. Young people are always looking for career advice. She turned it into an interview. I told her to start her career somewhere else. There were great opportunities waiting for her on the Western Shore, but she was adamant. I remember it even though it was about 18 months ago. She was so sure this was the place for her. It was close enough to Washington, Baltimore, and Philadelphia for big-city access, but small enough to do every kind of reporting. She wouldn't be pigeonholed here, doing one job. She wanted to cut her teeth here. Learn here. The way she did at college."

The Chief's brows came together as he listened carefully. "What do you mean?"

"She went to a small school, so she didn't get lost in the crush of students, had teachers who had time for her. It was a place where she could learn from her mistakes." He shook his head slowly. "She was eager to make her mark. That's probably what got her killed. She made a mistake she couldn't recover from."

The Chief's dark eyebrows came together as he stared at Nelson. "Why do you say that? Did she rub someone the wrong way? Catch someone in an illegal act? Discover someone in a compromising situation?"

Nelson shook his head with a chuckle. "No, Chief. Nothing like that. I monitored all the stories she was assigned. If... and I say if she was going into what could be a ticklish situation, I would have gone with her, or gone myself. I would never put any of my people at risk."

"Yet, she is dead." The furrows in the Chief's forehead grew deeper. "Okay, but maybe she was here for another reason? Maybe she was running away from something. Any ideas?"

The editor shrugged. "It could be, but I didn't get that impression at the time. Since she moved here, she has focused on her work, probably a little too much. I encouraged her to take some time off. Not to work such long hours. But she was committed, learning by doing. Racking up experience on her resume." Nelson lowered his eyes, avoiding the Chief's stare. "Okay, if I must confess to something, it's this: I've probably been taking advantage of such a dedicated reporter. It's hard to find someone like her to come to this out-of-the-way place. They want the big city, big stories, and the big bucks."

The Chief stared out the windows, took in a deep breath that filled his cheeks and blew it out slowly. In control again but not completely, he challenged the editor with a question. "You're already thinking about how you're going to replace her, aren't you?" The Chief didn't wait for an answer. He turned to the room and ordered everyone to finish their statements. He looked at his watch, then shot me a look with his eyebrows high on his forehead. I could almost hear his question, *Where is Detective Craig Mason?*

He noticed the photographer standing at the windows, his shoulders slumped with the heavy camera bag still slung over his shoulder, staring at the pastoral scene outside. He headed over to him and signaled me to join him.

"Young man? I'm sorry, your name is..."

The man didn't respond. The Chief and I exchanged glances. Neither of us knew what to say so we waited.

The bag slid slowly off his shoulder to the floor. "It's Robin." He mumbled his question. It was clear something inside him had broken.

"I'm sorry, son. Whoever did this, buried her with her red purse. Her driver's license was in her wallet. Her face and description match the license. We don't believe it was a robbery. Her money and credit cards were still there. I suspect the motive was more sinister."

The grief-stricken young man turned his back to us, too consumed with grief to do more than look at the pine woods and open area where the plantation overseer's house and slave quarters had once stood. Seeing his shaking shoulders betrayed his grief for the young woman, a colleague and probably a friend.

The Chief had once told me he had been in law enforcement for more than thirty years, plenty of time to make him almost immune to the horrible things one person could do to another. Almost. Somehow, he still had a level of compassion. It served him well now. He took a step forward and lowered his voice. "Young man, why don't you tell me your name?"

The photographer complied, but slowly. "My name..." He

stopped to gain control of himself and began again. "Cam, you can call me Cam. That's what Robin called me." He paused for a moment barely hanging on to control. "Everyone does. I'm the paper's news photographer."

"You're very upset, Cam." The Chief stated what was obvious to us all. "Are you alright?"

"Yes, I guess," he said though his voice cracked on the last word. He started to gulp air and tears sprang from his eyes, but he flicked them away before they could flood down his cheeks. "S-she was my friend."

I suspected he wanted to be more than friends with the reporter. Then I began to wonder...did he strike out at her when she rejected him? My suspicious mind was running at a full gallop. I had to stop and listen.

"That's alright, son. Tell me about your friend. Take your time," the Chief encouraged.

After a few moments, the photographer began again. "Okay."

"Did you know her well?" the Chief asked.

He shrugged. "I guess so. Better than most. She has been working really hard since she came more than a year ago. She wants...wanted to be an investigative reporter. That's why she worked alone, but I would go out on her stories if she thought there would be a good photo op. If it was a special event, I'd go along to get pictures of the organizers or the person receiving an award. You know, things like that."

"Those don't sound like stories requiring investigation," the Chief commented.

"They're not, but it's part of the job here. When you work for a small paper, you do a little bit of everything." He took a breath and looked away. "If she was working on an investigation, doing preliminary interviews, what she called fact-finding, she would go alone. I could always follow up later." He interrupted the Chief when he began to ask another question. "One more thing. We often attended public meetings, like the regular county and town meetings. We had a lot of ground to cover, especially the meetings of the commission council. She needed to go so she could keep up on what was happening." He glanced over at the editor-in-chief. "Some people would expect her to do a story by just summarizing what happened, but she always did more. After those meetings, she'd find someone to interview about some aspect of the agenda then we'd go back to the newsroom. She would write her story. I would go through the pictures I'd taken." A small smile touched his mouth, probably from a memory of a happier time. "Together, we'd pick out the shots to go with the story both in print and online."

The Chief frowned. "Why wouldn't you do that alone? You are the photo editor, right?"

He tilted his head to the side. "She liked to watch over my shoulder. She wanted to learn every aspect of the business. She came with a solid foundation—journalism degree and all—but she believed this kind of work she could only learn by doing. That's why she came here to our little paper. Like Nelson said, it was a place where she could make mistakes and learn before she went to a paper in a large market that was less forgiving. That was her goal. She said she had no life outside of work, but it was okay. She liked to say she could have a life later." He squeezed his eyes shut. A single tear escaped down his cheek. "Now..."

The Chief gave him a moment then asked, "Did you see her last night? Did you talk to her?"

The photographer Robin had nicknamed Cam, nodded, then shook his head. "No, it was two nights ago. He looked down at his shoes as he described what had happened. "I was working late prepping some pictures for upcoming articles. I was behind because I'd spent so much time out here at the site. When I'd finished, everyone else had left for the day, everyone but Robin. She was still at her desk in the newsroom."

"Was that unusual?" The Chief wanted to know.

"No, not really. I was often at the paper, working late, too. Sometimes, we'd talk." He turned his gaze toward the horizon, probably reliving one of those newsroom conversations. "She didn't care if she had to stay late. She said she'd come here to work, to learn. I finally found the courage..." He bit his lip. "She looked so beautiful when she was concentrating on something, but there were times when she thought no one was looking, she'd let her guard down. All the joy would drain from her face. That's when she could barely raise her eyes to look at the world."

"What do you think caused it?" the Chief asked.

"I don't know. I would have helped, but she held her feelings deep inside." His shoulders slumped, his head fell forward, and he sobbed. He had given the Chief all he could for now.

Almost overcome with his emotion, my teacher's instincts kicked in. I stepped forward to do what I'd done with so many of my little people, my students, who were crying their hearts out. I put my arm around his shoulders, drew him close, and mumbled some words that I hoped would bring him comfort.

It seemed to be what he needed. He was able to get himself under control and continue. "I went over to her desk and asked if she wanted to get a drink or a burger. I know it sounds lame, but it was hard for me to get up the courage to talk to her if it wasn't about a story. She was so..." He took in a gulp of air. "She smiled at me," he said in a small voice. "She smiled and apologized. She said she had gotten a message setting up a meeting with an important source. She said it could be the big break she wanted, and she was late. She grabbed her notebook and red purse—that was sort of her signature, the red tote. At the door, she said we could get together another time *if I don't have an accident.*"

"An accident?" the Chief said.

"Yeah, she was always afraid of a deer charging across the road running into cars. That's the last time I saw or spoke to her."

The Chief frowned. "Did she say where she was going?"

"She said she had to drive all the way down Route 33," Cam said.

"Do you know who she was meeting?" The Chief pressed.

His eyes dropped as if he was reliving the scene. Then he answered slowly, "She didn't say a name. She never liked to reveal her sources. She said it was the only way to build trust, to build a reputation to protect people who gave her information." Then he added with great excitement, "But she said she was going down toward Waterwood. She thought she might get information on *two* stories."

"Two stories?

"Yeah," Cam said. "There's the one about the hidden treasure supposedly buried on Waterwood land."

TJ huffed at the thought of the treasure bringing people to his place at all hours of the night. The Chief scowled at TJ then asked about the other story.

"I couldn't say exactly, but she said it might be the one to make her career," Cam said.

While we all tried to digest the comments, the editor piped up, "That's a common hope of every new reporter. They want to make their mark." He knitted his eyebrows together. "She said, Waterwood. Are you sure?" Nelson sounded like a reporter sniffing out a story.

"Yes." He looked down at his shoes. "I think so." I felt sorry for this young man who relied on what he saw in photographs, not on his memory for spoken words.

Nelson wasn't done. "And she didn't say who she was meeting?" Cam shook his head. "Was it a man or a woman?" The editor was grilling the young man.

"I don't know." Cam sounded desperate then his face brightened. "Wait! She said he had information. She said *he,* so it must have been a man."

"There are a lot of men down on this part of the peninsula, Cam," the Chief said, taking over the questioning, but the eyes of the editor and the photographer had all shifted to TJ.

Chapter Nineteen

"Dogs are such agreeable friends. They ask no questions, they make no criticisms."

— George Eliot, Novelist and Poet

"Okay, everybody, this is a messy business. I appreciate your cooperation," the Chief announced. "The detective will be here any minute. Just relax for now." When he turned and saw me, he said, "Emma, good. Come, talk to me."

"What about? I don't know anything, Chief. I didn't know the woman. My statement..."

"Emma, I know. But you may be able to add some information to the investigation. Did you hear or see anything last night, maybe something out of the ordinary? Did you overhear a comment someone made while the forensic anthropologist was working on the skeleton in the field?"

I shook my head. "I—"

"You may know something you don't realize you know. Just go along with this exercise. It might yield an important piece of information, because the first thing I have to figure out is *where* she was killed."

"Where?"

"Yes, there wasn't enough blood..." He took a moment and thought about how to phrase it. "Um, in the place she was found. It was a head wound and that bleeds a lot. She wasn't killed there. Think about it and let me know if you come up with something. Anything."

I nodded in agreement and went over to the corner where Ghost was curled up on his bed. He firmly planted his head in the palm of my hand, waiting to be petted. I complied while speaking the thoughts whizzing around in my brain. "You certainly started something, Ghost. But it's a good thing. It would have been awful for that poor woman to lay out there for years, unknown, the way the man had. At least her family will know what happened to her. When Craig figures out who did this and why, they can have closure. It won't make the pain go away, but it might help."

I stroked his long, muscular body and thought about the family of the man buried in the unmarked grave. Dr. Bergstrom's initial estimate put the time of his burial around the mid-1800s. His family was long gone as well. It made me sad to think they lived and died without knowing what had happened to him. I felt certain they would have claimed the body if they had known the truth. Would someone show up from Robin's family to take her home? There wasn't anything I could do to help Robin, but was there something I could do to identify the man?

Ghost lifted his head and started to get up as TJ walked toward us, but when he saw TJ hold up his hand with the palm facing the dog—a signal that meant stay—the dog crouched down, never losing his connection to the man.

"Thanks for staying with him, Emma," TJ said as he knelt

down to stroke the eerily white fur of the Labrador retriever. "He isn't used to having all these people, all these strangers, in his house. There is enough going on without upsetting my dog, too. Can you stay with him while I give my statement? It shouldn't take long."

"It's the best job you could give me." I glanced up at TJ and was a little alarmed by what I saw. Ghost wasn't the only one upset by having these people around. TJ wasn't happy when they were crawling over his field. Now, he watched nervously as they invaded Waterwood House. "After all this is over, maybe we could take a long walk around Waterwood, just you, me, and Ghost to kind of reclaim it. In the meantime, Ghost and I will hang out together."

"Thanks," he said and followed an officer into the dining room to give his statement.

Ghost and I sat together. The dog kept his eye on the doorway where TJ had disappeared. I continued to stroke his fur, watching the humans milling around the kitchen.

Cam came over and knelt down. "Hi, can I pet him?"

"Sure, he likes his ears scratched," I suggested without moving away from Ghost. Remembering what the Chief had said, I decided to see what I might learn from the photographer. "I'm sorry about your friend."

His hand stopped moving and he looked away. "Thanks," he said quietly. "She was a good friend."

"You two met at the paper?" I asked. If he talked about Robin, maybe it would comfort him in some small way. Also, he might remember something, something important.

"Yeah, yes, we did." He paused as his eyes lost focus for a moment, remembering. "Nelson hired her as a reporter, but she didn't know the area, didn't know the people, didn't know the issues. He threw her into the deep end alone without a lifeline."

"Wow! That seems a little extreme."

"Robin had me. Her first assignment was a commission council meeting. I had to go anyway, because the politicians like to see their pictures in the paper. They think it shows they're doing something. That day, someone was giving a major presentation about the sewer designed for a large new housing development."

He must have noticed a confused expression on my face. He continued immediately. "I know, it's not a spicy topic, but if you don't have a working sewer system and you have to—"

I held up my hand. "I get it."

"So did Robin. She knew if the developer didn't get approval, his project was dead. It was a big deal to him, the small town close by, and the people who had put down a deposit on a home before it was built. She understood it was a major deal, but she had no idea who the players were, or the issues involved."

I took a stab. "But she had you."

He nodded slowly, remembering. "The meeting got heated. As soon as it was adjourned, the members fled. They didn't want to talk to the press, to Robin," he corrected. "Fortunately, she had recorded everything and could pull quotes. It was all a matter of public record. We left, picked up some fast food, and headed back to the newsroom. While we inhaled dinner, such as it was, I briefed her on the basics." Suddenly, a bright smile lit up his face.

"What, what is it? Did you remember something?"

"Yeah, I did. As we gathered up the greasy papers from our dinner, she stopped and looked at me. It was the first time I felt the full impact of those blue eyes. I'd never seen eyes like that, except in fashion magazines. The color never looked real, but Robin's was."

I waited to give him time to enjoy the memory. Ghost groaned a little. I'd stopped stoking his tummy.

I got back to my job as Cam picked up his story. "She was embarrassed. She apologized all over the place."

"Why?'

"She had forgotten my name." He huffed a little. "I wish everyone would forget the name my dear parents gave me. Ignatius, Ignatius Sabin. Being good Catholics, they named me after a saint."

Ignatius Sabin, I thought. What an unfortunate name. Didn't parents consider how a name affects a baby trying to navigate his way through life before putting it on a birth certificate?

As if he read my mind, he said, "They thought the saint would make my journey through life easier, but he hasn't. How many people do you know named Ignatius?"

Thankfully, he didn't give me time to come up with an answer.

"Probably none. Do you know the nickname? It's Iggy. IGGY! It didn't take the kids in school long to start calling me Piggy or Icky! No girl in her right mind would spend time with a boy called Icky." He hung his head for a moment in frustration. When he raised it, his eyes were closed, and a smile spread across his mouth. "Not until Robin. She went right to the heart of the matter. She said she wouldn't call me any of those names. She said I needed a name that said something about my creativity, what I did with a camera. Nelson had told her I was a very good photographer, which surprised me. She ran with that and gave me the nickname Cam, for camera. But it could be short for Camden, Cameron..."

"Campbell," I suggested.

"Yeah, you get it. Those are all normal-sounding names. Robin did that for me." Cam bit his lip then said, "I know I'm not much to look at, but finally I had a name other people could accept... without laughing."

"She was kind."

"And so much more," Cam added. "We covered a lot of boring meetings together, but she always said, that's how the people's business got done. It became a routine. We'd cover a meeting. Grab fast food. She would write the story while I edited the pictures." He sighed. "I think she liked working in my cubicle better than at her own desk. Nelson tucked me far away from the rest of the newsroom. I don't think she liked to be in big spaces."

"Do you know why?"

He shrugged. "It might have had something to do with her past. I don't know. She didn't like to talk about where she was before she came here. We'd talk about the news and coverage and all, but never about her past." He touched his index finger to his chin. "In fact, one night, last week..." His voice faltered. "One of our last nights working together, there were several photographs she found interesting."

"Do you know what grabbed her attention?"

"No, but the last day I saw her, she told me to hold on to them. She might need them later."

I tried to ask my question calmly. "Um, Cam, do you know why?"

"I'm not sure." He was lost in his thoughts again.

"Cam, maybe you—"

"Okay, Mr. Photographer," the young police officer said. "You're next. Would you come with me, please and bring your camera?"

Forgetting all about me and Ghost, Cam got up and walked toward the dining room.

I called after him. "Cam, tell them---"

The officer moved between us, cutting off our connection. "We have this, ma'am." And he hustled Cam away.

I was distracted by the sudden commotion at the kitchen door. People were talking all at once. The officers became more attentive When I finally caught sight of the person, I felt a wave of relief. Homicide Detective Craig Mason had arrived.

Chapter Twenty

"A painting that doesn't shock isn't worth painting."

— *Marcel Duchamp, French painter, chess
player, and writer*

The Chief moved across the kitchen to greet Craig. The two men shook hands and when the Chief turned to the group, the lines of stress on his face were not so obvious. He raised his voice in his gentle, non-threatening way.

"Okay, folks, Let's settle down. I'm sure some of you have information to pass along to the detective, but I need to brief him first. He will call for your reports in a few minutes. Don't come to me. This is his investigation now. He is the man you want." And they headed to the front parlor.

I settled down with Ghost again who was anxiously scanning the room for TJ. I had just gotten the dog to settle down and eat one or two of his favorite cookies, when there was another fuss at the kitchen door. A technician came in carrying a kit that looked like a small suitcase. The Chief appeared at the door to the main foyer and waved him over.

The tech moved through the kitchen and followed the Chief. A soft murmur developed among the people left in the kitchen. Caught up in the theories they were weaving, no one noticed me working my way across the kitchen to the main foyer. Initially, the grand staircase concealed my presence from the people in the parlor at the other end of the long entry. I slipped around until I stood just outside the open doorway. Fortunately, the Chief and detective did not think it was necessary to modulate their voices, so I was able to hear what they were telling the technician.

"We were talking when we noticed it," the Chief said in his deep baritone voice.

"Yes, I was standing right there." Craig sounded a little peeved.

I couldn't see what Craig meant when he said he was standing *right there*. Where? I inched forward hoping I could peer around the doorjamb . As I moved closer, the edge of a window in the parlor came into view. Not helpful. I didn't want to look out. I wanted to look into the room. I held my breath and tiptoed closer, hoping the two-hundred-year-old planked wood floors wouldn't give me away with a squeak. Then I saw the edge of a large mirror hanging between the two front parlor windows. The silvered glass reflected a small part of the parlor, exactly where the men were standing by the massive white marble fireplace carved with a medallion in the center and two columns on either side.

"Do you smell that?" Craig asked the technician.

The man paused for a moment, inhaled, and his nose wrinkled. "Yes, it's bleach."

The Chief and Craig exchanged a meaningful look I couldn't decipher.

"Test it," Craig ordered the technician.

The man put his portable kit down on the floor. I could hear the latches clink as he opened it. When he stood, he was holding a spray bottle. It reminded me of some of the crime shows I'd watched on television, but...

"I have the Luminol right here, sir." The man paused for a moment and looked around. "Sir, could you close the draperies, please?

When I saw the Chief grow larger in the mirror's reflection, I scuttled back from the open doorway and plastered myself against the wall. There was no time to race back to the kitchen or up the stairs without being seen. Though my heart was beating so hard, I stayed where I was. I couldn't see what was going on in the parlor anymore, but I could hear the men moving around.

"Alright, give it a spray," Craig said.

I held my breath right along with the men in the next room, wondering what they would see, wishing I was in the room with them.

"Oh boy," I heard the Chief groan. "That's not good."

"Looks like somebody tried to clean up using bleach.," Craig indicated.

A voice I didn't recognize said, "I'll have to do a second verification test, sir, to confirm it is blood."

"What else could it be?" asked the Chief, sounding like he did not want to believe it could be anything else.

"Well, as you said, it looks like someone tried to clean this area with bleach based on those swipe marks lighting up, but that doesn't mean blood is present. When Luminol comes in contact with bleach, the short reaction will look like twinkling stars. When the chemical comes in contact with blood, the reaction will last longer, and the blue glow will be more intense. It will react to other substances as well."

"Like what?" asked the Chief.

"Don't laugh. Luminol will react with vegetable peroxide, horseradish sauce, and certain metals, and, of course, blood."

Craig struggled to stifle a laugh. "Well, I don't think anyone spilled horseradish sauce on this white marble hearth. I think we all know what we're looking at. Do the other test immediately, please."

"Yes, sir."

I didn't dare stay where I was crouched on the floor. It was no hiding place at all. I heard the Chief announce, "I think we may have found ourselves a crime scene."

Chapter Twenty-One

"It takes many good deeds to build a good reputation, and only one bad one to lose it."

— Benjamin Franklin

I almost stumbled when I heard the Chief's pronouncement about finding the crime scene. In Waterwood House? In the front parlor? I felt dizzy from the idea. Part of me wanted to escape to a lone corner somewhere so I could process it...or avoid thinking about what was happening. I couldn't go upstairs using the main staircase. Someone would see me. TJ had warned me about the dangerous condition of the backstairs once used by servants.

The Chief's words, *crime scene* echoed in my mind. My breath caught in my throat. Remembering TJ's reaction to the reporter's story in the paper gave me a chill. He'd been so upset. Had she come to Waterwood? Did they get into a fight? Did something happen? I shuddered not wanting to think what that something might have been.

No, stop it, Emma! TJ wouldn't...

But people sometimes reacted in ways no one would expect. Panic caused people to do strange things. Was there an accident? Did he panic then take her body out to the Point and bury it? No one would look there. The police had just finished an investigation in that area. He could leave the land fallow thus masking the presence of another unmarked grave.

Wait! What was I doing? Convicting a man of murder and a coverup? A man who was dear to me. *For heaven's sake, this is TJ!*

I grabbed onto the door jamb to steady myself. I didn't want to give away any hint of those dark thoughts. The police—the Chief and the detective—had to do their jobs. I trusted them. I had to be patient. Pushing my body away from the wall, I walked into the kitchen where more people were milling around, talking, coming up with theories about what had happened and why. I ignored them and let my eyes wander around the large room. It was the place people gathered for companionship, comfort food, and security. But not for me, not today. My eyes fell on TJ, feeding Ghost in a corner where the dog would be away from the crowd. He was doing what came so naturally to him, taking care of his dog. That's what TJ always did, took care of what mattered to him. Robin's newspaper article had upset him so much. Could TJ have acted in defense of all he held dear?

No, NO!

The Chief and Craig walked into the kitchen. It didn't take a magician to read the seriousness on their faces. I caught a flash of disappointment on Craig's face then it was gone. He clapped his hands to get everyone's attention.

"Okay, everyone. Thank you for your patience. If we have your information, you may leave." That statement sparked a murmur of conversation. "Please, try to make yourselves available if we need to contact you."

I glanced over at TJ as he stood up with Ghost at his side. He closed his eyes in relief. But it didn't last long. I tensed when Craig motioned him over. I moved closer. As Craig was about to begin, the more crime scene experts rushed in carrying their kits. The Chief led them out of the kitchen toward the parlor.

TJ's eyes flashed ahead then back toward the kitchen. "What's going on, Craig?"

The detective took a deep breath. I could only imagine the battle going on inside him. TJ was a dear friend. They had survived several curve balls life had thrown at them, together. But there was a body of woman on TJ's property demanding justice and a crime scene in a parlor only steps away. When the frown on Craig's forehead relaxed and his face became a mask, I knew the battle was over. He was the professional.

"TJ, I'm afraid we've discovered evidence of something very unsettling," Craig began.

"Ya think? The body of a woman reporter buried in my field qualifies as unsettling," TJ shot back.

Craig lowered his voice. "That's not all. We found blood on the marble hearth of the fireplace in your parlor."

TJ started. "Blood? How?"

A technician in a white suit called out to the detective. "We've found something."

After Craig asked TJ to stay in the kitchen, he followed the man out to the foyer. Everyone else was heading to the kitchen door, free to leave, but TJ was home and told to wait for the detective.

I, too, could leave. Regardless of the worries filling my mind only moments earlier, I couldn't, I wouldn't, leave TJ alone. He was my friend, my confidante, my champion, and someone becoming so much more.

"There you are," I said, trying to sound casual as I walked over to him. I wanted to ease away the worry distorting his face. "Everybody's leaving, that's a good thing." I hoped the positive idea would offer some comfort, but it didn't. That worried look seemed etched on his sun-kissed face. "What is it?"

"I don't know," he said slowly. "The cops. The techs. They're all congregating in the front parlor again." The lines of his frown dug deeper into his face. "Did they find something else?"

I wanted to help, but was it right for me to tell TJ what I had heard? I'd never lied to him. Well, maybe in those early days of my recovery when he'd ask about my leg and how I was feeling. That didn't count. Not in comparison to what was happening now. "What did Craig say?"

TJ shook his head, his features twisted in confusion. "He said there was some new evidence, and I should wait for him here in the kitchen." He turned to me, his hazel eyes clouded with uncertainty. "I don't understand. Why are they in my parlor? The woman didn't belong on Waterwood land. She certainly wouldn't have been welcome in Waterwood House."

"Has she ever been here?" I asked gently. "Maybe during the police murder investigation involving Stephani and her brother Josh?"

TJ shook his head. "No. The police had the press conference about the arrests in Easton. I went to watch, but I stayed in the background. But..." Suddenly, there was a hard edge to his voice. "That woman, Robin, caught up with me after it was over. She was going on and on about how she wanted to come out and walk Waterwood with me, get a feel for the place, write a story about it." He closed his eyes and shook his head slowly from side to side. "I told her it was private property, and I didn't need a story written about it. It was fine the way it was. Private property is private. She didn't need a visit to get a *feel* for the place."

"What did she say?" I asked.

"There wasn't much she could say. If the police thought it was important, Craig would have told me. He doesn't keep secrets from his friends."

At that moment, Craig entered the kitchen.

"Tell me what is going on," TJ pleaded.

Craig came and stood with us by the massive oak table where we'd spent many hours sharing stories, dinners, and bottles of wine or beer. Where, working together, we'd stopped a dangerous situation from spiraling out of control. Where we'd become close friends.

Craig turned to TJ. "Has anything out of the ordinary happened in your parlor lately? Has someone had an accident or—"

TJ's eyes grew wide. His mouth opened, but no words came out. He took a step backward. "This is all too much. No, nothing has happened in there. I barely go into that room unless I'm heading to the library for something. It's kind of embarrassing to admit I barely use many of the rooms in this big old house." He narrowed his eyes. "Why do you ask?"

Craig glanced down at the floor as he put his hands in his pockets. He spoke slowly and calmly. His voice was empty of accusation or threat. "When the Chief and I went into the parlor earlier, we thought we smelled bleach and had a tech check it out, not expecting him to find anything."

"But he did. Is that what you're trying to tell me?" No one could call TJ a fool.

"Yes, he found blood on the marble hearth. It glowed blue in the chemical spray. We could see by the swish pattern someone had tried to wipe away the blood and clean the area with bleach."

TJ gasped then pulled out a chair at the big table and plopped onto it. "You mean... you think the missing woman...Robin... was killed in my front parlor?" His voice rose with the horror his words represented.

Ghost worked his way over the stone floor toward TJ, the room was so silent we could hear his claws move over the stone floor. He sat by TJ, looked up at his human friend, and sensing his distress, softly laid his paw on his leg. It was automatic for TJ to stroke the head of his dog.

"I want to know how someone came into my house to—" Slowly, TJ raised his face to his friend. "You think I killed her." After a tense moment, he added, "I can't believe you..." He fell back in his chair and held up his hands as if pushing the detective and the whole crazy situation away.

Craig opened his mouth to speak, closed it, then began again. "I think we have some questions that need answers. That's why I'm going to ask you to come with me to Easton so we can dig into this situation and find the truth, okay?"

There was a tense moment when TJ did not respond to the request. Was Craig going to force him to go by arresting him and reading him his rights? What a nightmare. I knew how TJ felt. Anxious about what could happen. Angry, filled with indignation. Betrayed by a friend. The experience of being under suspicion when the professor was found dead on my patio was still fresh in my mind. An experience I wouldn't wish on anyone.

"Am I under arrest?" TJ asked in a thin voice.

"No."

"Okay." TJ looked down at Ghost and stroked his head. "Hey, Big Boy, I've got something to do, and I don't think you can come with me."

"He can stay with me," I blurted out. "until you come home."

TJ forced a big smile, but it was tinged with sadness. He pushed himself to his feet and pushed the chair under the table. That's when the tech came rushing into the room again.

"Detective, there's something else you should see," said the man in the white plastic suit and led us all to the parlor. This time I wanted to see things for myself.

The parlor was eerily quiet considering the number of people working there. The Chief stood at the far end of the room, his shiny black shoes spread apart on a patterned rug and his beefy arms folded over his chest, watching. One group of technicians was working at the far end of the hearth. They were gently scraping the white marble for what I suspected were blood samples, but it was crazy. The marble where they were working was white. There was no sign of red blood. Then, one of the workers picked up a spray bottle and sent a clear solution over the surface. Almost immediately, it turned blue. The scraping began again.

Craig and TJ were standing with the main tech who was pointing at the other end of the marble fireplace. "We were looking for blood splatter, trying to be as thorough as possible, and we got two different readings at the end. One, up here on the corner of the mantel," He pointed then sprayed the blood-identifying liquid. "And another place just below it." He used the spray bottle again on the raised marble hearth that extended out from the fireplace to the floor.

I squinted, not sure I could see anything. The tech must have noticed.

"It is faint but it's there." He called for all the heavy draperies to be pulled across the windows, making the room darker. "It's easier to see now."

163

He was right. There were places on the marble glowing with a blue light.

"Blood?" asked Craig.

The technician nodded. "But not from the incident you are currently investigating. We have to do some tests, but I think this blood is very old. That's the thing. Marble is porous. It will absorb just about anything, and it is almost impossible to get it out. It might have been scrubbed when the blood was fresh, but there really isn't any way to get it out of old marble like this." We all stood around, staring while the tech added, "Detective, I think you have another crime scene, a very old one."

TJ and I looked at each other and shared one thought: Emma.

Chapter Twenty-Two

"Dogs have a way of finding the people who need them, and filling an emptiness we didn't ever know we had."

— Thom Jones, American Short Story Writer

My eyes remained locked with TJ's while we silently shared the idea of an old crime happening in the front parlor. A crime so violent, it left enough blood on the white marble fireplace and mantel to be detected decades later. All kinds of questions filled my mind: When had the crime happened? Who was involved? Did Emma know?

I often thought the police assumed the worst possibilities and conclusions and now, I was doing the same thing. Maybe the blood wasn't from a crime at all. Maybe it was an accident. But long ago, someone with a bashed-in skull was buried in an unmarked grave on Waterwood land. Was the old blood residue connected to the skeleton? And to Emma?

Craig's voice penetrated my thoughts and brought me back

abruptly to today's murder investigation. "... won't take long. I'd like to sort through what we have so far on today's case, TJ."

I was relieved when no one read TJ his rights or put hand-cuffs on his wrists. But my relief was short-lived. When TJ said he had to get his keys, Craig said he needed to ride with him. Those words sent a wave of icy cold through me. All the coinci-dences, all the little details that had worried me evidently were worrying Craig. Part of me wanted to complain. TJ was his friend. How could he even consider the possibility TJ had hurt the reporter, let alone killed her? But maybe I was jumping to conclusions. If Craig really believed TJ had murdered some-one, he would be led away from Waterwood in handcuffs. No, I needed to help TJ in any way I could.

"I'll take Ghost back to the Cottage with me." I said, trying to sound light and unconcerned. As if it was the most normal thing in the world to have a homicide detective drive my friend to the police station for questioning. But I don't think I fooled anyone.

TJ turned to me, his hazel eyes darkening to a muddy brown. He was worried, too. "You'd better take some of his food... just in case..." I heard his unspoken words: *Just in case... they hold me.* TJ added, "You know where the keys to the truck are, right? Hanging in the kitchen."

A new fear gripped me. True, I had driven his truck from the field back to the Cottage. It was the first time I'd chosen to get behind a steering wheel since the accident. The idea I might drive his truck on a public road was unthinkable, but this wasn't the time or place to debate it. I barely nodded my head.

"Good." He turned to Craig. "Let me tell Ghost what is happening then we can go." He infused his words with too much enthusiasm. It was easy to see through his brave façade.

After a few minutes, we all walked outside. Tears burned my eyes as I stood outside with my hand on Ghost's collar, watching TJ get into Craig's unmarked police car and drive away. The dog laid down and moaned. He felt as sad and frightened as I did. I assured Ghost that TJ would be home soon. The dog moaned again. He must have sensed my uncertainty.

I urged Ghost back in the house, no easy feat. If I left him outside, I worried he might run off, looking for TJ. Inside, I offered him his favorite cookie, but he turned his head away. Maybe I needed to calm myself first. I tried to picture this kitchen back in Emma's time. It would be comforting to smell the aroma of fresh bread baking in the oven. Just the thought of it was making my mouth water. We should have something to eat. Wasn't that the best thing to do in an anxious moment like this? There were too many crazy things happening. Too many unanswered questions.

And a fresh concern popped up. When word got out—and it would—that TJ was being questioned, someone might take the news as an invitation to rob this beautiful home filled with lovely antiques. I knew TJ hated the idea of locking up, but if there was ever a time to set the locks, it was now. I walked out to the foyer to check the windows and door. I was shocked to see the yellow crime scene tape crisscrossed over the doorway to the parlor. There were so many lovely things in that room, the alcove, the library. It would be easy for someone to clear it out and make a quick visit to a pawn shop or a fence for a healthy reward.

Fragile figurines were displayed on an antique wall shelf. Delicate, they looked like they might be French antique pieces, but what did I know? I was only familiar with Hummels. Two massive silver candlesticks stood on the white mantel. I shuddered to think someone might sell them off to be melted down. The ornate but elegant lines would be lost. Workmanship like that should not be squandered but preserved. As an antique... or had one been used as a murder weapon? Each was big enough to smash someone's head. I shook off the thought. I had to concentrate on securing Waterwood House and that meant locking the first-floor windows.

I was tempted to break the crime scene tape. Instead, I shimmied around it and raced from one window to the next. Some were unlocked. One library window was open!

In the foyer, I glanced up at Emma's portrait, silently hoping for reassurance TJ would be back soon. She had waited patiently for parts of her life to change. During the long wait, life had taken a toll on her, but she had rebounded and thrived. I would follow her lead. This portrait was a testament to patience and resilience. An artist had painted it when Emma was in her later years. She was beautiful, not with the dewy look of a young girl, but with contentment shining from deep inside her heart. She had lived a life her father had not meant for her. After Daniel died, Benjamin returned to Waterwood from their trip south. Shortly after, he fell ill with a lingering disease. It must have been an alarming time. Benjamin knew if he died before Emma wed, Waterwood would be vulnerable. At that time, women were not considered worthy of land ownership or control of wealth. He must have worried his daughter was an innocent. He had given her a sheltered life, free of want and cushioned the loss of her mother as best he could. He knew she had learned much about the plantation but feared she would not be able or allowed to handle it on her own.

The poor man must have been desperate when he accepted the proposal from a neighboring plantation owner to unite their lands and their children through the joining of his son Joshua to Emma. Sadly, Benjamin hadn't survived long past the wedding, unable to guide or protect her anymore. He did not live to see the tormented life Joshua created for his wife, the daughter of Waterwood.

These thoughts weren't helping. A soft whine from the big white dog at my feet reminded me it was time to move along. After securing all the locks, I made another decision. No, I wasn't going to drive TJ's truck to the Cottage. This day had already brought enough emotional drama to overload my senses. The walk would do us good. I grabbed some dog food kibble and cookies, locked the kitchen door, and we headed down the drive.

I thought Ghost would romp around as he always did when on a walk with TJ. He didn't. He was walking in my footsteps, afraid I might disappear, too. I talked to him, tried to reassure him everything would be alright. TJ would be home soon. Life would go back to normal. All my words meant to comfort him didn't make a bit of difference. He didn't believe what I said. I didn't believe those words either.

I stopped trying to paint a happy face on what was happening and voiced the thoughts going through my head, even those tinged with fear and foreboding. It's what we both needed. He moved next to me and placed the top of his head in the palm of my hand. I remembered the moment I'd first met Ghost, how afraid I was of such a big dog. Now, I was grateful he was tall enough to make a physical connection with me as we walked home.

With all the upheaval, I'd forgotten to look for a reply from Emma. It felt like I had written the letter days ago instead of only a few hours.

"Ghost! We're going to take a quick detour on our way to the Cottage." I tried to make my voice light and full of fun. I saw the perfect throwing-stick by the side of the drive, scooped it up, and hurled it as far as I could. "Go get it, boy!" I guess the hope in my heart was reflected in my voice. It was just what

Ghost needed. He ran after it with delight. We played toss and fetch the whole way to the cabin.

At the open door, Ghost stopped short. He cautiously poked his nose across the threshold and sniffed madly then pulled back to the world he knew. Had he sensed something unusual inside? Could he feel the presence of Emma and Daniel? He looked up at me with those copper-brown eyes filled with uncertainty.

I knelt down and rubbed his ears. "It's okay, boy. You don't have to go inside." I glanced over at the desk and saw a letter sitting on the writing surface waiting for me. "You stay here. I'll only be a minute." Ghost sat and watched as I sprinted to the desk and returned with my prize in hand.

When we got back to the Cottage, I gathered some pillows and a blanket to make a bed for Ghost in the kitchen. When I put a cookie in the middle of the bed, Ghost understood. After downing it in a nanosecond, he curled up in a big ball and was snoring in moments.

Knowing he was content for the time being, I took a quick photo of her letter then sat down to read it:

Beyond Waterwood

> *My Dear Emma,*
> *Upon reading your most recent letter, I agree with your sentiment that people do not change. I guess preoccupation with money is universal. But it is not true for me.*
> *I never needed what you call treasure. While my father was alive, I felt safe. He did everything in his power to protect me. Thus, he arranged my marriage to the son of the family whose lands bordered Waterwood.*
> *I never wanted to locate and unearth the chest. Early in marriage, I began to suspect what kind of man my*

husband was. I did not want him to have the contents of the chest. It was originally meant for me. After my dear father's passing, I left the chest undisturbed as insurance against a dark day when I might need funds to take care of myself and my children. Fortunately, that day never came. To be honest, I quite forgot about its existence.

If you and my descendant feel it is needed, please do with it what you will. Of course, he—this TJ—does not need my permission. All that is Waterwood is his now. But to realize the depth of all it offers, he and those around him must consider all that has gone before and understand the spirit of Waterwood. To find it, you only need to look around you. The clues are there. They hang at its heart.

Yours with affection,
Emma

Postscript: What kind of a name is TJ?

I sighed with relief. This letter sounded like Emma, my friend. I was so glad I'd followed my instincts and written to her again without pressuring her for answers about the man-in-the-field. The upset hadn't festered. At least something had gone right today. But was it too much to ask her to answer clearly and concisely? I needed answers, not riddles right now.

I folded the copy and put it in my pocket. The memory of TJ being taken to Easton in Craig's car came back. Feelings of uselessness rushed back. Why couldn't I help TJ? This situation was all a misunderstanding, wasn't it? There were so many questions and no answers. What was going to happen?

Fear and uncertainty brought on a flood of tears. My sobs must have awakened the big dog. He came and pushed against my leg. It was his way of offering comfort, but I needed more. I needed a human being I could trust, who would care, give me guidance and comfort. I needed Maureen.

I took out my phone and dialed my dear friend's number. As soon as she answered, I was hit with a wave of guilt. She sounded so happy. Was she laughing when she said hello? I wanted to end the call, but it was too late. Sometimes, caller ID isn't your friend.

"Hello, Emma, dear heart. How are you?" she chirped.

"I'm fine." I tried to sound light and unconcerned, but my voice cracked.

Maureen's tone changed immediately. "Emma, what's wrong?"

I tried to respond but tears choked my throat. I couldn't even breathe.

"Emma! What's happened? Are you hurt? Where are you?" Her questions gushed through the phone. "Are you home?"

Finally, I squeezed out one word, "Yes."

"I'm coming over. Right now! Stay there! I'm coming."

"Please." My voice broke. That was all it took to bring on another rush of tears. But Maureen didn't respond. She was already on her way.

I sat on the steps that led upstairs and cried out the fear, foreboding, and uncertainty. Finally, the flood stopped. My sleeves were wet where I had tried to wipe away my tears. Now, I needed a tissue... or three. I walked to the kitchen, Ghost following in my footsteps, and took the whole tissue box back to the steps to await Maureen's arrival.

I heard the roar of an engine, but it didn't sound like her Porsche. Hearing the noisy trucks and noisy boats watermen loved was common on the Shore, but the source of this sound was different. I scrambled to the door and opened it. Ghost leaned against my leg and barked as a sleek sports car thundered up the drive, swung up to my steps, and stopped.

My breath caught. This wasn't just any sports car. It was a fancy convertible. When the sun hit its red metallic paint, the car glowed. The aerodynamic lines of the car made it look like it was speeding even as it slowed. The narcissistic driver was probably a treasure junkie or a newshound hungry for details about the murder. Well, whoever it was, he wasn't getting anything from me. TJ had left me in charge, to protect Waterwood until he got back. I was determined to defend all that was dear to him.

It was a good thing there wasn't a rifle in the hall closet or I might have grabbed it. Fancy car or not, this person didn't belong here. I marched to the top of my front steps, planted my feet, and put my fists on my hips. I opened my mouth to scream at the trespasser. Then stopped.

The passenger door opened, and a woman got out. It was Maureen!

Chapter Twenty-Three

"All good ideas arrive by chance."

— Max Ernst, French Painter

"Friends," I said to Ghost and ordered him to stay as Maureen stood for a moment next to the car. She was tall, about 5'8" with the figure of a woman half her age. She defied the notion a woman in her sixties was always overweight and frumpy. Her daily workouts were her religion. Even on a casual afternoon, she looked chic in a pair of slate gray chinos and a silk blouse of pearl to set off her silver hair shaped in a pixie cut. The woman raced over and engulfed me in her arms, sputtering her concern in my ear.

"Are you ill? Tell me what's wrong. You know you can." Then she thrust me away at arm's length and eyed me from head to toe. She frowned. "You look alright. Is it your leg? Should you sit down? What..."

I lost track of what she was saying, because my attention was drawn to the man unfolding himself from the sleek sports-car. He was about medium height with closely-cut silver hair that shone in the sunlight. His chest and arm muscles filled his deep blue polo shirt and...

"Emma!" Maureen gave me a little shake.

The command in her voice snapped my attention right back to her. "Maureen, I'm sorry."

"Tell me what's wrong, Tell me now!" she demanded.

"Maureen, I'm fine."

Her body sagged a little, probably from relief, then her eyebrows drew together. "Then why am I here?" she asked slowly.

"It's TJ."

She looked around quickly, searching for the man. When her eyes fell on Ghost standing patiently at the front door, she murmured, "Oh, no."

"No, no, TJ is fine." I gave my head a little shake, hoping to clear my thinking. "I mean, he is fine, physically. But he isn't. The police have taken him in for questioning."

"Why? Illegal farming? Is that even a thing?" She tried to cover her concern with humor. "The man is the most honest, law-abiding person I've ever met."

My jaw clenched as reality hit me again. It took me a couple of tries to get even a few words out of my mouth. Finally, the most important and dreaded one passed my lips. "Murder."

Maureen put her arm around my shoulders and turned me back toward the Cottage. "We'll go inside, sit down, and you can tell me what's happened. Here we come, Ghost." She turned her head a little and spoke to the man. "Logan, would you get her a glass of water please? The kitchen is at the end of the hallway."

It was just like Maureen to rally all available resources and put them to work, even if it meant using someone else's house.

She must have noticed my hesitant reaction as I looked at the man. "Emma, it's okay. This is Logan. My friend." The little quivering emphasis on the word *friend* gave the word extra meaning. "He is here to help."

"Hello, Emma," the man named Logan said in a voice low and soothing. "Let's get you inside. Forgive me for saying, you look terrible."

Suddenly, I was exhausted. And maybe a little weak from relief. It felt like the stress and worry had passed from me to my friend. Even if it was just for a little while, the transfer would allow me to rebuild my strength. Barely able to put one foot in front of the other, Maureen and her friend supported me up the steps, through the front door, and into the living room. Logan delivered a glass of water into my hand, and, after Maureen motioned him to a chair, he sat down. Ghost kept an eye on the stranger while he took up a position at my feet.

"Okay, would you start at the beginning, please?" Maureen asked softly.

"Do you know... they found the missing newspaper reporter." The words came tumbling out in a rush. No details, just bare facts. "She was murdered and buried on Waterwood land. They found the place where she was killed." My throat threatened to tighten up again, so I drew in a quick breath. "They think she was killed in the front parlor of Waterwood House," Tears prickled my eyelids. I struggled to tell her the last awful truth I had to share before the dam burst. "T-They think TJ did it." And now, in the safety of my own home, cushioned by the comfort and caring of my friend, the tears gushed out.

Maureen held my shuddering body and a box of tissues magically appeared at her elbow. I thought the sobs would never stop coming. Until I felt a paw on my knee. Through the blur of tears, I saw the sad eyes of TJ's best friend. I had the comfort of Maureen, but I was Ghost's only trusted source of reassurance right here, right now.

I had indulged my fears enough. It was time to pull myself together, if not for myself and TJ, then for Ghost. I pulled myself out of Maureen's embrace, leaned forward, and put my arms around Ghost's thick neck. His body trembled, another sign of his anxiety. Nuzzling my face in his silky fur, I whispered words of comfort and encouragement. Slowly, the shuddering stopped, and I could lean back against the sofa cushions. Ghost kept his head on my knee. I put my hand on top of his head to complete the circle of caring.

Once the waves of emotion stopped, all of us took a deep breath. Both Maureen and her friend Logan wanted details, not out of morbid curiosity. They wanted to help. I learned Logan was born and raised on the Eastern Shore, right here in this county. He had known TJ from almost the first moment he'd moved to Waterwood full-time. Logan's family owned a huge farm, too. Their connection began as a business relationship and rapidly grew into a friendship.

After addressing their questions about what was happening at Waterwood until I ran out of answers, Logan spoke to Maureen as if I'd disappeared from the room. "I don't like it. This situation sounds serious. Craig is a good guy, but he has to do his job. I don't like the part about Craig taking TJ to Easton in his car. I just don't like the whole thing. Are you okay here?" Maureen nodded. "Then I'm going up there..." He pulled out his phone. "And I'm not going alone."

"Who are you calling?" Maureen asked.

"Only the best attorney on the Shore." He turned to me. "Emma, don't worry. I won't come back without TJ."

He pressed send and a male voice answered his call. "Hey, my man, it's Logan. I need a favor and..." His words drifted away as he walked out of the room and out of the Cottage. It was only a moment before we heard the roar of his car engine, and he took off.

Alone now, I motioned for Ghost to come up on the sofa and put his head on my lap. "So, Maureen, tell me about Logan."

She seemed to be startled by the question, but only for a moment. I could see joy spread across her face. "What would you like to know?"

I laughed. "I want to know everything!" The distraction would be just what I needed.

"Well, he used to be a waterman then he became a crab broker, but he's stepping away from the business so his son can take over," Maureen said.

"Is he married?" I knew how things could get complicated. I had to ask.

With a lilt in her voice. "Oh, heaven's no. Not anymore." She hurried on. "He's kind and fun and interesting to talk to and..." A little blush of pink began travelling up her neck to her cheeks, giving her a youthful glow.

I tried not to smile when the color reached her cheeks. This woman, who had managed millions of dollars, earned the trust of powerful clients, and shepherded some of New York's most creative minds, was having an attack of the shys.

Excited, she continued, "You've seen him." He is handsome."

I nodded slowly. "Yes, he is very attractive in a relaxed and confidant way."

"I love his moustache and goatee. He keeps them perfectly trimmed and they're so soft. When he gets a little nervous, he reaches up to pull down on the brim of the cap he wore for so many years when he worked the water. Not finding it, he covers that automatic reaction by running his hand over the top of his head or down his goatee. I don't think he realizes he does it. It's so cute."

I was enjoying her description of the new man in her life until she talked about his cap. TJ almost always wore a cap. He too had a reaction when he was nervous. He'd take off his cap and smoothe his hair back. TJ. I fought down my worry and said, "That's nice." Go on."

She looked down for a moment. "The first time he smiled at me, I was distracted by the little crinkles around his blue eyes. I remember thinking, this man must smile a lot and I've learned he does."

I leaned back against the cushions. "So, you really like him?"

She giggled. "And I like his car too. When he first showed it to me, it was straddling two spaces but in the far end of the parking lot. He protects his car, and he should. It's the latest model of the Chevrolet Corvette Z51. I'd seen pictures, but it was a whole different experience to see it in person. It looked like it is racing down the road while it was parked."

"So, you fell for his car..." When I saw her blue eyes darken with worry, I added, "I'm teasing." To help restore the lightness of our conversation, I asked, "Did he offer to give you a ride?" I wiggled my eyebrows.

She drew herself up, looking prim and formidable. "I'm a New Yorker, born and bred. I'm smarter than that. I waited until we had a dinner date and I had asked a few friends about him."

"Ever the wise lady." I patted her hand. "You obviously enjoy his company. And he likes being with you, too."

She lightly slapped her knee. "Emma, I tell you, I'm too old for love."

"Never too old, Maureen. This all sounds good to me."

"Yes, it is, isn't it?" There was that self-satisfied smile again.

Finally, she looked up and caught me looking at her. "What?"

My lips stretched into a smile. "You're happy and I'm delighted for you."

She returned the smile for a few moments, then we both sank back into the pool of worry, worry about TJ and what might happen to him. Our concern closed over us the way water does when a body is sinking.

Finally, Maureen wet her lips and asked the question that was like an 800-lb gorilla sitting in the corner. "Emma, do you think he..."

She didn't complete the question, but I heard every unspoken word. Hinting at the possibility TJ could kill another human made my chest tighten. I got up and tried to walk off the fear. "How could you think... TJ wouldn't, couldn't hurt anyone, not..." I stopped in mid-step and my shoulders sagged as I turned to her. In a voice so soft, I could barely hear my own words, I admitted, "I don't know, Maureen." I plopped down on the sofa again next to Ghost. "He was so upset at the woman for resurrecting the story about the family's hidden treasure chest. And he was mad at the paper for putting the story on the front page. You should have seen him. He was livid."

"Did you hear him threaten her?" she asked softly.

I really didn't know where to put myself, I got up and moved over to the armchair. Maybe it would give me a better perspective. "No. He was white-hot angry when he saw the article, came here to the Cottage, and blew off steam about it. He felt violated. Thought it would send another wave of strangers over Waterwood, looking for the treasure. He caught a lot of trespassers during their coverage of Kid Billy's murder. He didn't want to go through that again."

"But did you hear him threaten her?" Maureen wouldn't let it drop. "Did he call her? Did he—"

"STOP! Yes, he was upset. Yes, he wanted to tell her to stop, tell her the effect her stories were having on him and Waterwood, but I never heard him utter a threat. Not even when he was here ranting in the safety of my kitchen."

Without an expression on her face I could read, she looked at me for the longest moment. I felt like she was sifting through what I'd said, looking for a flaw in my argument. Finally, she stood. ""I was with Logan when I got your call. He saw I was... well, rattled by how you sounded. He didn't think it was safe for me to drive myself so..." She held her arms out at her sides then dropped them. "Here I am." She looked at me with such a sad, concerned expression. "Are you better now?"

"Yes, I'm fine." Her weak smile made me feel guilty. "But I'm sorry I upset you. I shouldn't have—"

"Nonsense, of course you should have called me. It was the right thing to do. And you get the bonus of getting TJ some legal help." She ruffled her alabaster silver hair. The professionally trimmed strands fell back into a perfect pixie cut. I could only make a guess at her age based on her accomplishments. She lived as if the years didn't matter. Her spark of life burned brightly.

"Make me some coffee, please. I need a cuppa your darkest roast." We hugged then I led her into the kitchen with Ghost following close behind.

Chapter Twenty-Four

"The past, like the future, is indefinite and exists only as a spectrum of possibilities."

— *Stephen Hawking, English Theoretical Physicist*

S pending time with my mentor who was guiding me in my first attempt at novel writing gave us the opportunity to talk about something other than murder as we lingered over more than one cup of coffee. I caught her sneaking glimpses at me. Maureen knew me too well. I'd tried to assure her I was fine, but we both knew I wasn't. Normally, I'd be fascinated by Maureen's stories and advice, but our hearts weren't in it. My ears were focused on any new sound coming from the driveway. I was concentrating so hard, hoping to hear the rumble of Logan's car engine, it didn't sink in right away when the sound became real.

"They're here!" Maureen announced as she bolted from her chair and headed to the front door.

I followed slowly. I too was eager to hear the latest developments. And there was my main worry. I almost wept with relief when I heard Logan's voice in deep rich tones boom out the words, "We're back!"

We. He had kept his promise to bring TJ back.

Ghost was ecstatic. After he jumped on TJ, almost knocking him down in his excitement, the dog walked in TJ's footsteps everywhere he went. He was not going to lose track of his man-buddy again.

We all settled in the kitchen. It was the natural place to be though I sort of wished at that moment it was a little bit bigger. But no one seemed to mind as four adults, including two big men, and one very big dog maneuvered around as we put together dinner for five. Yes, Ghost deserved something special.

I silently sent a huge thank-you out to Maria for filling my fridge, freezer, and cupboards with delicious foods, everything from crab dip and crackers to chocolate chip cookies, full of chips and nuts. We warmed up the dinner in the oven while I quickly gathered up my notes and research on 19th century portraiture from the dining table. Then we ferried everything to the dining room so we could eat in comfort. I was finally using the table for its original purpose: good food and conversation with good friends. As we passed a platter of crab dip, mouth-watering fried chicken, and bowls of steaming mashed potatoes, gravy, stewed tomatoes Eastern-Shore-style, the men told us about what had happened in Easton.

"You should have seen your face when we found the room where Craig had stashed you." The crinkles around Logan's eyes deepened as he teased TJ.

"I couldn't believe it when I saw you." TJ playfully slapped the man's well-developed bicep.

"Nope, it wasn't me who surprised you," Logan said with a humble laugh. "It was my secret weapon."

TJ was shaking his head in disbelief. "Yeah, I think you're right. I haven't seen Louie Byers in years."

"I like to *get up and down* with him from time to time," Logan admitted, using one of the local phrases meaning staying in contact with someone.

"I hear you keep in touch with everybody," TJ chuckled. Being with friends was having a positive effect.

"Yeah, well, you never know when you'll need a friend. He spent some time in D.C. at some big-time law firm and handled some major cases. Got himself in front of the Supreme Court. Even has the framed certificate to prove it. It's huge!"

"And now he's back on the Shore? Why?" TJ asked.

"Because it's The Shore! You should understand. Did you see Craig's face when he walked in and saw Louie sitting in the chair next to you? I thought he was going to –"

"We get the picture," Maureen assured him.

TJ looked down at the empty plate where the cookie crumbs and smears of melted chocolate chips lay. "I don't know what would have happened if Louie hadn't been there. I—"

Logan interrupted. "Don't go there, buddy. Nothing happened. And nothing's going to happen," he insisted as he reached up to pull on the brim of the cap he no longer wore. Instead, he ran his hand down to smooth his goatee. "Louie knows you're innocent. He has an uncanny ability to pull the truth out of the messes we create and put the spotlight on it. You'll be okay."

"Thanks to you. I'm grateful—"

The hitch in TJ's voice almost reopened my floodgate of tears. I knew the events of the last days and hours had deeply affected him. Here was the proof. To see the hurt, the fear, the—

Logan said quickly. "It's getting late." He put his big hands on the table and pushed his way to his feet. "We need to help—"

"No, you don't," I said quickly. "I'll handle the cleanup."

"If you're sure..."

When I nodded, Logan gestured to TJ who followed him to the door. Ghost trotted along behind him, his tail wagging. "I'm going to run TJ up to Waterwood House to get his truck then come back to take you home, Maureen."

I was confused. "Why do you need your truck? Where—"

Logan interrupted to explain. "He can't go home until the forensic investigation is finished. Craig wants him back at the station in the morning."

"Why?" I wanted to know.

The two men exchanged looks. I felt like there was something they weren't telling me.

Logan looked at TJ. "She's not going to drop it, is she?"

TJ shook his head. "No, she is relentless. When she gets her teeth into something—"

I finished his sentence for him. "She doesn't let go easily. So, save time and tell me."

TJ came over and touched my arm. "I'll tell you, but listen to everything I have to say before you react, okay?"

It was hard, but I nodded and braced for bad news.

"I got a text from Robin, asking me to meet her at the newsroom in Easton that evening. I answered I was on my way. I didn't want to go, but I thought she might listen and understand without all her colleagues standing around and Nelson hovering. So, I went. Only no one was there. The place was dark. I wasted time trying to get inside, thinking she was in a back office. The place was locked up tight. I gave up and came home."

"Okay." I searched his face for any sign he wasn't telling me the whole story. "Why should that upset me?"

"Craig asked me for my phone. He said he needed to see the texts. Then he asked me for my password."

"Okay, so he could access your phone." I was trying to stay calm.

"That's when we ran into a problem," Logan clarified.

All eyes focused on TJ. "I don't use a password." He leaned over and swiped up on the screen and the apps appeared. "I never wanted to deal with all the security password stuff. I swipe and my phone is ready." TJ took a breath and let it out slowly. "The texts weren't there."

"WHAT?"

"Emma," Maureen cautioned. "Let him finish."

I pressed my lips together and forced myself to listen.

"I told him somebody must have deleted them." TJ shifted his eyes down. "Believe me, I wasn't as calm as it sounded. I was angry. I got the vibe that Craig didn't believe me."

"He didn't?!" To me, the story was getting worse and worse. "He is your—"

"Emma!" Maureen barked. She took a moment then asked, "What about the phone records?"

Logan answered. "They're getting the paperwork done for the order, but it will take time for the phone company to comply."

"If your phone isn't password-protected, someone could have deleted the texts," I stated as fact.

"Who would do that?" Maureen wanted to know.

"The killer!" we said in unison.

"So, I think it's best TJ stay with me tonight," Logan finished calmly. "Thank you for this dinner, Emma. I think we all needed to catch our breath and be together." His watery blue eyes sparkled. Then he turned to TJ. "I'll meet you outside. Don't take too long." Logan winked and ushered

Maureen out the door, giving us a private moment after an eventful day.

"You know," I said, "you have some really good friends."

"Yes, yes, I do and I'm grateful, especially for one friend in particular." TJ leaned down and scratched Ghost's ears.

"Ha!" I said, only half-kidding. "I thought you meant me!"

He straightened up and put his arms around me. "I did."

I smiled. "Are you going to rub my ears, too?"

"No, I'm just going to look at you and think how lucky I am to have you in my life."

In the next moment as we stood with our eyes locked, so much passed between us, more than words could have communicated. Then I saw what energy was left in the man drain away. Afraid the weight of all that happened in the last days was going to bury both of us, I tried to lighten our last few minutes together to avoid an emotional meltdown.

"Oh! There is something you must do before you leave," I proclaimed.

His lips spread into a mischievous smile. "And what would that be?"

"I need you—" I began.

"I know, I know. You don't want me to be mad at Craig."

"You?" Playing the indignant woman, I put my fists on my hips and pursed my lips. "I am the one. I can be mad at him. He scared me today. He didn't have to do that."

"I know he was doing his job, Emma."

"Well, if that's what *friends* do, I'd hate to—"

TJ cut off my words with a kiss.

The tingles chased away the anxiety, uncertainty, and anger that had consumed me all day. It would have been so wonderful to fall into this feeling of warmth and caring. His arms around me made me feel so safe.

Afraid this feeling of security and happiness would dissolve into a flood of tears when he leaned away, I tried to be cute and funny. "There is something else." I continued.

His eyebrows knitted together. "What else?"

"Do I need to worry about your good friend, Logan?"

TJ laughed and squeezed his arms tighter.

"No, really. I'm entitled to worry about Maureen. This new man, Logan, is spending a lot of time with her. I don't want her to get hurt. Besides, I have enough to worry about already." I smoothed his sun-kissed hair that had fallen over his forehead.

Now, it was his turn to inject a little light humor. "You sound worse than a teenage girl's father." My concern must have shown on my face. "Okay, okay. The short answer is Logan is good people. Born and bred on the Eastern Shore, he bought a boat and worked on the water instead of working on the family farm. He made a bundle and now, he's enjoying life. You don't have to worry."

There was no way I would stop worrying about the possibility of TJ being charged with murder and thrown into a jail cell. But I felt better about Logan and Maureen.

TJ loosened his hold on me. And speaking of Logan..." TJ glanced at the front door. "I'd better get going." He leaned down and rubbed Ghost's ears. He straightened up and stretched out his back. "It's been a long day." He drew me near again and kissed me on the nose. "Are you sure it's okay for Ghost to stay with you? It will only be for one night."

"He'll be fine." I kissed TJ on the tip of his nose. "We'll keep each other company and I'll spoil him silly with lots of treats."

"No, you wouldn't! And ruin his handsome figure?"

The distinctive Corvette horn sounded, and he gave me a quick kiss. Then he got down to Ghost's level, put his arm around the big dog, and spoke to him quietly. He was trying to reassure Ghost who wagged his tail madly. When the door closed leaving Ghost inside with me, his tail dropped and he stood like a statue, waiting for TJ to return.

While I put the Cottage to bed as Uncle Jack liked to call it, I paused at a window overlooking the creek and the Lone Oak on the far shore. I turned off the lights and marveled at the canopy of stars in the night sky. I hoped the upset and fears of this long day would vanish like the stars at dawn.

When it was time to go upstairs, I tried to get Ghost to follow me, but he wouldn't leave the front door. He expected TJ to walk in at any moment. I offered him a cookie, always a surefire enticement, but he left it on the floor. I sat on the bottom step and explained what was happening...or not happening. He looked at me with those golden-brown eyes, searching for truth, then flicked his head back to the door. Nothing I could say could get him to come upstairs so I left a night light on in the kitchen and put a blanket on the floor by the door. At least, he could be comfortable while he waited.

Sometime in the night, I woke up with a wet nose under my hand followed by a silky-soft furry head. My heart must have registered the arrival of Ghost before my brain reacted. After petting him and cooing reassurances, I realized he wanted more. With a quick pat on the mattress, he leapt into the air and curled up next to me. A little surprised, I tried to inch over to give him more room. A mistake. He moved closer to keep in contact. I smiled when I realized his predicament. He had misplaced TJ. He wasn't going to lose track of me. My last thought as I fell asleep was gratitude for the queen-size bed. I don't know what we would have done with a twin or double bed. I suspected we would have slept together curled up on the floor.

Chapter Twenty-Five

"What a business this is of a portrait painter! You bring him
a potato and expect he will paint you a peach."

— *Gilbert Charles Stuart, America's foremost
portraitists. His best-known work is an
unfinished portrait of George Washington.*

I must have forgotten to close the curtains the night before.
The warm rays of the sunrise nudged me awake. I wasn't
the only one. Ghost moved to the floor and stretched out his
muscular body. I needed to get up, let him out and prepare his
breakfast. This was good. While my body was healing, I had
spent too much time lolling around in bed. It felt like a waste of
time. Then I had a curious thought. If I had a dog of my own, I
would have a reason to get up early. A dog would be great.
Having Ghost for company felt good, but I sighed and fell back
on the pillow. I needed a better reason to get up in the morning,
a way to be productive and accomplish something that
mattered.

I still had to decide what I was going to do and where I would live—here at the Cottage or back at condo in Philadelphia. I'd learned the schools on the Shore – both public and private –needed teachers. I had the option to stay. If I went back to Center City Philadelphia or one of the suburbs where there were jobs, I could still come down to the Cottage on weekends... and see TJ. Being in his arms, feeling his lips on mine the night before, made my heart sing more than I ever imagined. Once again, I was overwhelmed. Blaming it on the need for a cup of coffee, I tabled the decision-making again and swung my legs over the edge of the bed.

On my way to the shower, I caught a glimpse of my face in the bathroom mirror. I stopped in mid-step, shocked. The face was looking back at me had colorless cheeks, drawn skin around the eyes, chapped lips, and weary eyes like an old woman who had seen too much. No wonder Maureen kept stealing looks at me and asking if I was okay. Obviously, the circumstances of the lives of two different people—one past, one present—being buried on the Point had taken a toll on me, too. I closed my eyes not wanting to remember how TJ had fallen under suspicion. No, I couldn't think about how the murder of the reporter might upend his life—and mine now that I was beginning to admit how important he was becoming in my life. I shuddered at the thought of how devastated I'd felt.

No! Don't think about what could happen. Don't let fear and anxiety define you. Get back to being yourself before all that stress is permanently etched on your face, girl!

A hot shower and a little blush on my cheeks went a long way to reviving my body and my attitude. It would also have a good effect on those around me, those I cared so much about.

Starting my second cup of a delicious Kona-blend of coffee, I dawdled at the kitchen table. Taking time to relax, rejuvenate, just taking deep breaths helped. All the dishes from dinner the night before were clean and put away. Ghost had curled up in the corner, catching up on his sleep.

I wandered into the dining room and picked up my tablet. And put it down. If Nelson had run an article suggesting TJ had hurt Robin, even in some indirect way, I did not want to read it. Yet, I wondered how a newspaper handled the loss of one of its own. I couldn't resist. I sat down and brought up the site.

The announcement was at the top of the front page. A large color photograph of a smiling Robin Hunter was surrounded with a thick black border and a message.

It is with a heavy heart that I announce the passing of a young, vibrant reporter, Robin Hunter. In all my years in journalism, I have never had to announce the passing of a colleague who was valued and so accomplished at such a young age. I know many of you, our loyal readers, have followed her reporting with keen interest and enthusiasm. Her dedication to the truth meant we could rely on the facts presented in her stories. Her tenacious attitude uncovered situations in our communities that warranted our attention. She will be truly missed.

--Nelson Jennings, Editor-in-Chief

Next to the box was an article with the larger than normal headline:

Local Reporter Found Murdered

I began to read the article electronically, then skimmed the rest of the paragraphs. It made me feel like I was reliving the moments that began when Ghost found the poor girl's body to the discovery of blood on the marble mantel in the front parlor of Waterwood House to memory of seeing Craig taking TJ to his car for the ride to the police station in Easton. I guess I wasn't surprised to see a separate paragraph reporting TJ was taken in for questioning. I jumped to the last paragraph of the article where I found the promise that the paper would follow the murder investigation every day on the front page until the killer was apprehended and punished.

Oh good, that's all we need. Let's whip up the locals, especially curiosity seekers, who will swarm over Waterwood land looking for who knows what.

If I'd had the newspaper in print form, I would have wadded it up and had the satisfaction of stuffing it in the trash basket.

Instead, I closed the site, put the tablet down, and paced. I tried to focus on something I could control. But I didn't feel I could make any good decisions about my life, not now. Not until this situation with Robin's murder was resolved. As I continued to pace, it felt like the memory of the skeleton, the forgotten man-in-the-field, followed me. I needed to do something, something to calm my mind.

I stopped. Of course. I turned and headed to the den. All the uproar and indecision had distracted me from the one simple thing I often did to calm my mind and, during a raucous time in the classroom, the little minds of my students.

I pulled out my box of origami papers of many colors. There was no one color or one figure to deal with all the things affecting my mind. I decided to deal with the sadness connected with the forgotten man. After I did a little research online about death and funeral in the origami world, I selected a sheet of blue paper to represent the broad expanse of sky above his resting place. Then I began to fold a crane. It was often the shape used to express love and hope, but it could be used to let your message of compassion fly to the person who had departed. I couldn't figure out why I felt some kind of connection to this man. Maybe because he had lost his life here at Waterwood and couldn't get back to the people who loved him?

As I made one fold after another to create this familiar shape, my emotions settled, and my resolve strengthened. When TJ was safe and Robin's killer was behind bars, I would try to identify the forgotten man-in-the-field. The answer might lie at Waterwood House. I felt a smile creep across my lips and my mood lighten as I remembered the alcove off the main parlor at Waterwood House. That's where I'd seen the writing table with graceful lines. I wondered if Emma had sat at the Davenport desk to write her letters. The desk was originally designed with built-in secret hiding places. I wondered what she might have kept there. I wasn't sure what to do with Ghost. He was sleeping so peacefully on his makeshift bed in the kitchen, I was tempted to leave him at the Cottage, but he didn't need to be left again.

The walk up to Waterwood House was good for both of us. Even though I explained to the dog TJ wasn't home, he ran around checking every room just in case I was wrong. Finally, he took up a position close to my every step.

I remembered the first time I'd walked inside Waterwood House by myself. It almost felt like I was trespassing. In the city, a person didn't walk into someone's home alone unless she was a relative, and even then... That wasn't the case here on the Shore. People left their houses unlocked, trusting their neighbors, friends, and family would respect their privacy and possessions. After the time I'd spent on the Shore and here at Waterwood House, I felt so comfortable, I called out a greeting to Emma's portrait and hesitated only at the entry to the front parlor. It hadn't been too long since the police had removed the yellow crime scene tape. They must have decided there was nothing more for them to do.

Finally, I could get a close look at the white marble fireplace and hearth that lay just above the oak floor. There were no signs of blood. The evidence Luminol's chemical reaction had uncovered had long since disappeared. There was no obvious sign of Robin's blood or the violence that had taken her life, but Dr. Bergstrom had assured me it was there. He'd said it would be almost impossible to remove every trace of blood from marble. I shivered knowing it would probably be there forever though we couldn't see it.

My eyes wandered over to the place at the other end of the hearth where the modern technicians had found faint traces of blood. They did not believe it belonged to the reporter. They suspected another act of violence had happened a very long time before the modern murder. One tech voiced an opinion it was from a head wound which would explain the amount of blood picked up by the chemical reactive spray.

Head wound. The skull found in the field showed a severely damaged skull wound. It wasn't the skull of Emma's husband. He had drowned during an ice boat race. Could the man have been a visitor here at Waterwood House? Was there an altercation, a disagreement between the man and Joshua, Emma's husband? Accidents happen. The man could have died as a result of his injury. But why would he have been buried in an unmarked grave located on the edge of a planted field?

I had come to Waterwood House looking for answers. One fine house, one marble fireplace. All I'd found so far were more questions. It was time to check Emma's desk to see what might be hiding there.

Ghost curled up in a corner of the parlor's alcove where the desk was tucked away from the main activities of the household, conversation, and guests. The wall of windows gave Emma a vista of Waterwood. The antique desk itself was a gem. I ran my fingers over the satiny finish of burled walnut. Its condition was perfect. Even though it was pushed against the wall, it appeared to be a Davenport desk. I could identify it only because Craig and I had attended an auction hoping to uncover evidence leading to the killer of the striving college professor. When a Davenport desk was offered for bid, I'd perked up. The discovery of Uncle Jack's plantation desk had made me curious about other types of desks. Might there be another desk with intriguing capabilities?

The auctioneer took time to show us the intricacies of the Davenport desk. It was named after a ship's captain of the late 1700s. Small and finished on all sides, it could be carried from ship to ship and placed in a cabin, looking as if it was made to be there. It became a popular piece of furniture in 19th century homes in both Europe and the United States. Its compact size made it easy to use in one room or another. But the real genius of the desk design was its many cubbyholes, storage slots, and drawers.

Known for its secret compartments, could Emma have stashed something away in her Davenport desk? Something to provide a clue to the man's identity? I'd settle for anything.

I took a few steps back and considered the little desk. Its size and design suggested it was nice, but unassuming. I wondered if TJ's Aunt Louisa, the family historian, had dismissed its importance or had already cleared out Emma's belongings. I dearly hoped not. I wanted to find something to help identify the unknown man-in-the-field. It was a long shot but worth a try.

On the top of the desk was a highly ornate frame with gilt columns and three-dimensional leaves across the top sitting on a small easel. In the frame was a small painting of a young girl with pinchable rosy cheeks. She had a mess of blonde curls. This was a watercolor painting of Emma's daughter. The child's eyes were the same deep blue color as her mother's, matching the waters of the Chesapeake on a bright summer day. Considering the tall windows of the alcove, it was amazing the sun hadn't bleached out the Wedgewood blue of her little dress with a pale pink sash. As an accent, she wore a necklace of coral beads around her slightly pudgy neck. I looked on the back, hoping to find a name to identify the child. Instead, I discovered a crude mechanism so the painting could be worn as a lady's pin. There was no identification of the child or the artist. I peered closer and saw tiny numbers inked in the lower right corner: 1869. The artist was talented but lacked the skilled technique of a highly-trained artist of the time.

Young ladies, even those who lived on plantations distant from the bustling towns and cities, were often given music and art lessons. Emma must have preferred the canvas to sheet music. Access to fine artists and teachers at that time was often limited to big cities, but some talented young painters took to the road to establish their reputations and build their financial cushion. Some established portrait painters would accept commissions in a particular area or region and travel to their subjects. These artists were lodged in the fine family homes, given comfortable work spaces, and celebrated throughout the neighborhood. The artist's presence enriched the prestige of the host family and gave the artist a respite to recharge his body, ego, and creativity. The benefit to his purse could not be ignored.

As I recalled lessons from my art history class, the fine portraits hanging along the main staircase here at Waterwood House became even more significant. The portraits. Carefully, I lifted the child's portrait from its small easel and went in search of the one family portrait we'd found including Joshua and Emma, their sons, and daughter.

TJ had stashed it in a dark place upstairs because Emma looked so worn and unhappy. It took a few minutes to find it, but I finally stood in front of the painting. The daughter was leaning against her mother's skirt. These two females along with the baby sitting on Emma's lap were relegated to the far-right side of the painting, separate and apart from Joshua and the boys prominently positioned toward the center.

I focused on the little girl. She was older than the child in the small frame, but she had the same soft blonde curls. The term rosebud lips applied here. They were small, delicate, and perfectly formed. A lovely child to delight any mother.

Alone, I spoke to the portrait. "Hello, young Anna Grace. Did your mother paint this picture so you could be with her while she was working on aspects of plantation management and the family's social connections? You were so young, not yet ready for her to teach you about being the mistress of a plantation." I felt a wave of sadness. This sweet girl had succumbed to an outbreak of measles, an often-deadly disease at that time. At least Emma had captured her daughter's face, filled with innocence and hope.

Back in the alcove, I carefully returned the painting. It was time to get back to the search for a possible secret lurking inside the desk.

A key was lodged in a keyhole at the center locking the slanted desktop into place. An invitation to look inside. I took hold of it and turned. A satisfying click sounded in the quiet house, quiet except for random creaks and groans that came from age. Carefully, I raised the cover to find three small drawers. Inside the first was a pair of reading glasses in a narrow metal frame, popular today as granny glasses. Next to them was a small knife with an ornate silver handle. Almost too small and too delicate with its blade made of mother-of-pearl to be a letter opener, I put it on top of the desk next to the portrait of the little girl, promising myself to research it later.

Finding a small box in the center drawer made my heart race, but it only contained stamps from Emma's century. There were several two-cent black stamps featuring Andrew Jackson with a melancholy expression and a few five-cent stamps with flourishes engraved around a portrait of Thomas Jefferson. The design was the same on several stamps, but the colors varied from red to buff to several shades of brown. As I opened the last drawer, something rattled inside. The source of the rattling was a twisted stick of wax used to seal an envelope. Next to it was a small dagger-like piece made of bronze with a sharp end, perfect for breaking the seal on an envelope or slitting it across the top. Used to open a letter from family or friend, it could have also been used for protection. Looking closer, there appeared to be a small dent in the handle.

Emma, I ordered myself, *you must stop romanticizing everything you see. The little dent could have been the result of constant use. One slip and a close encounter with the floor could have created it.*

Carefully, I returned it to its place in the drawer.

In the center section below the writing cover was a small stack of personal stationery with Emma's name engraved at the top of heavy cream-colored paper. I lifted out the sheets and set them aside. They belonged in the plantation desk at the cabin now. I wanted to give Emma the opportunity to use her own personal paper.

Along the right side of the desk was a knob. When I pulled, a long, thin section came out holding two delicate crystal inkwells and several antique pens waiting to be used. One was a long, slender cylinder made of silver with an etched design toward the top. I could imagine Emma using it in her later years after the death of her husband, when she was no longer forced to deny her elegant nature. Next to the pens, there was a small section for nibs, many caked with black ink.

Sunlight coming through the windows of the alcove glinted off a small square of silver, the top of an antique inkwell. Carefully, I lifted the cut-crystal bottle, only about one inch square. Inside was a black pile of flaked India ink, now long dried out. While all these things were fascinating, they were not what I'd hoped to find. I pulled over a stool with a padded seat and sat down. It was time to bypass the obvious, in search of the hidden.

My eyes wandered over the desk, wondering where the switches or pins meant to release hidden compartments might be. Nothing was obvious to me. The time to be gentle with the desk was over. I'd have to run my hands over every square inch. I moved the child's portrait to a safe place and returned the mother-of-pearl knife to its drawer to protect it. My finger rested on the drawer's knob while I considered where to go next.

Wait! Was that a click? My finger was still on the knob. Had I pushed down without realizing it? Yes, the knob moved though it should have been stable. Something had happened. The writing surface had moved, as if it had been released. I pulled it toward me opening a small space. It was large enough for two fingers, room for me to lift the leather-covered writing surface away. Two sections that could have been doors to compartments appeared, embedded deep in the desk. But what caught my eye was a little door that had popped away from what appeared to be a solid piece of wood. Had I broken something? Holding my breath, I pushed the little door back into place and it latched. Not a broken piece. A cleverly designed hiding place. Hoping I had uncovered its secret mechanism, I touched the little knob on the open drawer again. Nothing happened. Disappointed and mad at myself for closing the little door, I pressed, pushed, and clawed at the place where the little door had appeared. Nothing happened. It looked like a solid piece of wood.

Frustrated, I ordered myself to calm down. I hadn't slept well the night before. Worry about TJ and fear that a killer might be roaming the county were making me impatient. I needed a break. I replaced the writing surface and pushed the drawer closed, but before closing the cover of the desk, I touched the knob one more time.

Click!

So, everything had to be in place for the mechanism to work. Energized, I opened the desk again and discovered the little door was open. This time, I opened it as wide as possible. I peered into the small space but couldn't see a thing. With my eyes closed, I reached inside with two fingers, hoping to feel more than the wooden walls of the enclosure.

I did.

Chapter Twenty-Six

Clara Peeters was a talented Dutch still-life artist in the 17th century. In one painting , she rendered a self-portrait in the reflection of a ceramic goblet's pewter lid to prove a woman's technical prowess in this difficult genre.

My fingers extended into the secret compartment of Emma's desk and felt something that didn't belong there. It was a tiny space making my effort to retrieve the item from its dark place challenging. It wasn't made of something hard like wood or metal. It was soft. My fingers felt pudgy in such a narrow place. I could almost pinch what felt like fabric, but I couldn't move deep enough to reach it. I needed a pair of tweezers, but that would mean a walk to the Cottage and back again. I was sure TJ had tweezers somewhere here at Waterwood House, probably in his bathroom, but I wasn't about to go poking through his things. I considered the old pens in the desk but worried they might damage the hidden treasure.

Okay, one more try. I jammed my index finger into the space as far as I could until it hurt then curled the tip, so the fabric was pressed against the side. Then I pulled my hand out ever so slowly. Nothing appeared. Frustrated, I brought up the flashlight app on my phone and shone the strong beam into the narrow opening to reveal a bit of shimmering rose-pink satin stuffed in the opening. I inserted my index and middle fingers like a pincer, grabbed it, and pulled out a small pouch. Its weight suggested something was inside.

I put the pouch on my lap and carefully loosened the thin cord pinching it closed. With fabric pulled open, I peered inside. It was difficult to see anything. I turned the pouch upside down over my left hand and an object fell out. Gold intertwined initials *GM* appeared on a disk of lapis lazuli. This was the missing mate to the cufflink found in the unmarked grave.

I felt like the breath had been kicked out of me. Emma had lied to me. No, she hadn't really lied in so many words. She had lied by omission. I had proof she knew something about the man-in-the-field in my open palm. What was so awful to make her lie? I couldn't imagine after all the achingly terrible things I'd uncovered already. This cufflink represented something worse, but what? Not willing to think about it now, I bundled the cufflink, a link in more ways than one, into its storage pouch and put everything back in its hiding place.

Having it out of sight helped, but I still needed to clear my head. The scene at the front of Waterwood House always rejuvenated me, so I headed to the front door. That's when I noticed a small oil painting on the foyer wall opposite Emma's portrait. It was a small landscape, about 8"x12", mounted in a simple wood frame painted black. It looked familiar. The name of the painting was etched on a small plaque attached to the bottom of the frame:

Witches Point.

Emma's initials in the corner showed she had created the painting of the same place where TJ had found the skeleton in the unmarked grave.

I tried to match up my visual memory of the Point with the perspective Emma had chosen more than 150 years earlier. She must have set up her easel in the shade once offered by the line of trees now lying broken on the ground. Back then, she had painted a bright, sunny day. The water beyond the shoreline reflected the deep azure blue of the sky. A few feathery clouds drifted through the center of the painting. The field from the trees to the shoreline wasn't cultivated for crops. Nature had covered the soil with short green plants and wildflowers in a riot of color—red, orange, white, yellow, even blue. But there was something curious about the land and its flowers. I took two steps back, facing away from Emma's portrait, and noticed something was wrong. There was a small area where the flowers were not vibrant as in other areas of the painting. Their colors were flat, almost grayed out. As I stepped up to the canvas again, close enough to smell the flowers, the effect had disappeared. It was subtle and could only be seen when standing a distance away.

It felt like something was terribly wrong with this painting. Carefully, I took it down from the wall. It left behind a rectangle of darker blue which showed it had hung in that spot for a very long time. It felt lighter than the other paintings I'd moved around. Why had Emma framed it in a cheap wood painted black? In order to solve this puzzle, I felt I had to go to the actual place where Emma had created the artwork. With it cradled in my arms, I headed out to the farm road that led to the Point, Witches Point, the place the bodies were found.

All of the vehicular activity going to and from the Point had made a rough road through the trees to the field. The forensic team was still working at the new gravesite. The crime scene tape still flapped in the breeze. The police were still nervous about people walking in the area. I didn't need to step onto the field. Emma had hung back in the tree line and so did I.

First, I tried to identify the vantage point where Emma had set up her easel. At the right time of day, the trees would have offered her shaded relief from the afternoon sun. Now, sunlight beat down on the old oil painting. I tried to block the light and moved into the original tree line. After taking several steps to the left, I felt like I'd found the right perspective. I rested the painting on a fallen limb and shielded it for two reasons: to prevent the paint from fading and to make the grayed area reappear. Using a branch with brown needles, I filtered the light to make the difference in the color intensity more noticeable. My eyes flipped back and forth from the painting to the real-life excavation of the unmarked grave area. Yes, the grayed area in the painting matched the location of the place the man was laid to rest all those years ago.

Emma had known about the burial. She hadn't lied to me, not directly. Why? What could have happened?

"Hello, Emma." The voice of Dr. Bergstrom made me jump.

The painting teetered on the limb. Dr. Bergstrom sprang forward and prevented it from crashing to the ground. Then he propped it up again.

"Oh, I'm sorry I startled you," he said. Are you alright?"

I nodded.

The doctor let his gaze wander over the surrounding landscape. "I was taking a break. It's rare for me to work in such a lovely spot and I wanted to walk around, taking it in. I saw you and wanted to say hello." He shifted his gaze to the painting. "This is quite good. Are you the artist?"

"Oh, no," I said quickly. "I've been helping TJ sort through some of the older things at Waterwood House, including the paintings. This one reminded me of the Point."

He held it up to study the artist's interpretation of the real place. "Yes, whoever painted it did a nice job." He paused as his eyes flicked back and forth from the scene to the painting. "Except there is no tree over there." He gestured to the right of the unmarked grave.

I was so preoccupied by the muddied colors in the one area of the wildflowers, I hadn't noticed. "Maybe there was a tree there when it was painted. The person who signed the painting lived in the mid-19th century."

"That would explain it," he said as leaned in closer to the painting. "That's odd."

I sprang up from the limb and peered over his shoulder at the painting. "What is?"

"It's such a bucolic scene, peaceful, lovely. Why would the artist put a vulture perched in the tree that no longer exists." He shifted the framed canvas, so I had a better view.

"Yes, there is a black bird there, but there are a lot of—"

The doctor interrupted. "—large black birds, yes, but there is really only one with a red head."

I leaned closer and saw he was right. "How did you notice it?"

He chuckled. "I'm trained to be observant, to notice the smallest detail." He anchored the painting on the limb and stepped away. "The artist painted from this spot."

"Yes, that's what I thought, too."

He kept staring at the painting, deep furrows forming on his forehead.

"Are you noticing this area among the wildflowers." I pointed. "The colors are less vibrant..." I pointed to the unmarked grave. "right in the area of your excavation."

It took him a moment to confirm. "Yes, you're right. That

makes two fascinating elements in this painting." He took another step back and stared at it.

I kept quiet until I couldn't wait another moment. "Do you see something else?"

"It may be nothing."

"Tell me," I insisted.

"It looks like there are some red flowers in the area of the grave. They aren't placed close together as one would expect but if you connected them, they would form a shape."

Yes, I could see four red flowers separated by others in muted shades. I hoped the doctor could decipher the meaning.

He stepped back, considered the picture again, then moved up close to it. He ran his finger about an inch away from the canvas this way and that. "I'm not sure, but I believe they were placed to form an X. Considering the red color to denote danger, was the artist warning people from visiting this spot?"

We stood together, silently considering the painting. Then he made a soft harrumpf sound, stepped closer to the frame, and ran his index finger over the nameplate. "Witches Point."

"TJ always refers to this piece of land as the Point. Maybe back in her time, it had a more specific name," I suggested.

"It makes sense, considering the symbol she painted into the clouds."

"What? Where?" I watched as he made a circle with his finger over a section of the sky. "Yes, I see a shape of some kind. What is it?"

"Considering the name once assigned to this piece of land, it is a very appropriate shape. I believe it is a pentagram, a shape assigned to witchcraft."

My jaw dropped. After all the years this painting had hung in Waterwood House, it was astonishing no one had noticed the shape. Surely, someone interested or frightened by witchcraft must have visited at some point. There was so much more going on here than I'd initially thought.

Finally, Dr. Bergstrom brought me back to reality. "Seems you have more research to do."

I took a deep breath and let it out slowly. "I may have already begun. When I was talking with the Maryland Room reference librarian last summer, he mentioned stories about witches living in this area. I'll have to dig out my notes."

"I'd be interested to learn what you find. Maybe a little quid pro quo for the DNA sample?"

I smiled. "You have a deal." I thanked the forensic anthropologist and he returned to his crime scene. I picked up the painting and set off for Waterwood House with more insight than I could have ever imagined.

When I got back, I took the painting directly to the foyer and when I was about to hang it in its spot, I stopped. Something was odd. It felt like the Witch's Point painting was too small for the grand foyer of Waterwood House. Based on the small size of the canvas, especially in comparison to the impressive portraits hanging on the walls of the entrance and running up the walls of the stairway to the second floor, it felt wrong for it to be here. Someone had hung it across from Emma's magnificent portrait. It had been there for a long time as shown by the dark rectangle. The place must have been chosen on purpose, but who would notice such an insignificant landscape? I didn't. My eyes were always drawn to the painting of Emma.

I returned the picture to its rightful place and stepped back to consider what I knew. Emma had painted the landscape. Thanks to Dr. Bergstrom's powers of observation, I had a better understanding of the messages she had hidden there. If Emma meant the painting as a warning, having the landscape there would remind someone leaving through the front door to avoid

Witches Point. But when the door was opened to welcome guests to Waterwood House, the mysterious painting would be blocked from view. Now, knowing what she had hidden in the scene with careful brushstrokes, the warning was as obvious as if set in neon lights.

A stab of cold ran through my body. It was time for me to leave. There was a lot to take in. Since I'd moved to the Cottage, I had uncovered a lot of information about Waterwood. I'd learned about Emma's emotions and family secrets when I read her diaries and gone through the valued possessions she had stored in her hidden attic room. But this time, I felt an uncomfortable weight from the discoveries Dr. Bergstrom and I had made. Part of me was grateful he was so observant, though part of me wished Emma had not been complicit in the burial of an unknown man. A man of substance and position. A man once loved as evidenced by the engraving in the case of his pocket watch. How was she involved? What was she hiding after all these years?

Chapter Twenty-Seven

"What could be more simple and more complex, more obvious and more profound than a portrait."

— *Charles Baudelaire, French Poet and Art Critic*

I walked out the front door of Waterwood House and sat down on the porch. I needed to think, and this was the place to do it. The painting had distracted me from the need to find the real killer. It was Craig's job, but I couldn't just sit and wait. I needed to do something to help. Finding the treasure like TJ wanted would go a long way to keeping strangers away from the farm. I had Emma's clues, but they were hard to decipher. Still, I should try.

I took the copy of Emma's letter out of my pocket. The key sentences were:

The clues are there. They hang at its heart.

Not much to go on, but it lightened my outlook to know I had something to work with though it might take a very long time to find the chest. The thought of me as a very old lady, bent over with a cane, tromping all over Waterwood with a shovel made me laugh. With a lighter attitude, I went to work.

The second sentence-- *They hang at its heart*—was critical. I figured the heart of the plantation, as Emma knew it, was Waterwood House. So, the clues were *hanging* there. Thankfully, I hadn't seen a noose anywhere though the thought gave me a chill. In our recent letters, Emma and I talked about paintings. One did hang paintings.

Could that be the clue? The paintings hanging at Waterwood House? There were landscapes, portraits, paintings. *Her* paintings. I thought of her painting of Witches Point and how she had embedded a message there. Could she have done the same in another painting? Where were they?

In my excitement, I jumped up and almost lost my balance. When the world stopped spinning, I dashed inside and headed up the main staircase. My idea was to begin in the attic where so many treasures, secrets, and surprises lay. As I climbed, I glanced at the portraits lining the wall. And stopped.

The second sentence was critical. *I left the clues hanging at its heart.* One *hangs* paintings. There were landscapes, portraits, paintings and *her* paintings. She had embedded a message in the painting of Witches Point. Could she have done the same in another painting? Where were they? Probably not in the attic. They could still be hanging somewhere on the walls of Waterwood House.

All the paintings hanging around me were large, full-length portraits and landscapes in oils. I rejected them as possibilities. She probably didn't have the luxury of endless hours to work on a large canvas. Her responsibilities at the plantation were too demanding and time-consuming.

As I slowly worked my way down the steps, I wondered where I might find her paintings. Thankfully, neither TJ nor his uncles nor earlier relatives had made many changes in the family possessions here in the main rooms of Waterwood. Where...?

The alcove.

I hustled through the main parlor, fighting the distraction of what had happened there. In the alcove, I stood in front of Emma's writing desk and, beginning with her daughter's portrait, I slowly moved my gaze in a circle around the room. There were several paintings and framed mementos. I checked the artist's signatures and rapidly became discouraged. My approach seemed logical and correct, but there were only three paintings left. Then two.

I let out the breath I'd been holding. The small landscape in the ornate gold gilt frame was signed Emma Elizabeth Ross. I could feel the frown scrunching up my forehead. Something was wrong. I looked at the signature again. She had left off her married name, Collins. She had stayed in her marriage in life, but she had divorced her heart and creativity from him after he drowned.

Okay, Miss Emma Elizabeth Ross. Did you hide our clues somewhere in this painting?

I hoped so, because I hadn't found any other painting by Emma still hanging on a wall.

When I looked closely at this landscape, there was something tucked into a grove of tall pine trees in the background. I didn't recognize the place, but something felt like it didn't belong. I took the painting to the window, but I still couldn't make it out. Whatever it was didn't fit and it wasn't the only thing. The creek was on the *left* side of the canvas.

I remembered Dr. Bergstrom's suggestion to step away from a painting to get a clear and comprehensive view of what it contained. For a different perspective, I propped it against a wall and stepped back. I squeezed my eyes a little to focus on... What was a sheath of corn doing in the middle of the woods? There was something else there on the right of the canvas. As I moved closer, it blended into the low-lying plants. I stepped back and the shape reappeared, dark, as if a shadow. It was low, almost level with the ground. A shadow with straight lines? What could cast a shadow like that? Could it be the top of something *in* the ground? Something like a large strongbox? And what was in front of it? At first, I thought they were small pearl white flowers, but they were round. They had no stem. Just three white circles sitting on the ground.

My mind was whirling. I covered my eyes and drew in a deep breath. This had begun as an emotional journey. Now, with these clues and notes, it was time to approach this search logically. I ran to the kitchen for paper and pencil then made a crude sketch of the place represented in the painting. If I had to rely on plants, my quest would be in vain. Plants die. Trees topple over. But I had to try. This was the last step. I just knew it. I couldn't give up now.

I picked up my sketch along with the painting itself, because I wasn't sure a picture taken with my phone would capture an optical clue like the one hidden in the Witches Point painting. If I was going to follow a clue lurking there, I need to go to the Cottage, grab Daniel's notes and my boots. I had no idea where my quest would take me.

When we got back to the Cottage, my tummy rumbled, I glumped into the kitchen, glumped because Uncle Jack's boots didn't exactly fit me. I grabbed some of Maria's chocolate chip cookies then felt guilty. If I kept snacking like this, I'd blow up like a blimp. Plenty of time for a diet later. It was time to start my hunt.

I looked out at my starting point: the Lone Oak on the other side of the creek. It was too far to walk around the water. I decided to take the row boat across. Armed with Daniel's notes and my sketch of the painting, I set out. Ghost watched my every move from the Shore after I'd reassured him I would be back.

Pleased I hadn't lost my skills of handling the little boat, I stood under the heavy limbs of the old tree where I thought Daniel had indicated and started pacing off the steps. The ground was no longer dug up as it was on the night Stephani and her gang had threatened me.

I changed my direction as Daniel dictated and counted again… then stopped. I had walked into the creek up to my ankles and was still directed to take more steps into the water.

This can't be right. I must have made a mistake.

The creek was here in Daniel's time, right? Did they bury the treasure under water? No, he would have mentioned it and it would have been too difficult for Emma to retrieve it. I checked the notes again. Did his instructions call for enough steps to take me to the other side of the creek? But how would I pace them off correctly?

Emma would have to help me. After I made my way back across the creek and secured the boat in the little cove, I made my way to the cabin and pulled out a fresh sheet of paper.

The Cottage

Dear Emma,

I am sorry to be a bother, but I need your help in my quest to find the treasure chest. I know it has lain undisturbed for centuries, but with all the attention it is getting today along with the advanced ways of finding lost things, TJ and I are afraid the chest your father left you will fall into the hands of strangers. To avoid such an unhappy occurrence, we both feel it is vital to find it and keep the contents in the family.

With your help, I found your landscape painting. You are one clever woman. I retrieved the instructions Daniel sent during our correspondence. With this information, I ended up in the creek. Is it possible I made a mistake? I tried to be careful.

Would you please offer me more guidance, so I don't dig up all of Waterwood.

Thank you for your help.

With great affection,
Emma

I'd put out the call for help. Now, all I could do was wait. I wiped away the thin film of dust building up on my typewriter. The pages of my novel's first draft were collecting dust, too. Once again, I promised myself to take the time to set up a work area in the den. Up until now, I'd go to the cabin and work on my novel using the typewriter, because there was no power to recharge the computer there. It wasn't going as fast as I would have liked. But I assured myself, the reading I was doing about the craft of writing was laying a foundation for the work I wanted to do. We hadn't had a writer's group meeting in a while. The flu was jumping from one to the other.

We'd decided to take a little time away to allow the bug to die out, but we had our assignment: WRITE! Gretchen, the unelected leader of the group, had decreed. She warned we would be expected to share ten pages with everyone for a critique at the next meeting, whenever that might be. I'd grown accustomed to those meetings, even though I vehemently refused in the beginning and had to be cajoled to attend. I'm glad I did and now, I missed the meetings and discussions about writing. I had suggested using Zoom, but the idea was rejected immediately. Soon, I hoped, life would get back to normal.

Before I could leave the cabin, my phone rang. Caller ID said it was Craig. Normally, I would have answered immediately, but today, I paused. Craig had always been an ally. He had been a close friend of TJ's for a long time. I thought he could be trusted, but after seeing him drive TJ away in his unmarked car, I wasn't sure. My hand hovered over the ringing phone. Was he calling with some new piece of evidence to condemn TJ? Was he calling to boast about his investigative skills? Had he found something that would hurt TJ? About to decline the call, I wondered if he had some good news, something to remove any doubt of TJ's innocence. There was only one way to find out. I steeled myself and answered the call.

Craig sounded relieved. "I was afraid I wouldn't reach you, Emma."

"I'm here." I cringed a little, sure I sounded distant and dismissive. *Stop it,* I ordered myself. "And what can I do for you on this fine day?"

"You're right, it is a fine day. Spring is just about here," he said, sounding relieved.

I couldn't hold it in any longer. "Craig, I know you're working the case, but if you have time to call me and talk about the weather, you have time to answer a question."

"Okay." He sounded leery.

"Why are you giving TJ such a hard time? Taking him to Easton for questioning and not believing him about the texts..." My voice went right up the scale. "Come on, Craig. He told you he didn't do it." I couldn't, I just couldn't use the word murder in the same sentence as TJ's name.

Craig switched to his reassuring voice, the one he used with victims and their families. "Emma, please. It will be all right, I'm sure, but you have to understand—"

"The only thing I have to understand is TJ is innocent. Why are you putting him through this? Look at Robin's phone. It will show you he is telling the truth."

Craig drew in a long breath. "We can't locate her phone. The battery is probably dead."

"Or somebody pulled the SIM card," I said. "You need to find her phone, Craig."

"I've asked for a court order to get the phone company to pull her records. I just hope she had an Android phone. It will make things so much easier."

"Do whatever you have to do, but you should know if TJ said they exchanged texts, they did."

The phone went silent. Had we lost the connection? Then he said softly, "Emma, he could be lying. People do, even friends."

I couldn't speak. I could barely breathe. He wasn't just saying TJ could be a liar. He was saying it was possible his friend could be a murderer.

Craig used my silence to regain control of the conversation. "Emma, you want me to do my job. You want me to find the killer, right?"

I tried to say yes, but the word came out like a squeak.

"Good. To do that, I could use some help. Help only you can give. Will you help me, Emma?"

I cleared my throat and was finally able to form some words. "Yes, of course."

"Good. There's someone I want you to meet."

"What? You're trying to *fix me up* with one of your cop friends?" I said, filled with indignation.

"What? No, no. It's about the case. I want you to meet Robin's roommate Fred."

I sprang on this new piece of information. "She had a boyfriend? Maybe—"

"Fred is short for Frederica. No romantic interest. I know her, but I can't get a good read on her. I'd like your take."

Finally, there was something constructive I could do. I put aside my concerns and focused. "But you're so good at reading people. And you have so much experience. I don't know what I—"

"She is holding back, but there is something..." he trailed off.

"Do you think she's a suspect?" Another possibility sharpened my attention.

"I—I don't know. Probably not, but maybe... That's why I called." His voice strengthened as he declared, "I'm not putting you in any danger. I'd like you to talk to her at her place of work."

"Oh, wouldn't that be awkward?"

"Wouldn't you like a glass of wine and maybe an appetizer or something, courtesy of the police department?"

"Yes, but—"

"She is a bartender and good at her job. Likes to talk with her customers."

I relaxed. "Nothing more normal than a casual conversation with a bartender." I chuckled.

"You should trust me, Emma." He didn't pause for a response. "Can you go this afternoon? I can't get away to pick you up, but I can meet you at the pub around three. She'll be there but the place doesn't start getting busy until 4:30 or so. I could introduce you, if you could find a way to get there."

I heard the roar of an engine getting louder then it stopped outside my door. "I think I can arrange it."

Then he suggested, "You really need to think about driving again."

"Let's solve one problem at a time, okay? I'll text if there's a change in plans."

Chapter Twenty-Eight

When having my portrait painted, I don't want justice, I want mercy.

— *Billy Hughes, Television Actor*

The engine sounds were replaced with laughter. The sense of fun in everything Maureen and Logan shared was contagious. I opened the door to bright smiles. I'd grown close to Maureen in a way I hadn't done—hadn't allowed myself to do—in a long time. When I had been so hurt by my husband and friends who said I should forgive him since we were perfect together, my psyche had blocked access to the inner me for protection.

Somehow, Maureen had gained my trust with a gentle touch and now, I could enjoy and appreciate her advice, counsel, and the pleasure she took in life. Yes, it all got down to trust. I could see this man delighted in Maureen's company and brought new life and energy to my friend. She was shedding years in front of my eyes. If he could make her happy, more than happy, I would be thrilled to have him in my life, too.

Knowing these two people were always willing to do something spontaneous, I proposed a trip to Easton for some pub food and conversation as Craig had asked. They jumped at the idea, ready to go.

Ghost padded up the hall, his head hanging low.

"Poor Ghost. This must be very confusing for him," Maureen said as she rubbed his right ear. He leaned against her.

"He isn't eating much. I even put his favorite delicacies on his kibble—small chunks of fresh carrot and frozen green beans, cut, not French style." I wiggled my eyebrows. "He is a very discerning eater." But I grew seriously concerned as I looked at the dog. "He's showing no interest in anything."

"He doesn't understand why TJ left him behind," Maureen concluded.

"TJ didn't have a choice," Logan said.

Maureen raised her eyebrows. "We know that, but Ghost doesn't get it."

"He's been following me everywhere. I guess he is afraid I'll disappear, too." I had to chuckle "This morning, while I was taking a shower, he poked his nose through the shower curtain to make sure I was there. Scared me to death. I'm not used to having a dog, especially one who checks up on everything I do."

Maureen's cracked a sneaky smile. "I have an idea. Isn't TJ meeting with the detective?"

"Yes," I responded slowly, beginning to catch on to her idea."

"Let's reunite this big boy with his buddy."

I began to protest, but she overrode my objection. "You said it yourself, Ghost doesn't understand why he's been separated from TJ. He needs some time with his friend." She put a fist on her hip. "Craig asked you for a favor. Now, it's time for a little quid pro quo. You know, a fair exchange. We'll go talk to his bartender if he'll let Ghost spend some time with TJ."

I stared at her. I couldn't admit I had just accused him of being a false friend. I was too embarrassed.

Maureen gave me a questioning look. "Emma? You only have to text him. Tell him we'll bring Ghost to him on the way to the Pub."

I had no choice. My hands shook a little as I tapped out the text. I felt such relief when he responded.

"OK! Let's go!" I grabbed my wallet and stuck it in my pocket with my phone and headed toward the door where Maureen and Logan stood stock still. "What's wrong?"

Maureen pursed her lips and frowned.

Logan pointed to his car. "That's what is wrong. We came in the 'Vette."

The three of us stood and stared at the car. It had everything: sleek lines, power, comfort... and room for only two people.

"I know, Maureen," Logan said. "I'll give you the keys and you drive the 'Vette. I'll stay here with Ghost, if it's alright with you, Emma?"

"Drive your car?" Maureen screeched, horrified. "No way. I'm smart enough to know it's too much car for me to handle. Maybe someday, but not now."

"Emma and I are not going on an adventure without you," Logan pronounced. "Ghost needs another idea."

I made a tentative suggestion knowing the arrival time could be more than an hour and a major assault on the wallet. "An Uber?"

"No," Maureen announced as she turned to the new man in her life. "You take me home where I'll pick up my car. I'll zoom back here, pick up Ghost, and follow you to Easton."

"No, I couldn't ask you—" I began.

"It's not that far," Maureen said. ""Besides, my SUV has plenty of room in the back for Ghost."

"And it's a brilliant idea." Logan declared. "That solves all the problems, right boy?"

He gave Ghost a vigorous rub on his back. I could have sworn the dog purred. Every time the man smiled, his whole face lit up and brought something special to everyone around him. I could understand why Maureen was taken with him.

Maureen skipped down my front steps. "Come on, we've got places to go. People to see."

"We'll be back in a flash," he said to me with a light squeeze on my arm.

And they were. I'd barely had time to brush my hair and put on a little makeup when I heard two car horns outside my window. Quickly, I explained to Ghost what we were going to do and how I needed him to be a good boy in Maureen's car. I was amazed when he sat and gave me his paw. Who says a dog doesn't understand?

Rushing out to Maureen's Porsche with Ghost on my heel, I held out an old sheet. "He sheds a bit. We could put a sheet down—"

"No bother. The car is detailed on a regular schedule." She held one hand up high in the air in triumph. "And I found something we can use as a leash."

We sprang into action. I put a bag of treats on the front seat. Ghost watched our every move. I kept talking to him, telling him what was happening, the way TJ would have done. Before coming to the Eastern Shore, I would never have talked to a dog the same way I would reassure a child. At first, I felt a little funny, but when I saw his reaction—up on his feet, listening attentively—I knew I was doing the right thing.

It was time for him to get in Maureen's car. I was a little

nervous he would balk, but when Maureen opened the door, he leapt inside, sat, and stared out the front window, ready to go. Maureen opened the windows in the back so Ghost could stick his head out and take in all the smells. I'd never seen a dog whose nose was always twitching, as if he was afraid, he would miss something.

"Maybe I should ride with you?" I said, worried how Ghost would act.

"Don't be silly," Maureen said. "I know a lot about dogs."

"You had a dog in New York?"

"Not exactly. We had a big dog food account for years. I loved going on the shoots to get my dog-fix. I learned a lot from the trainers. We'll be fine, won't we Ghost?" A resounding bark came from the back in response. "See? Now, go get into that luscious car for a ride you'll never forget."

I took my seat in Logan's amazing Corvette and felt embraced. The thought made me chuckle, but it was true. The beige seat of softest leather supported my back, head, shoulders, every part of my torso. There was plenty of headroom so I didn't feel hemmed in, and I could stretch out my legs easily. The controls were directed toward the driver. Was this what the cockpit of a fighter jet looked like? Maureen whispered to me not to be afraid. She closed my door. Her last comment had the opposite effect. I grabbed the chicken bar, and we were off.

Chapter Twenty-Nine

Car and Driver Magazine — Since 1955. "In addition to sharp and unbiased reviews, our features and columns allow our readers to ride shotgun with the world's finest automotive writers."

B ut I didn't need to hold on. As Logan steered down the Waterwood drive, through the curves and all, my body barely registered the movement. Was it the suspension absorbing the changes? There was so much I didn't know about cars. When Logan turned onto the main road, with no one around, he went through the gears. My logical self said I should be afraid, but there was no jolt of acceleration to unsettle me. Just a smooth ride. We cruised to a stop before making the turn onto Route 33 where a grove of cherry trees had burst forth with their white blossoms. People always think of the pink cherry trees around the Thomas Jefferson Memorial Tidal Basin in Washington, D.C. The white ones seemed to bloom first, as if Mother Nature favored them.

As we made our way through St. Michaels, Logan was careful to avoid jaywalking tourists and the speed limit changes then he opened her up outside the village. I felt uncomfortable riding to Easton without any conversation, especially since I was burning to ask a question... so I did.

I started with, "Maureen and I have become good friends over the past months. TJ told me how you two have been friends for a long time, but I have no idea how you and Maureen met." I turned to him, hoping he would tell me the story without me having to prod him for details.

He responded with a happy chuckle. "Oh, we laugh about it all the time. We met at the library in Easton of all places. They have this huge section of magazines dedicated to cars. I love reading them, sitting in one of the upholstered chairs in the library's reading room. Their writers are very thorough. They know just what drivers like me want to know."

"And Maureen?"

His smile lit up his suntanned face. "I went to the library one day, walked up to the display shelves and all the current issues were missing. I couldn't believe it. Not just one, but all the car-related issues."

"Wouldn't it be easier buying your own subscriptions?"

"I guess, but I like the ritual of going to the library. It gets me away from distractions so I can concentrate on the articles and specs. Even living alone, you'd be surprised how many interruptions there are at home."

Believe me, I could relate. "Then what happened?"

I marched over to the information desk to ask what had happened to *my* car periodicals." He shook his head slowly at the memory. "She didn't say a word. She just pointed to the place where a group of upholstered chairs were arranged for the comfort of patrons to sit and read. That's the first time I saw the sassy lady named Maureen sitting there as calmly as you please, reading my favorite one with the rest of the car publications stacked on a small table next to her. When I looked back at the librarian to confirm what I was seeing, she raised her eyebrows and shrugged. I asked her if she could help, but she said the lady was there first. I was going to have to handle this situation myself."

"What did you do?" This was a story even Maureen couldn't concoct.

"I didn't know what to say or do. She was unlike any woman I'd ever seen on the Shore. I was a little surprised at myself when I realized that she was more interesting to me than the latest issues."

"Well, something must have happened to bring you two together."

"I knew I couldn't exactly walk up to her and demand the magazines. I was trying to figure out what to say without offending her. I'm not so good at talking to strangers after working so many years alone on the water. I guess I was pacing back and forth—I think better on my feet—when she lowered the issue she was reading, looked over her glasses, and asked if I wanted something." He blew out a little puff of air. "Promise not to laugh? I almost blurted out I want to buy you dinner and get to know you."

I had to choke back a giggle. The last thing I wanted to do was embarrass this nice man who was bearing his heart. "So, what did you say?'

"Nothing brilliant, I assure you. I asked if she was finished with any of the magazines."

"And?"

"She looked at the stack and a little blush spread over her lovely face when she realized she was hogging them all. She

227

grabbed the stack and offered them all to me, except the one she was reading. I told her I never realized I had such competition for the motor magazines. I felt my own face grow hot when I added, *Lovely competition at that.*" He swung his head around to face me. "Emma, I never say anything like that."

Realizing he was looking at me, I gestured at the windshield. "Eyes on the road, please."

In the little bit of time I'd seen these two together, I knew there was a whole lot of flirting going on. "Then what happened?"

"I sat down in the vacant chair next to her and we swapped issues. But I have to admit, I wanted to know more about the woman than the cars being reviewed. So, I invited her for a coffee as a thank-you for sharing. We found we had a lot in common."

"Let me guess: Speed."

He let out a hearty laugh. "You know her too well. If I'd known she was on land, I would have gotten away from the water a lot sooner."

"What do you mean?" I wanted to know.

"I spent a lot of years as a waterman, then a broker, spending most of my time with others like me. I love everything about working on the water: The smells, the tastes, battling the challenges nature throws at you, even the history and folklore. The land was never my first love like my father and brother. Can't stand getting all muddy and dealing with beasties like ticks."

"But working the water has its own dangers and—"

"Yes, it's not work for the faint-hearted, but I love it, even coping with the surprises my finicky engines would throw at me. Above all, I love searching out that elusive Blue crab when the rain changes the salinity of the water or heat drives him to change his behavior. It's so much better than watching plants grow!"

His laughter was infectious, and I joined in.

But he did add one more thing. "Now, my attention is firmly on land."

Chapter Thirty

"In front of the model, I work with the same will to repro
duce truth as if I were making a portrait. I do not correct
nature, I incorporate myself into it; it directs me. I can only
work with a model. The sight of human forms nourishes and
comforts me."

— *Auguste Rodin, Artist*

I t took longer to find a safe, protected parking place for the
car than to drive to Easton. I sent a text to Craig that we
had arrived while Maureen parked nearby and opened the door
for her passenger. In moments, TJ burst out of the police
building with Craig not far behind. I had to fight back tears as I
watched the man and his dog. Ghost jumped up on TJ, something he never did, and pushed the man to the ground. They
wrestled then, with Ghost standing over the man licking every
inch of his face.

Craig turned to me. "TJ has got this. Now, you need to

keep your part of the bargain." His tone was cold, but then warmth crept in. "I'll walk over to the Pub with you."

No one started a conversation as we headed up the hill to the main street through town. When we pushed through the heavy doors made of leaded glass of the Pub, the atmosphere was warm and welcoming, with a sense of home. The wood paneling and hand-carved details of honey-colored oak set the tone of the impressive bar area. Shelves backed by mirrors on one wall were framed in detailed wood moulding were filled with bottles. Liquor bottles of all descriptions, colors, and shapes. Tall chairs with red leather seats were drawn up to the bar where a tall woman, almost six feet, was polishing glasses.

According to Craig's description, the woman had to be Fred. Her looks and the way she carried herself, she could have been a model on any runway or fashion magazine cover. Her long blonde hair that accentuated her caramel skin was pulled up in an artfully formed messy bun. I envied women who could apply makeup that didn't scream *makeup* but made the most of their natural features. Fred knew how to accent her high cheek-bones, well-formed lips, and amazing eyes that were more copper than brown.

Maureen, Logan, and I stood together in a tight circle to get our bearings then followed Craig over to the heavy wood bar polished to a high sheen. We watched as he tried to talk to the bartender who was avoiding him by making busy work. Logan took in the situation immediately and dipped his head so we could hear him over the jazz playing on the house speakers.

"You two go with Craig. I'll sit with my buddies over there. Take your time. Those guys can talk my ear off." And he headed to a corner table.

Craig waved us over. After what I felt was an awkward moment, Craig called out to the bartender. "Fred, I want you to meet two friends of mine. They can have whatever they want. It's on me."

She casually cast a look over her shoulder to check us out. Then she put a smile on her face and greeted us like long-awaited new friends. I spotted the technique bartenders use to make people feel welcome. People who felt comfortable spent more money. One of my college roommates clued me in on some of their tricks. She'd made a lot more working at a local bar than I did at the college bookstore.

After chatting about the weather and checking out the menu, Craig loaded up our order with stuffed potato skins and onion rings. Fred headed to the kitchen.

"I don't want to eat all that food," I hissed at Craig.

He leaned toward us and lowered his voice. "It was the only way to get Fred to leave for a minute. Ask her about Robin. She won't talk to me. I'm the police now, not just a friend. She is pretty rattled about what happened and might open up to the two of you ladies." Craig leaned back suddenly. "You're gonna love the potato skins. They do something special with them here. Fred, I've got to get back to the office. Let me settle up with you."

They conferred over the bill, he paid, and left with a wave.

Fred set us up with silverware and napkins. "Your orders will be up soon."

We nodded and thanked her, but she didn't move away.

"Are you really friends of his?" she asked.

"Afraid so," I said with a crooked grin. I had no idea how this conversation was going to go. We'd either become new friends or she'd freeze us out.

She started wiping the bar top with a white towel, the way I'd seen so many bartenders do. Then she stopped in mid-movement. "I suppose he told you Robin is – was my roommate."

Maureen and I both offered our condolences.

"It must be difficult losing a friend... and in such a terrible way." Maureen said. "Are you okay?"

Fred paused and looked at Maureen in surprise, her perfectly formed eyebrows high up her forehead. Had Maureen said the wrong thing? I held my breath.

Then Fred's shoulders sagged. "Thank you. No one has bothered to ask me how I'm doing." She went back to buffing the already shiny bar top and snarled, "Like I'm not affected by all this? I just shared my home with the woman for over a year."

Maureen knew what to say. "I'm sure people are still in shock. Their brains will catch up."

Fred folded the towel. "It wasn't like we were longtime friends or anything. She came to town more than a year ago and needed an affordable place to stay. I have a big apartment with an extra bedroom I rent out. We talked and seemed to have the same values. Plus, I figured Nelson wouldn't hire a serial killer," She stopped suddenly and groaned. "That was inappropriate." She raised her eyes to us. "I'm sorry. I better check on your order." And she shuffled off to the kitchen, her head down.

I whispered to Maureen, "You're good at this."

"You need to jump in. You have things in common with her that I don't...like your age."

"Oh, got it. I thought for a moment you meant I know about what's in all those bottles." The display on the mirrored wall was impressive. It was hard for me to imagine knowing what to do with each liquor and what to mix with what.

Fred was back with our food and drinks. Craig was right. The 'skins were hot and delicious with Amish apple bacon and chilled sour cream. When she came by to check on us, we raved about everything, and she lingered.

I thought she might want to talk, so I asked, "What was Robin like? Did she get along with people?"

Fred waited for a moment and got a faraway look on her

face. I was afraid I had gone too far, but she started talking. "She was a great roommate. She was neat and clean. Never had late-night visitors so I didn't feel awkward. You know, she was the kind of person you like having in your home. And she was focused on her work. She said she'd come here to learn her craft, you know, being a journalist." Then she pressed her lips tightly together and cocked her head a little. "But I think there was more to it."

"Any idea what it was?" I asked.

Fred raised her shoulders and dropped them. "Nothing real specific. A little bit of everything." A contented smile spread over Fred's lips as if something had come to mind.

"Did you think of something?" Maureen asked softly.

"There was that time shortly after she moved in when I asked about her Twitter handle. I was stunned when she said she didn't have one. I'm all about social media. It's brought me customers, created a little community centered on the Pub... and me." Her eyes sparkled. "And it passes the time when things are slow. I told Robin if she posted, it would help grow her following and might get her noticed in other markets, the ones where she dreamed of working."

I tried not to let my excitement show. "Did she ever get on Twitter?"

"Twitter, Facebook, Instagram—but she didn't have a lot of pictures until she started working with the newspaper's photographer. What's his name?"

"I think you mean Cam, short for camera. I met him at..." Oh, I didn't want to say the place where Robin was buried and switched. "He was with Nelson one day."

"Yeah, that's right. Cam. The two of them worked really well together. I wish I knew..." She looked past the customers in the Pub, out the windows to the street. "I think she was holding something back. I didn't push. Maybe if I had..." She cleared her throat and carefully enunciated each word, giving me the feeling she was trying to control or hide her emotions. "It's a shame what happened to her. She was a good person, on her way to being a good reporter, good enough for a big city paper. That was her dream. She started teasing me, saying I might be looking for a new roommate soon. I'm sorry she never got the chance to move on."

"That makes this even harder," I said, and we paused, each inside our own thoughts and feelings.

Fred took a deep breath and shrugged. "Oh, well. Time to find a new roommate. Not for the first time."

"It must be hard carrying a big apartment on your own," I suggested, knowing Craig would want to know if there was a financial aspect that would put Fred on his suspect list.

"No, I make good money doing this job. You'd be surprised. I can carry it on my own, but I like the company and help with the rent lets me sock away more for the future."

Maureen grabbed the lead. "Really? What are your plans if you don't mind me asking?"

Fred put an elbow on the bar and planted her chin in her hand. She seemed to appreciate our interest. "I'm not sure. Maybe own a bar though I'm not sure about adding food." A man came in and took a seat on the other side while loosening his tie. "Oops, gotta get to work."

Fred greeted the new customer like an old friend. His haggard face quickly relaxed, and he perked up to wave to friends sitting at a table and to check out the sports news on the big screen TV. Fred chatted with him for a few minutes when she served up his beer in a chilled mug. When they were joined by someone, Fred slipped away and came back to us.

"I really like talking to the customers." She looked at us with those eyes of liquid chocolate. Fred was intent on making us feel like the only people in the bar and that we mattered to her. I could understand why she was successful.

"Some bartenders don't like to listen, but I think it's part of the job. I've gotten to know some of them really well. I've thought about going back to school to get certified as a therapist, but I hear the take-home pay is lousy compared to what I make here. Maybe I'll do something in art."

"Art?" I was a little embarrassed how I blurted out the word.

"Yeah, crazy, isn't it?" It was good to hear her laugh. "There's a gallery next door. I've gotten to know the owner pretty well. She's taken me under her wing, taught me a lot about paintings and all. I've even taken a few classes at the Art Academy. The teachers there say I have talent. Just need to take classes and practice. That's nice, but the important thing to me is I like it." Her roving eye, always on the move, picked up a couple entering the pub. She winked at us and was off to take care of them.

We were about to finish our appetizers when a big hand reached in and stole an onion ring. Maureen slapped Logan's hand. "You are incorrigible."

Fred was back, standing with her hands on her hips. "Logan, you ole reprobate, are you bothering these nice ladies?"

"Sure am! And how is my favorite bartender?" he said, teasing.

I almost choked on my drink. The man knew Fred and hadn't said a word.

Fred shrugged. "I don't know."

"It will get better," he said with absolute assurance. "Hang in there, and if you need anything, you have my number. Anything."

Fred's eyes began to glisten.

Maureen spoke to head off the tears that threatened to ruin

her shift. "It's been great to talk with you, Fred, but before I go, I *must* ask why a lovely woman like you has the name Fred? There must be a reason."

The woman who wouldn't look out of place in New York or Paris rolled her eyes. "It's not as romantic as it may seem. I wish it was."

"Tell us." Maureen insisted. "I want to know."

Fred began with a sigh. "My mother named me after my great-grandmother who had come over to America from the old country. Her name was Fredericka. The kids always teased me growing up. They called me Freddy. I never liked it. I almost went back to my real name when I went to work as a bartender, but it sounded too pompous. Who wants to talk to or tip a Fredericka? But everybody loves Fred!"

"I think it's perfect," Maureen announced. "And I know how mothers can saddle their children with unbelievable names. It must have something to do with being pregnant."

"Did your mother..." Fred began to ask.

"Oh, yes, she did. Give me your pen." Maureen wrote something on a napkin and turned it for us to see. It read *Siobhan*. "That's my first name."

Fred peered closely and tried to sound it out.

"See?" Maureen said quickly to put Fred out of her misery. "Nobody can say it. Thankfully, the good woman, may she rest in peace, used the feminine version of her French father's name, Maurice."

"You mean, like Maurice Chevalier in the movie, *Gigi*?" Fred asked, her eyes wide.

Maureen nodded.

"I love that movie!"

"I do, too," Maureen smiled. "So, Maureen is my middle name and that's the one I use."

Fred pointed to the napkin. "But how do you pronounce—"

Logan said, "Siobhan. It's pronounced *Shiv – awn.* Say it fast and you get *Shivawn,* a good Irish name. "

Maureen turned around slowly and stared at Logan. "You know how to pronounce it!"

He put the palm of his hand on his chest. "I am a man of many talents. And I'm going to have to drive like it is the Indy 500 race to get Emma home and get us to Annapolis—"

"Oh, no! I totally forgot." Maureen slipped off the bar stool. "Forgive us for leaving so abruptly," she said to Fred in a flurry.

As I grabbed my purse, I looked at Fred. "Oh, do you remember Robin's handle, what she used on social media?"

"Sure, that's easy. I set it up so they're all the same: RobinHunterNews."

"Thanks."

Maureen touched my arm. ""Come on, Emma. We'll have to come back soon when we have more time." She turned to Fred. "I was enjoying myself so much, I lost track of time. It was lovely to meet you. We'll see you again."

Thanks to Maureen, we left Fred with a big smile and laughter instead of tears."

Chapter Thirty-One

"Only humans can be accountable."

— Mark Walport, English medical scientist and Foreign Secretary of The Royal Society

I didn't know if my fight with Craig about TJ's innocence had made an impression, but, when we went back to his office to reclaim Ghost, he announced TJ could go home to Waterwood House. But he added, "Don't leave the county." A broad smile took the sting out of his words.

The next day, I walked out to the Point to see what was going on. As I made my way to the shallow grave, I could see I wasn't the only one who couldn't stay away. The Chief was there, watching. Cam, the photographer, moved around just outside the tape, trying to get a good shot destined for the front page. I wondered how he was doing. Was he having trouble covering this story about the murder of his friend? As I watched him change lenses, his hands seemed to shake a little. It must be challenging for him as well, because it was very different from coverage of council meetings, award ceremonies, and store openings. One man was standing back with his arms crossed, watching everything that was happening: Nelson, the editor. His gray eyes were watching everything intently.

TJ had come with Ghost close on his heel. Seeing them here, together, made it feel like all was right with the world. But it wasn't. There were still many questions to resolve. He seemed calmer today as they walked over to me. "Hey, I want to thank you for taking such good care of my buddy here. I don't know what I would have done without your help." I was about to say something, but Ghost barked just like the dogs on TV shows do and we laughed. He touched my arm. "I want to tell Nelson I think his paper did a nice job with the announce-ment about Robin. I don't want to do it after what he's said about me, but... Be right back." He headed over toward the man frowning at the forensic team who were concentrating on their work.

I watched as TJ spoke to Nelson, then I looked closer. Something was going on there. The editor had taken a big step away as if TJ had the plague. He dropped his arms and stomped away to another place, away from TJ, where he could continue his observations. Was Nelson adding drama to a tedious process law enforcement had to follow maybe in hopes of stirring things up to sell more papers. The last thing I wanted to do was spend more than a nanosecond guessing what moti-vated that man.

When TJ came back, dragging his feet a little, I asked what had happened.

"I don't know. I tried to be nice and that's what I got. Look, I have to meet the tire guy. Do you need a ride or are you going to stay for a while?"

I noticed Craig walking toward the team at the gravesite. "No, I think I'll stay for a little bit and watch."

TJ talked to Craig for a minute then went to his truck.

"Why are you ignoring me?" Nelson's words made me jump. "Do you have a problem, too?"

My teeth ground together. I didn't want to talk to this man. He had allowed the reporter to write the treasure on Waterwood land and put it on his front page which upset TJ. That's how this mess all began.

"TJ was trying to be nice," I spat at him. Why couldn't I hide my feelings?

"Ah, well, maybe that's what he told you, but I know I'm not on his favorite-friends list." His mouth was sounding wet as he tried to push all those words out of his mouth. His speech impediment certainly didn't enhance his image. He assumed a nonchalant, casual attitude and leaned over in my line of vision so I had to look at his gunmetal gray eyes. "Tell me, why are you upset?"

I turned slowly to face him head on. "And why would I want to say anything to you?" *You, who has suggested in both subtle and overt ways, that TJ could be capable of killing your reporter.* But I kept that to myself.

He answered as if I had truly asked a question. "Because I'm a newspaperman and a good listener."

Anger and frustration boiled up and words erupted from my mouth. "This is all your fault." There was something about this man that brought out the worst in me. I was about to apologize when I caught him smirking. My blatant accusation had pleased him. "Forget it. Just leave me alone." I turned and walked away as quickly as I could on the uneven ground. Then groaned when I saw I was walking right toward Craig who was coming my way. Too late. I closed my eyes, wishing I had never said anything. I stood still and waited. Would Nelson embarrass me in front of Craig? But I peeked around and saw he was walking back to his car.

"Anything wrong, Emma?" he asked.

"No, what could be wrong?" I snapped. My mouth was out of control. "I couldn't be better."

"Wow, everybody is on edge today. Must be something in the stars."

For once, I kept my mouth shut. As a result, there was an awkward silence between us.

Finally, he said, "I have something for you."

Great, some mindless gesture I have to pretend is meaning-ful. "And that is...?"

"A package from Dr. Bergstrom."

Now, I was boxed in by my own impulsive behavior.

"Emma?" Craig said tentatively. "I think you'll want this." He held out a plain white cardboard box. "It's the bone marrow sample he took from the body found in the unmarked grave."

I swallowed. "Which one?"

"It's from the skeleton, your man-in-the-field. Do you really want to try to identify the poor man buried there?"

I'd been so preoccupied by the threats to TJ, I had forgotten about the possibility of tracing the identity of the unknown man. "Yes, I do."

"He said he did an analysis and called in a favor from one of those gene-mapping, build-your-family-tree companies. He sent me an email to forward to you so you can get in touch with them to start your search."

I couldn't believe what I was hearing. "Yes, yes, please send it along," I said in a rush. "I'll do the research and maybe, just maybe, we can put a name to the unknown man."

"Emma, I can't ask you to do this officially, but would you keep me in the loop."

"I'll do that, by email, so I won't be a bother. You're busy right now."

Craig sighed a little. "You're right about that, but you will call me if there's a big breakthrough, right?"

I had been so upset with this man who was just doing his job, but now, my friend put a smile on my face. He knew me so well. "Yes, of course."

My phone soon chimed with an incoming email. Craig had wasted no time forwarding the email. I read it quickly and ran to my computer, ready to begin my search. The email gave me the information about the account Dr. Bergstrom had set up for me. I only had to wait for the initial report of possible matches. I was grateful he had expedited the process. Now, it was up to me to follow through with the investigation.

In the meantime, I wondered what I could do from my end. My best source of information was Emma herself. The first casual question I'd put in a letter had brought back a curt response with a warning. I decided to give her another chance to be clear. I hustled back to the cabin. All this walking was paying off. I felt stronger. I was careful but no longer tentative about walking. At least there was a positive side to this messy business.

Soon, I was sitting at the plantation desk in the cabin with pen in hand. I'd stopped at the Cottage and brought along the sheets of Emma's personal stationery and laid them on the corner of the desktop.

The Cottage

Dear Emma,
You asked about the name of my friend and your descendant. His given name is Thomas Jefferson Ross, but he prefers to be called TJ. He told me your family has a long-standing tradition. Every firstborn son is given the name of a famous person, a hero. That way, if the boy ever

falters, ever second-guesses himself, he'll remember what the family expects of him and what he should expect of himself.

TJ thought the tradition dated back to your father who was named after the great American politician, diplomat, and inventor Benjamin Franklin. I guess the idea of using a nickname or initials wasn't popular in his era. In my time, people shorten everything, like a cousin is known as a cuz. Our name isn't shortened very often, but someone I knew tried to call me Emmy all the time. After gently correcting her, I stopped spending time with her group of friends.

Speaking of names, the authorities here are trying to determine the name of the poor soul buried at the Point. Their chances of success are small.

I looked at the Davenport desk you placed in the alcove off the front parlor. There were some pages of your personal stationery in one of the slots. I brought them here to the cabin. I'll leave them on the plantation desk if you wish to use them.

There isn't anything big happening here. The world is about to pop into spring. Light green buds are on the trees. Daffodils are standing about a foot tall with flower buds growing fatter each day. It won't be long before the spring flowers will fill the world with color and scent. TJ will be able to plant the part of the field known as the Point. The skeleton has been removed and the space made whole again.

So, Waterwood has settled into its normal rhythm, getting ready for the demanding schedule of preparing and planting fields for a summer or autumn harvest. TJ and I have talked about reviving your kitchen garden. I will let

*you know what we decide. Perhaps you could offer some
guidance in selecting the best plants.*

With deep affection,
Emma

I read the letter, careful that it offered only a gentle nudge
or two. I thought my description of her family's naming tradition would reinforce our connection. The update on the arrival
of spring was a natural thing. The fact TJ would be cultivating
the land called the Point was a normal update of what I'd
written before. At least I hoped she would consider it a natural
comment. The only part making me consider a rewrite was the
part about people trying to identify the man. It was a quiet
appeal for information, but I hoped it wasn't too obvious.

I couldn't decide. My uncertainty was the result of what
had happened to TJ and what Craig might do. I got up from the
desk and walked around the small cabin TJ had rebuilt for this
special piece of furniture and the two lovers. A little form of
crimson paper nestled in one of the cubbyholes caught my eye.
I had folded the origami butterfly to honor Emma and Daniel,
to symbolize a soul set free, and a bond of love meant to last
forever.

Finally, I put my fancy and beloved fountain pen in the
stacked pen holder and moved the letter into the center of the
writing surface. I would have to wait for her reaction and hope
for the best.

Chapter Thirty-Two

"Good people do not need laws to tell them to act responsibly, while bad people will find a way around the laws."

——*Plato*

Later, my ringing phone jolted me awake. I'd fallen asleep on the sofa. The screen showed an incoming call from Craig. I began to reach out to answer it but pulled my hand back. His calls were never friendly chats, especially when he was on a case involving TJ or me in some way. I was emotionally drained by everything that had happened since the morning TJ had hammered on my door waving Robin's article about the unclaimed treasure somewhere on Waterwood land. So much, too much. But...

I tapped the green button and said hello. Craig was almost out of breath. Immediately, I thought something had happened to TJ. It's amazing how fast the brain can process and jump to conclusions when under stress. Then I remembered TJ had said he had to meet a guy who was going to fix one of the tractor's tires punctured by an antler lost in one of his fields. He had no idea how long it would take, hopefully it would be done before dark, but if I needed anything, he had his phone.

"Hey, is everything okay?" I asked, while dreadful possibilities came to mind.

"I'm fine," pausing to draw a breath. "But our friend Fred isn't."

Did Robin's killer go after Fred? My hand tightened on the phone case.

"Someone broke into Fred's apartment and ransacked the place."

I was so relieved I almost laughed. Instead, I cleared my throat. "Is she okay?"

"She was at work. She is pretty shaken up though."

"Thank goodness she wasn't home. Um, does that mean the person who broke in knows Fred and her schedule?"

"That crossed my mind, and I came up with a vague connection. The person only has to know she is a bartender at the Pub then pop in to see if she is working and he's good to go to her apartment."

"He... or she," I suggested.

"That's always a possibility, but if this break-in has any connection to Robin, I still think we're looking for a man."

"Unless..." I paused, not wanting to voice my suspicion.

"Go on."

"Unless Fred wanted to throw suspicion in another direction. If so, she might have staged the break-in."

"Emma!" Craig barked. I could hear his quick intake of breath. "I'm sorry. This case is getting to me."

"No, *I'm* sorry," I said quickly. "Look, I know she is a friend of yours. Maureen and I liked her, too. We've even talked about finding a time to go back when she is working. But Craig, you said yourself, she was reluctant to talk to you because you are with the police. Or..." I waited, but he didn't push back. He was listening. "Fred probably knew Robin better than anyone else in the area. Maybe she had an inkling of what Robin was working on. Maybe more than an inkling and it was something that directly affected her or someone important to her. Don't be distracted by her pretty face. I bet she is strong enough to move Robin's body." There was silence on the line. "Craig, are you still there?

"Yes, I'm here." Craig sounded irritated. "I have had the same thoughts." He drew in such a deep breath I could hear it. "This job must be getting to me."

In the silence that followed, I felt like Craig was fighting demons only he could identify. "I thought of all those things and buried them. I don't want to believe she had anything to do with Robin's murder."

"But you believe your long-time friend is capable of murder?" Oh, no! Those words flew out of my mouth before I realized what I was saying. There was no way I could claw them back.

The silence between us was like ice.

Finally, I pushed out the words, "I'm sorry.

Cold and deliberate, the detective, a member of law enforcement, was back. "I will keep in mind what you said. I called so you'd hear the news from me."

"Good luck with your..." but I was talking to the tone that indicated our call was ended.

I hadn't asked him what was taken from Fred's apartment or if he had any idea who had broken in. He hadn't said anything about Robin's laptop, tablet, or phone. But then again, I hadn't given him the opportunity. The only thing I'd accomplished was to insult a friend and the lead person who had TJ's future in his hands.

I am such an idiot!

I wanted to call him back and grovel with my apologies. If I did, I suspected he would send the call to voicemail. I didn't think I could express myself adequately in a recorded message. Look what a mess I'd created in a live conversation. No, best to leave things alone for now.

There were times Craig's job of solving puzzles and figuring out motives was fascinating. The wide array of facts and information about seemingly random things amazed me. But the emotional toll of seeing what human beings do to one another was staggering. No, I wouldn't want Craig's job for the world. At school, seeing a child fall and scrape her knee on the playground was enough drama for me. At least I could offer comfort and dry her tears.

My head jerked up as I thought of something I might be able to do to help. I grabbed my phone and sent Craig a text and mentally crossed my fingers he would respond. I asked:

Have you looked at Robin's social media yet?

It wasn't more than a few seconds before I had an answer:

No. Too busy.

Finally, something I could do to help. There was no guarantee I would find anything, but it was worth a try. So many reporters babbled online about the stories they were covering, it was a wonder they found time to do the work.

I went to my laptop, got online, and began my search for RobinHunterNews. I went to Twitter first since I'd heard it was the preferred site for journalists. If she wanted to become known and eventually move to another news outlet, it was the site where she should post. Also, the paper had online e-editions. I went back about three weeks then began to read forward. She'd posted about some annual event at the Chesapeake Bay Maritime Museum in St. Michaels and an art show opening in Chestertown. All newsworthy to locals, but not the type of thing to get the attention of a big city editor. I kept going. Her other social media followed along the same lines, but her posts on Instagram, the site requiring pictures, included two shots of Waterwood shoreline. She must have taken one on the day she showed up at Witches Point to cover our discovery of the unmarked grave. The other one ... it looked familiar. I zoomed in on the picture. Yes, it was blurry, but Waterwood House was there. Had she taken the picture while looking for the buried treasure?

Then I came across a post about a public hearing on climate change. Then more about proposed new rules about setbacks and use restrictions being considered by the Council Commission along with hints about an investigation she said *would change your mind about leading citizens and how decisions are made.*

That sounded dangerous to me. Maybe she had angered the wrong person or people? I scrolled on.

I shook my head in disgust as I read her post meant to reignite interest in buried treasure on Waterwood land. That is what started this whole mess.

Well, not really. TJ would have found the skull and that story would have grabbed her attention.

I set my speculation aside and reread the post. Buried in it was a suggestion of a tie-in between treasure and her investigation of the proposed new rules. It didn't make sense. She had gone missing before she could follow it up. There was one post of a photo on Instagram with a caption about a Council Commission meeting. It didn't seem important. Why would she post such an innocuous picture of three community award-winners grinning at the camera? What was newsworthy about it beyond the obvious? I looked at the date. It was posted a couple of days before she went missing. There must be something about...

My phone rang again. I felt like my head was going to explode. So much was happening, so fast. With a sigh, I saw it was Craig. Our conversation was brief. There had been a development. TJ was going up to Easton. If I wanted to come, I needed to contact him right away.

I did.

At the police building in Easton, we were shown into an antiseptic interrogation room containing a cheap table and two chairs. The strange color paint on the walls—a medium pea green—made me fight down the urge to be sick on the worn linoleum floor. This environment sapped energy and hope out of me.

Alone, we had little to say, almost afraid to speculate about what was happening. The only sound was Ghost's rhythmic breathing with his head on TJ's knee. He had brought him because he knew Ghost wouldn't let him out of his sight anytime soon unless they were home together. Fortunately, we didn't have to wait long for Craig to reappear.

"There is an interesting development. Come with me."

Chapter Thirty-Three

"If I am a painter and I do your portrait, have I or haven't I the right to paint you as I want?"

— *Oriana Fallaci, Italian journalist and author, famous for her revealing interviews with many world leaders*

TJ and I exchanged a look, totally mystified, and followed Craig down the hall. When he stopped in front of a closed door, he said, "It seems my murder victim had a brother. The man walked into the building and told the officer on duty that he had a present for me. You two can watch from here."

He opened the door into a small, dark room where we could peer into another interrogation room at two men and two uniformed officers standing guard. One man, seated at the table, had brown shaggy hair that needed a good washing. His skin was brown from constant exposure to the natural elements. His body was in constant motion—foot tapping, hands clenching and unclenching, tongue wetting his lips again and again. It was obvious he would bolt if given the chance. The man wanted out of that room.

A second man stood in the corner, watching. He looked like a normal person you'd see in a restaurant or movie theater. He was clean cut. His shirt and slacks were casual. He leaned against a wall with his head hung low. He held his hands at his waist, his fingers folded together as if in prayer. He was ordinary looking, except for one thing. His short hair was platinum blonde. Just like Robin's hair.

I turned to Craig, who was leaning against the wall, watching the two men. "Robin's brother. No question."

Craig nodded slowly. "Sam Preston."

As if he knew he was being watched, he released his fingers and gave a little push of his body off the wall. The officers reacted, but Sam waved them off. They relaxed but were vigilant as Sam began to pace, far from the man at the table. Built solid, he watched the seated man, ready to pounce if he tried to stand or even do more than breathe. The scene made me nervous. Robin's brother moved like he knew how to use his strength, but the other man sitting at the table wouldn't be a pushover. The only word I could think of to describe him was massive. His shoulders and upper arms would have strained the seams of any tee shirt. His thick neck suggested he'd played football at one time. He raised his beefy hand and ran it over the black stubble on his face.

"Who is the Nervous Nellie?" TJ wanted to know.

Craig turned toward the door. "That's what we're about to find out." He pulled open the door and left.

TJ and I took a step closer to the glass window to watch and saw Craig enter the room.

"Mr. Preston?" Craig said as he extended his hand.

"Call me Sam, please." The voices came through a tinny speaker.

Seeing the way Sam's hand gripped Craig's, the phrase *killing machine* popped in my head though I wasn't sure if Craig or the man sitting at the table should be worried.

"First," Craig began softly. "I want to say, I'm sorry for your loss."

Sam inclined his head a little in acknowledgement. Then he raised his eyes to the seated man. "I just want you to arrest the man who ..." His voice cracked and he stopped.

"Hey, HEY!" yelled the man at the table. "Don't look at me. I didn't do nothin'..."

"Shut up!" Sam commanded.

In the silence, Craig shot them both a look that screamed *Stand Down*. Then he asked the seated man, "Who are you?"

The massive man raised his chin a little and declared in a deep voice rubbed raw, "I am Tim Turner, but folks call me Buck." He cast a sidelong look at Sam filled with resentment then flipped his gaze away and directed his full and congenial attention to Craig. "This lug and I have been friends since childhood." He shook his head of unkempt hair. "But we ain't friends no more, I guess." His eyes were sharp as needles as he turned to Sam. "What happened to you over there?" Buck slammed his hands flat on the table.

We all jumped.

The uniformed officers leapt forward, but Craig waved them off. "Sit down!" Craig's tone put him in command of the situation. He picked up an extra chair and slammed it down on the other side of the room. "You, too." Sam complied. "Now, I ask the questions. You answer. Got it?"

Buck looked away, failing to hide his disgust. Sam's quiet "Yes, Sir" suggested a military background.

"Okay, gentlemen. This is what I've got. Sam Preston, brother of Robin Hunter, and Tim—"

"Buck, call me Buck," he said with a huff.

Craig paused for a moment. Was he going to assert his authority again? "Alright. Buck," Craig said without a trace of emotion.

I was impressed by how the detective would pick his battles.

"Buck, what is your relationship to Robin?"

"She is my woman. I was gonna make her my wife..." He mumbled, "As soon as I found her."

"Found her?' Craig asked, confused. "You didn't look very hard. She has been on the Shore for what, a year? She even posted on social media."

"I don't look at that stuff," Buck announced. "It's all lies and manipulation by the government."

"Okay," Craig continued. "Why weren't you together?"

"She ran away from him," Sam said.

"No, no, she was just taking some time to build her career. I was letting her get this journalism thing out of her system."

"She left you 'cause you hit her, you moron." Sam's voice rose as he began to get out of his chair.

"SIT DOWN!" Craig's command could be heard through the cinderblock wall.

Sam slowly lowered his body back on the chair.

"Buck, is that true?" Craig asked.

I wondered if we were getting close to a motive to hurt Robin. Maybe a confrontation that went terribly wrong?

"Not exactly." Buck's voice was barely above a whisper.

"HA! Really?" Sam bellowed. "Why did she get a restraining order against you?"

"Is that true, Buck?" Craig asked calmly.

Buck looked away and gave him a little nod. Then he turned back to the man sitting across the table. "What did you expect me to do? I was working real hard to get us out of the apartment and into a house with a fireplace."

I looked at TJ with an unspoken question. *A fireplace?*

"It was real important to me. Robin was helping though she wasn't making much money at her little newspaper job. Then she said they had cut her pay. I told her to find another job doing something else, but she refused." His nose went up in the air to show he was affronted by her reaction. "I'd have that house now if she hadn't taken off."

Craig scowled. "Are you saying she took money from you?"

"Yeah, she tried to steal everything from me, but I had a few tricks up my sleeve to protect myself. She couldn't hide from me."

Craig asked the most important question of all as if he was asking about the weather. "Mr. Turner, did you kill Robin?"

Buck started to come across the table, grabbing for Craig, but the officers' hands clamped on his shoulders, forcing him back in the chair.

"What an animal," I breathed.

Craig took a deep breath and rose. He motioned to his officer. "Mr. Turner, we're going to offer you free accommodations for the night while I—"

"You can't do that," Buck screamed as he tried to lunge at Sam "This is your doing."

Sam was on his feet in a shot, knees bent, hands out, arms and fingers tensed. Ready.

"STOP!" Craig examined the two men who had frozen in place at his order. "Sam, sit down. Mr. Turner, go with the officers." The raised voices had brought backup rushing into the room.

"You can't arrest me. I ain't done nothing," Buck bellowed.

"I'm not arresting you. I need to detain you for a short time while I follow up on some details." When Buck started to open his mouth again, Craig carefully declared, "And I have the authority to do that." Staring at Buck, he slowly shook his head. "Don't give me a reason to arrest you."

It took a moment for the words to sink in. Then Buck's shoulders sagged. He was led out by the officers without difficulty. The room was silent while Craig and Sam stared at each other.

"What now?" TJ breathed. "Is he going to detain Sam, too?"

I had no clue. Everybody waited without saying another word. Another officer entered the room and Craig sat down.

"Officer, would you get us two coffees, please?" Craig turned to Sam. "Or maybe you'd like a bottle of water?"

"Water would be great. Thanks."

Refreshed, Craig began. "Okay, how about you tell me your story?"

Sam examined his bottle of water closely for a few moments, took a deep breath, and sighed. "I wasn't excited when Robin took up with Buck." He shrugged. "I figured she would grow out of her infatuation. It didn't happen soon enough. I found out what was happening with my sister while I was on my second tour in Afghanistan. He worked hard to control her then beat up on her when she resisted. She finally ran away and got a restraining order."

Craig raised his eyebrows. "Buck doesn't strike me as the type of man to let a little restraining order get in his way."

"You're right about that."

"Why didn't you do something about the situation when you got home?"

Sam raised his eyes to meet Craig's unspoken accusation with clear determination. "I was ready to fix it. I needed to talk to my sister, but she had disappeared. She knew Buck wouldn't give up and wouldn't let a piece of paper stop him from getting what he wanted. And he wanted her." He shook his head in resignation and dropped his eyes back to the water bottle where his fingers were busy stripping off the label. "I looked for her. Drove my wife crazy. I had no idea Robin had changed her name. She always said she wanted to be a TV reporter. That's where I looked. I had no idea she had opted for the anonymity of newspaper reporting. I didn't know where she was until..." He took a ragged breath. "Until a buddy of mine saw her picture on the news and called me."

Craig waited until Sam got his emotions under control and continued. "Then you contacted us and came here."

"Yes, I needed to confirm..."

"And sadly," Craig said quickly. "You were able to make the identification. Again, I'm sorry for your loss."

Sam slowly raised his head and looked directly at Craig. "I came here for another reason, Detective. I wanted to see if Buck was anywhere in the vicinity. Apps are great tools." Sam raised his chin a little and huffed. "If he thought he could hide, he was wrong. I found him here, in the area. I tracked him."

"Why?"

Sam's left eye narrowed. "I wanted to look him in the eye. I was sure I'd be looking into the heart of a murderer," Sam said with an edge to his words.

"But you brought him in. You are a —"

"A trained killer. You're right. The United States Army taught me some skills and right along with those skills, it taught me to have respect for the rule of law. That's why I brought him to you. It's your job to finish this."

TJ and I looked at each other, amazed.

Not long after we'd observed everything that had happened in the interrogation room, Craig came to ask us a favor. Sam wanted to see where his sister had been found. I wasn't sure it was a good idea. It would be one thing to see the body of a loved one, but quite another to see where it had been dumped in raw earth. There was no talking him out of the idea. Instead, I came up with a plan to help balance the horror with support. I ducked down the hall and made a call.

"Maria, I'm so glad I caught you. Are you still at the Cottage?"

"Yes," she answered cautiously. "Why?"

"I have a huge favor to ask. Is it possible there might be enough food prepared to feed four people tonight? I have to warn you, three of them are men who might have big appetites. It's been a tough day." There was silence from the other end. "It's okay if there isn't enough. We can get pizzas or go out to eat in St. Michaels or Easton—"

"NO!" The strength of her response made me gasp in surprise. "No, you want to eat here with your friends, you bring your friends. Maria's dinner is better than those restaurants," she said with a glint of disdain.

I quickly agreed and was ready to tell Sam, TJ, and Craig we could look forward to a fantastic dinner, but Maria wasn't finished. "I am going to set the table in the dining room. This dinner doesn't belong in the kitchen."

What had I left on the table? So many times, I spread my research and historical items there. I didn't want to lose track of—

"Stop, I can hear what you're thinking," said Maria, with a smile in her voice. There is very little on the table. I will carefully move everything into the den. Tomorrow, you can return them to the table and get back to work. I must go." She ended the call abruptly.

It was always an adventure talking with Maria. At least I had a plan to offer, a plan to help ease the sadness of the brother's errand.

Chapter Thirty-Four

"When we are tired, we are attacked by ideas we conquered long ago."

— Friedrich Nietzsche, a German philosopher
and cultural critic

I was so relieved to see the drab steel gray clouds had been blown to the east toward the Atlantic Ocean which was not far away. The wide dome of the sky was filled with lavender, orange, red, and yellow to celebrate sunset and lighten the mood of this sad errand. I wondered if this show of natural beauty reminded anyone of a power greater than any of us and in that, brought solace and comfort.

We parked on the other side of the trees and the four of us walked out toward the water, toward the portion of land where the yellow crime scene tape still flapped.

Sam looked at TJ. "Is that where...?"

TJ nodded.

I could hear Sam choke back tears and he set off to walk those last yards of ground alone.

The three of us backed away to give the grieving brother some privacy. As I looked at the beauty surrounding us—the azure blue sky, rich brown earth nurturing pale green shoots of new growth, a flock of geese in the V-formation overhead—it was hard to reconcile such a violent act could happen in such a peaceful place. It was more than I could handle, watching Sam standing by the tape, hunched over, his shoulders shaking. I turned around and looked at the river calmly flowing on its way to the Bay. Nature took everything in stride and went on with life.

After a short time, Sam came to the place where we were waiting, but there was something different about him. It was the way he was walking. His military training was showing. He was marching and he marched right up to TJ.

Sam looked him straight in the eye and barked, "Did you kill my little sister? Did you kill Robin?"

We were all shocked at Sam's outburst. Craig shifted his position in case he had to prevent a physical confrontation. I opened my mouth to defend my friend, but we didn't have to do or say anything.

TJ didn't flinch. He looked Sam in the eye. "No, I did not kill or harm your sister in any way."

"But how could she have been murdered here in your home, right under your nose unless you...?" Sam's voice choked with tears. Desperate for answers, he had followed the situation to a logical conclusion.

But it was wrong. TJ pulled the grieving man into a hug and hung on while Sam's body was pummeled by sobs.

I stepped back to give the poor man some privacy. I figured this was a guy moment. Having a woman involved would only make it worse. Instead, I turned back to the place where someone had buried Robin, evidently hoping her body would never be found.

"We'll take care of him," I whispered into the wind.

When the men moved toward the line of trees, I followed. Once again, I was amazed by men's ability to rebound from an intense emotional moment.

As I approached TJ's truck, Craig called out to me. "I hope you're going to make good on your promise."

"Promise?"

"One of Maria's dinners," TJ clarified. "We told Sam all about her fabulous..." He threw his hands up in the air. "...everything!"

"It's all waiting for us at the Cottage," I assured him.

"Great! I'm starved." Craig announced.

I got to TJ's truck, shaking my head. Wasn't it just like a bunch of men to find comfort by thinking of their stomachs! I hoped Maria had some bottles of beer in the fridge. This didn't strike me as a wine-drinking meal.

In the few minutes it took us to meet at the Cottage, we had become a subdued group. The men milled around in the entry hall and living room, not knowing where to settle, even TJ and Craig who had been to my little house loads of times were uneasy. The energy we'd felt earlier had drained away, leaving behind emotional exhaustion. I wanted to create a comfort zone, a place and time where we could all recharge. My first stop was the fridge. When I opened the door, I sent up a silent prayer of thanks to Maria. She had made sure there was enough cold beer for the meal and had left a split bottle of Prosecco on the door for me. Maria was a gem!

I should do something nice for her, something for the woman, not the person who takes care of everyone else. Maybe a nice Pashmina shawl or...

Later. It was time to get this group into a better mood. "Okay, who wants a cold beer?" I sang out.

That was the call that gave them direction. Suddenly, my kitchen was filled with big male bodies. I'd never get dinner on the table at this rate. So, I put them to work. After sending things to the table, pulling enough meat loaf for an army warm from the oven, serving up a big bowl of fluffy mashed potatoes, heating the peas, and whisking the gravy into shape, we all sat down. As I looked around the table, I realized—yet again—Maria was right. I should use the dining room for friendly gatherings, not just solo research projects.

At first, we all focused on our great dinner, but as our appetites were satisfied, eating slowed down so I asked Sam a question. "Did Robin email or mail you, I don't know, anything that might have been notes for a story?"

Craig shot me a look but remained quiet, hoping for a positive answer. Sam took a long time to consider what I'd asked.

Finally, he said, "I don't think so. Our email servers are reliable. No, I would have remembered if I'd seen anything. Like I said, her contact with me has been sporadic in the past year or so. I thought she'd be happy about our baby coming, but she barely talked to either me or my wife. I didn't even know this area existed or that she was living here." He pushed back from the table. "Bathroom?" His voice cracked.

I directed him down the hall and he had no sooner rounded the corner then Craig said, "Way to go, Emma? He was getting calm, and now, you upset him all over again."

"It wasn't my fault. His sister was murdered. He is going to be emotional. She was working on a big story which might have led to her death, and we don't know anything about it, except what she put on social media. That's just weird."

"She's right," Sam said as he came and sat down. "I'm sorry I'm ... as she said, emotional. Ask me anything. I want to help."

Craig set the tone and direction. "Sam, I understand you and Buck grew up together. Can you tell me what that was like?"

Sam moved his empty plate away and pushed back from the table with his beer in hand. "When we were little, he was fun and nice. Mom liked to have him over because he was so polite. He even helped with the dishes." Sam turned to me. "This was such a great dinner, Emma. Just what I needed. And I'll help with the dishes when you're ready."

"You're welcome, Sam." I made it obvious when I looked toward Craig that Sam should continue to answer his question.

With a deep sigh, Sam did. "We did everything together, built forts, raced our bikes, all the things boys do. He was even okay with Robin trailing after us sometimes. You know, most guys would want to ditch a little sister." A weak smile crossed his lips at the memory. "Heck, he even invited her along when we went to get ice cream at the local Dairy Queen." His smile died. "But we weren't always together. His dad was into hunting big-time. Not big game or anything like that. Dove, deer, goose, mostly. They even went up to Canada once. His dad gave him his first hunting rifle when he was, I don't know, really young. He would go out on what he called *hunting expeditions* with his dad. Just the two of them. They were close."

"Was that part of growing up where you lived?" Craig asked.

"Not really. His family was into it. Mine wasn't."

"I know what that's like," TJ added. "Did it strain your friendship?"

"No, we were really tight. What tore us apart was when puberty hit. He went into testosterone overload. It was the same for all of us, but Buck's dad died at about the same time. Looking back, I guess Buck buried his emotions. He didn't know how to grieve. He acted the way he thought his dad would act, all tough and macho. The man never showed his feelings, even when he was proud of his son. It was a slap on the back and on to the next. Buck must have thought that was the way he should be. He didn't realize there is more to life, and I guess there wasn't anybody to teach him how to be a man."

Sam drained the last of his beer. "Buck did everything his dad told him to do. When the man finally went to the doctor about his constant cough, lung cancer had taken hold and he was gone in a matter of weeks. Buck tried to show he wasn't affected by it. He said, dying is part of life. His dad had taught him that when they went hunting on the Michigan Upper Peninsula or up into Canada. He thought it was no big deal.

"How did he get the nickname Buck?" I had been wondering since I first saw him at the police station. It was appropriate, but I had wondered where it had come from.

"That one time they went to Canada, they saw a huge buck. His dad told him he had to get a buck like that, one with a big rack." Sam glanced at me. "Antlers."

Glad for the little comic relief, we all smiled. Then Sam went back to his story.

"To stay focused on his goal, he wanted us all to call him Buck. To be honest, I think he is obsessed with finding and shooting the Big Buck, calling it his holy grail. His goal in life is to hang those antlers over a fireplace. Keep in mind he doesn't have a fireplace or even a house yet, but he has the guns to bring down the big stag. He has always been afraid people will see him as weak, the boy without a father. When he got mad, he would stomp and snort just like a buck. He figured if he got the buck, it would prove how strong he was."

"You two are so different. How did you stay friends?" Craig asked.

"We didn't, not really." Sam took a little breath and his lips tightened. "When we got to high school, he started paying more attention to Robin, not as my little sister, but as a girl, if you know what I mean. Made her uncomfortable. She spent more time with friends her age and avoided Buck. So, I did, too."

He shrugged and picked up his empty beer bottle.

"Would you like another?" I offered.

"No, I've had enough." He took a deep breath. "I guess you need to hear the rest of the story."

Craig nodded.

"Those last years, I got okay grades, but when it was time to apply to college, I knew it wasn't for me. I joined the Army. The night before I left, Buck came over and promised me he would look out for Robin. The thought made me cringe, but..." Sam cocked his head to the side and stared out the window. "I hoped he would be the boy I'd grown up with. He became a mechanic. Figured he could always find a job after he got the rack and went west to go after elk and moose. He trained and got to be a good one. Letters from Robin told me how he took care of her. Even loaned her prom date a spiffy convertible. When she went to college, he would drive to campus, take her out for dinner so she could avoid the dorm food. She wrote about those kinds of things she thought I would do if I were stateside. At first, I was a little jealous, then grateful." He played with the empty bottle, getting lost in memories.

Craig kept the conversation going. "Then what happened."

"You know, nature took its course. The time they spent together, strengthened by the memories they shared of growing up. When I came home, they were a couple. She was working at an entry level job for a weekly paper. He had his cars. When he went on a hunting trip, she stayed home and worked on some in-depth story. She was really driven. It was all good. I signed up again and went back overseas for another tour. About a month later, that's when things got weird."

"What do you mean?" Craig wanted to know.

"The tone of Robin's letters changed. She was religious about writing to me, but they got shorter and focused on her work. There was very little about Buck." Sam's hand became a fist as it rested on the table. "I knew something was wrong, but I was too far away..."

We all stayed quiet to allow Sam to regroup. I tried not to watch but it was hard not to notice his changing expressions as memories left tracks across his face. After several minutes, he began again.

"She wrote about her plans to leave the Pittsburg area. She was trying to figure out where to go. She could have gone out West, but she always wanted to be close to the action. She liked politics, national politics. I don't know why, but she gobbled up everything about it. She wanted to be a TV political reporter and do in-depth stories. Called them investigations." He shrugged as he played with some crumbs on the table. "I guess with the state of things the way they are now, she'd had a lot of work opportunities. But she needed more experience. She thought about going to New York City, but decided it was too big. If she wanted to cover politics, Washington, D.C. was the place to be. There was no mention of Buck and, when I asked, she said she was going alone. Then the letters came with no return address on the envelopes. She said she would send it when she found a place." His hand squeezed into a fist again. " I should have known!"

He slammed his fist on the table. The dishes leapt up in the air. I caught my wine glass as it wobbled.

"Sorry." His meek voice spurred me into action.

I bounced up, grabbed my dish and glass and said with energy I really didn't feel, "Okay, gentlemen. Time for coffee and some dessert."

Craig looked hopeful. "Maria's Chocolate Chip Cookies?"

"And brownies. Grab your dishes. It will make things go faster" and I led them to the kitchen.

"That must have been when Robin got the restraining order," Craig whispered to me. "She wanted to make sure Sam didn't mention where she was, but she didn't want him to know why she'd left. Tough spot for her."

"Do you think Buck killed her?" I asked in return.

"He has a temper and likes to get physical. I don't know. Maybe."

The chocolate and coffee did little to revive us. I think we all felt the burden of the story of what brought the young journalist to the Eastern Shore. Sam had given Craig the background he needed. Now, he had to find her killer.

Chapter Thirty-Five

"Yesterday is history, tomorrow is a mystery, today is a gift of
God, which is why we call it the present."

— *Bil Keane, American cartoonist, known for
the newspaper comic, Family Circus*

The weekend had finally arrived, though for TJ during the
spring planting season, it was a regular workday. Early in
the morning, Craig sent a text to both TJ and me, asking if we
wanted to join him for a pancake breakfast at the Cove in St.
Michaels. I had heard a lot of good things about it, but I hadn't
managed to go and sample the delicacies people were always
talking about: stacks of flurry pancakes that arrived at the table
with pats of butter already melting over the golden-brown
stack, warm maple syrup—*real* maple syrup, not sugar water—
perfectly fried slices of thick bacon cooked to order as crispy or
limp, and a side of hash browns. And the coffee, not fancy or
foamed, but soul-warming good. It sounded like heaven. I sent a
text accepting the invitation and closed my eyes, hoping TJ

would say yes, so I would have a ride. He answered fast and I had just enough time to shower and dress.

At the Cove, tucked in the back of the pharmacy, it seemed like half the town had come for breakfast. It was a like a small diner, serving simple but delicious food, tucked in the back corner of the drug store. We had to wait for a table to open up for us, but Craig promised it would be worth it. Craig and TJ talked sports. We couldn't talk about the case. There were too many ears around us, all perked up for tidbits and gossip they could carry to friends and family. I let my eyes roam over the room that could have been twice the size to accommodate customers and the fleet of waitresses taking orders, delivering food, filling coffee mugs, and busing tables. Waitresses, yes. There were no men in sight. Waitresses based on their simple coral uniforms with white half-aprons and a fan of coral print fabric held in place by their name tags. It felt like we had traveled back to the 1950s. Nobody seemed to feel this was a sexist setup. The four women worked the tables in concert. If someone had time to grab the coffeepot, every mug at every table was refreshed. Every time an order was delivered to the kitchen window, steaming hot, ready for pickup, a little bell would be tapped, like the one in old movies used to call a bell-hop. This morning, there was a constant tinkling of the bell serenading the customers. A large mural high on the front wall reminded us of where we were. It was a scene where the land, water, and sky met. A waterman was tonging oysters from his bay-built boat. Tall, wooden markers stood as guides for safe passage through the channels of deeper water. Simple buildings cozied up to the shoreline where families lived and thrived. It represented the Eastern Shore.

It wasn't long before we were pointed to a vacant table against the wall set for three. The waitress was there carrying three mugs and a coffeepot just as we sat down. Craig waved away the offer of menus and with a nod from us, ordered. The only change to the food I anticipated was orders of scrambled eggs for the men. I had no idea where I would put so much food.

While we settled in to wait, Craig asked if I had checked Robin's social media. When I nodded, both men leaned toward the center of the table to hear what I had found.

"I sifted through posts about local events and all, what you would expect from a reporter for a small-town newspaper Only, there were two things you may find interesting." I pulled out some pages. "I printed out the posts I thought were relevant. During the week before she was—" I casually checked the people at nearby tables and the waitresses bustling around near us, then whispered, "before she was murdered, she was promising some surprising revelations."

I waited while Craig and TJ scanned the posts. Craig let out a low whistle.

TJ raised his eyebrows in surprise. "Whatever she was talking about sounds like a possible motive to me."

Craig thought for a moment then shifted his gaze back to me. "You said there was something else?"

I glanced at TJ then looked away saying, "You're not going to like this." I had no choice. I had to plunge right in. "You're familiar with Instagram, the site where people post pictures and add a caption." I had printed out the two pictures Robin had posted and laid the pages on the table.

TJ grabbed one, then the other. "This is Waterwood!"

"Keep your voice down," Craig snapped. He took the pages from TJ's hands and looked at them carefully.

"I swear to you, Craig," he hissed. "That's Waterwood. How in heaven's name did she—"

"And here we are!" announced Annie, the waitress with red hair done in long braids. Breakfast is served!"

271

I reached across the table and took the pages. Talk of murder and trespassing was not going to ruin the sumptuous food in front of us. In the next minutes, with no discussion to interrupt the yummy tastes and delicious aromas, we enjoyed a breakfast to remember.

As I chased the last drops of real maple syrup around my plate with the last bite of pancake on my fork, there was a subtle shift in the lighting over our table. I had a strange feeling and looked up. A tall figure was standing next to my chair, looming over us. I would recognize the woman anywhere. Her jeans and light cotton pullover sweater gathered at her waist fit her perfectly. Fred was gorgeous though she wore little or no makeup. But makeup wasn't the only thing missing. Her friendly smile, always ready to flash at a friend or customer at the Pub, did not appear when she said good morning.

"I see you're enjoying your breakfast." Her words came out like bullets from a gun.

My greeting died on my lips. This wasn't about me. Fred was blasting holes into Craig with those copper-flecked eyes.

Craig quickly used his napkin and pushed back his chair to get up. He was ever the gentleman, but his courtesy was being wasted in this confrontation, for it was a confrontation.

Fred's body tensed. Her shoulders were almost drawn up to her ears. She was digging her fingernails into her hands. "No need to stand on my account." She leaned forward just enough to use her height to intimidate us, especially Craig. "I wouldn't want to disrupt this happy gathering." Waves of fury rolled off her. "I just have one question for you, Mr. Detective. Have you found the person who broke into my apartment?"

"Actually, Fred," Craig began to stand up again. "We can go outside, and I can explain—"

"I don't want an explanation. A simple yes or no will suffice. But I can assume from your reaction, your defensive reaction, the answer is no." She waved a hand in our direction, dismissing what we were doing. "Don't mind me. Go ahead, enjoy your Cove breakfast..." Every word was clearly enunciated. "I'll just continue to live in fear. Maybe whoever broke in and threw everything around will come back. Maybe he will lie in wait in the dark when I come home from work. Maybe he will come in and sit on my bed while I'm sleeping. No problem, Mr. Detective. I'll be fine."

She wasn't fine. Her eyes glistened with unshed tears. She was grieving and frightened.

Her eyes shifted to me, and I felt myself wilt a little under her gaze. "You should be more careful who you spend time with. Time shouldn't be wasted. Robin's murder has taught me that."

She took a step back, her eyes shifting back to Craig, and she slowly shook her head from side to side. "I've known you for a while. I always thought you were good at your job." Her eyes were filled with tears ready to burst free. "I hope it won't be an inconvenience if you have to dig *me* out a field somewhere. She added with emphasis as if she was throwing down a gauntlet. "I Thought You Were Better Than This!"

As the tears escaped and gushed down her cheeks, she made her way through the customers, silent and staring, and charged out the front door.

Chapter Thirty-Six

"It is for the artist...in portrait painting to put on canvas something more than the face the model wears for that one day; to paint the man, in short, as well as his features."

— *James Whistler, American Painter*

The mood was spoiled, and the restorative effects of breakfast were compromised. As we rode back to Waterwood in silence, I was grateful my tummy was happy. TJ dropped me off at the Cottage with a *See you later* and drove off. Inside, I pulled the papers with the printed pictures Robin had posted of Waterwood out of my tote along with my phone. Feeling a little annoyed by Fred and her offensive interruption of our breakfast, I remembered I wanted to show both Craig and TJ one more thing: the curious picture Robin had posted, the one with random people milling around while three smiled at the camera. The caption read, Council Commission meeting. That was all. There must be some significance I was missing.

I brought it up on my computer, made the picture large, and moved it around. Maybe I would recognize someone or... Wait, there in the background. In the corner was a man I recognized. Nelson Jennings. He was standing, no, leaning close to another man, poking him in the shoulder with his index finger. I zoomed in closer. The face of the editor-in-chief was in profile, but I could tell he wasn't happy. As written in *Alice in Wonderland*, this post was getting curiouser and curiouser.

I went for a walk to clear my head and to try and figure out how the pieces of this puzzle fit together. The air was sweet with the scent of early spring. Here and there, the first flowers bloomed. They had been planted naturally by birds and industrious squirrels. My walk took me past the cabin which reminded me I was waiting for a letter from Emma. I went to the cabin and popped open the lock and peered around the door. Yes, a letter was waiting for me.

Beyond Waterwood

My Dear Emma,
You are the clever one! Congratulations.
I hope you do not have angry thoughts of me as you proceed on your quest. Let me explain. My husband's selfish actions taught me if a person only grabs the prize, one misses the journey. There is little joy in living in such a way. Life is a journey. There is so much richness as one steps along the path of life. Along the way, I hope you have learned more about me as a woman and the caretaker of Waterwood.

Allow me to tell you about the landscape you found. I painted it for my daughter Anna Grace so if she ever needed money, she would know there was a legacy waiting for her, passed down from her grandfather. Sadly, I lost her to a devastating outbreak of measles. When she was gone forever, I wanted to destroy the painting, but then I remembered my baby daughter. When I found her, I promised myself I would give her the painting. But I never did. Nurturing hope until the last, I hung the painting in my personal alcove, where I hope you found it still.

There is one more clue to help you find the exact place to dig. I will show you where you will fulfill your quest.

Have patience, dear Emma. Your goal is in sight.

With great affection,

Emma

Post Script. Thank you for the stationery. Putting an empty sheet of that lovely snowy white paper in front of me always inspired my pen and instilled the hope that the person reading my letter would value my words.

That was curious. *I will show you where you will fulfill your quest.* How would she...

The last clue must be in her portrait! Back at the Cottage, I pulled off my clumsy boots and half-ran to Waterwood House. There, once I caught my breath, I looked at Emma's portrait. At first, I didn't see anything that looked like a clue. Then I noticed most of the fingers of her right hand were gently curled into her palm, leaving her index finger pointing downward.

Had Emma chosen to stand on the spot where the strongbox or chest was buried?

There was only one way to find out. I grabbed a bottle of water out of TJ's fridge and headed back to the Cottage and down the path toward the cabin to a place where I could see Lone Oak. I tried to gauge where I had stepped off Daniel's instructions then moved down toward the creek where I would have emerged from the water. No, this angle wasn't right. The Lone Oak was in the background of the painting. I moved around and... yes, this was the right perspective. But was it the right spot?

I held up my amateur sketch still tucked into the pocket of my jacket. There were more trees in her painting than existed today, but some had been replaced naturally. Could it be that the very young one in the painting was now the pine towering over my head? Well, nothing else seemed to fit so I walked toward it... tripped and fell flat on my face.

When I caught my breath, I looked around and found not a vine or branch, but something made of iron sticking out of the ground.

Chapter Thirty-Seven

The cellphone holds today's portraits.

I'd found something or at least, I thought I had. But I didn't have any tools with me to help my investigation and my knee throbbed. Fortunately, it wasn't my knee that was hurt in the accident. I hobbled back to the Cottage, my knee complaining every step of the way.

While I iced it, someone started knocking on my front door. I shook my head trying to clear my brain. So much had happened in the past days, I must have zoned out while sitting still, focusing on making the pain go away. I hadn't even noticed the sound of tires on the gravel drive, something I always heard.

Another knock. More insistent this time.

I was tempted to stay very quiet. Whoever it was might give up and leave me alone.

Another knock. "Emma? Are you home?" TJ's voice.

The one person I couldn't ignore. "I'm coming!" And I

limped down the hall. When I opened the door, he didn't charge inside the way he had several times since the newspaper article had first appeared. Something had changed. I hoped he was only tired, not broken.

The wind had picked up as it often did in the spring. A lock of hair escaped from under his hat. He reset it to keep the hair out of his eyes. As he did, the sun's rays highlighted the deeper lines across his forehead and the bags under his eyes. I really hadn't noticed the change, hadn't had time, until now. He was trying to keep his commitments to other farmers for the spring season as well as preparing his own fields. If there was one thing I'd learned since coming to the Eastern Shore and knowing, caring, for a farmer, the work never stops. At least, as a teacher, I could take the summer off if I could afford it. TJ didn't have that luxury. Plus, he'd been dealing with dead bodies on his beloved land and accusations. The least I could do was offer him a cup of coffee and a gentle ear.

"This is a nice surprise! Come in. Coffee?" I said with a smile.

"Hi." His voice was flat. "I don't think we have time for coffee."

I had to suppress a sigh. Things must be happening again. And all we wanted to do was catch our breath. "What's up?"

TJ lumbered through the door, headed to the living room, and sat on the edge of a chair so he could see the front drive through the window. "Craig sent me a text. Said he is on his way and would meet us here at the Cottage. He has something to tell us."

"Any idea what it is?"

TJ looked down at his hand gripping his knees. "No idea. I'm getting a little tired of all these surprises. I just want to plow the fields, plant the..." his words trailed off into a sigh.

I went and sat on the arm of his chair and rubbed his shoulders. "I know. And you will again, soon., just not right—" We both sat up straight at the sound of the gravel growling under Craig's car tires.

Craig came in like a whirlwind and we settled in the living room. No coffee. No social chatter. Just down to business.

"The court order finally came through," Craig began. "We have Robin's phone records. finally. We use these Call Detail Records in investigations, and they are accepted in court. Robin used an iPhone but fortunately, TJ has an Android smartphone."

"Why is that good?" I wanted to know.

"The iPhone uses iMessage with end-to-end encryption, but TJ's Droid phone doesn't, so the text became an SMS message. No encryption to keep the contents locked."

I closed my eyes and felt a headache coming on. "Craig, you're giving me information overload. I guess if I sat for a while to consider all that, I'd understand what you're talking about... and what it all means."

"I'm with Emma," TJ added.

Craig licked his lips and leaned forward. "Sorry, It's good news. We've got the wording of the text asking you to meet her at the paper's newsroom in Easton." He sounded triumphant. "This is the breakthrough we needed in this case.

"How so?" TJ asked.

"First, we have evidence TJ wasn't lying. We have the incoming text from Robin's phone to prove it."

Looking at Craig from under my eyebrows, I stated quietly but firmly, "I always knew he was telling the truth."

Craig lowered his head then raised his eyes, filled with remorse. "In my work, I need proof. Personal feelings don't enter into it." He cleared his throat and continued. "And we have location information."

My interest was piqued. "You know where she was when she sent the text?" Craig nodded. "How?"

"Location information is included in the Call Detail Records from the cell phone service provider. Well, that isn't exactly right. We know which cell tower handled the texts."

"I hope she sent the texts from Easton," with an ironic chuckle. "We only have one tower down in this area. It has to cover a lot of territory."

"That's not exactly true anymore."

TJ and I both perked up.

"What has changed?" I wanted to know.

"A new tower was installed recently to help cover this area," Craig explained.

I frowned. "Now that I think about it, I've had coverage more often than not lately."

"The new tower," Craig said with a little nod of his head. "And this is where things get interesting." TJ and I leaned forward listening intently. Craig focused on TJ. "There were two texts sent the night she was killed. The first one asked you to meet her at the newsroom in Easton. He replied he would meet her and would leave in a few minutes. A second text came from Robin's phone confirming the meeting. *Thanks*, she wrote."

"Okay, how does that..."

"Hold on for a minute. I'm not done. The first text was sent to TJ at 8:40 P.M. but the autopsy showed she was killed between 4 and 7 P.M. Dead fingers don't type text messages."

That sharp intake of breath was mine. "That means..."

"The killer sent the message," Craig confirmed.

"It was meant to get you out and away from Waterwood House... to set the scene in your front parlor. It would suggest you lured Robin there, killed her in the front parlor by bashing her head on the fireplace, used bleach to clean up the blood—in a very clumsy way, I might add—and TJ would be walked away in handcuffs."

I couldn't sit still any longer. I began to pace. I had to move, struck by the enormity of it all. And the devious nature of the killer. "This all took planning...

"and the ability to pivot quickly," Craig speculated. "Not every perpetrator is this smart."

"I stopped pacing and folded my arms across my chest. "But who..." The word trailed off as I tried to think who would be so devious to almost succeed at framing TJ for murder.

"That new cell tower was turned on at the right time for this case. Remember, those two texts were sent from Robin's phone before it was disabled? According to the cell phone coverage map and the latitude and longitude information supplied by the cell phone company, the first text came from the old existing tower and the second text came from the new one."

"Okay," I said slowly.

"That means..." TJ said to urge Craig to go on.

"There is one place, a very small area, where the coverage from the two towers overlaps."

"And that's important because...?" Was Craig dragging this out or was I too exhausted by events?

"The texts came from that small area. It includes part of Waterwood..."

TJ's words dripped with defiance. "So, you still think I—"

"TJ, listen for once, will you? Both texts registered on the towers covering that small area overlapping Waterwood... and Windswept Farm."

"Nelson's place?" TJ said, surprised.

"Yup," Craig said as he pulled himself out of the chair. "I think it's time to have a conversation with the newspaper editor, your neighbor, Nelson Jennings."

Chapter Thirty-Eight

"I use memories, but I will not allow memories to use me."

— *Deepak Chopra, an Indian-American author*
and alternative medicine advocate

"**C**ome on." Craig led us to my front door.

A little gust almost blew the door out of his hand. If it was this windy here at the Cottage, it would be worse at Nelson's farm.

"Wait a minute." I went back inside to find something to keep the hair out of my eyes. No time to find a hat, I grabbed the birthday scarf and went outside.

"Follow me," Craig ordered as we rushed to the vehicles.

TJ and I made our way to his truck and drove down the Waterwood drive to the main road then turned onto the very next driveway marked by a carved wooden sign with goldleaf letters spelling out Windswept Farm. As we made our way up the long road to the main house, I heard a vehicle following us. Was it Nelson? Had he found out what Craig had suspected?

Was he going to block our one narrow avenue of escape, if we needed it? With trembling hands, I pulled down the visor and flipped open the mirror.

"What are you doing? Want to look your best for the big confrontation?" TJ teased me.

Through tight lips as if Nelson could hear me, I said, "TJ, check out who is following us."

His eyes went to his rear-view mirror, and he gasped. He checked his big side mirror "Holy crow!"

I madly tried to see who was behind us using my side mirror. "Wow," I breathed.

"He is serious," TJ declared. He must have called out everybody but the national guard.

TJ was right. A line of marked police cars from St. Michaels and the county snaked along behind us.

"Man, I wish I had left Ghost at home." In all the uproar, it hadn't registered that Ghost was sitting in the back seat of the cab, enjoying the ride. When we stopped, he said, "Ghost, be a good boy and *stay in the truck!*" TJ commands were clear so there would be no confusion about what was expected of him. "Good Boy! Stay!" he repeated when we pulled up at the main house behind Craig's car.

The line of law enforcement vehicles spread out and stopped. Officers moved quickly but were not in a rush. Craig paused to confer with an officer with stripes on his uniform shirt. I didn't grow up in the military so I had no idea what his rank might be, but there was no question, he was leading the uniformed officers at Craig's direction.

"Spread out." The ranked officer kept his voice down as he deployed his people in different directions using his arms. The men and women moved almost silently since this was supposed to be a surprise visit. He sent one particularly large man to knock on the front door.

We waited. There was no answer. The mountain of an officer knocked again and called out. No response. Craig conferred with his man and decided to try to find an open door on the water side of the house. Craig followed and so did we. It was a tense moment, but I couldn't help myself. I glanced around at the beautiful spot. The house was large with lots of interesting architectural features, windows, and balconies. The weathered gray shingles were trimmed with wood painted bright white.

Craig led us around the water side of the house on a stone pathway bordered with a short hedge of rich green leaves, tiny white flowers, and a heavenly sweet fragrance to chase away the stench of arrogance and betrayal. Craig kept moving forward, his head constantly moving this way and that. TJ followed then stopped, looking straight down.

"Craig, look at this." TJ pointed.

Craig backtracked, still alert to any changes in our surroundings. "What is it?"

TJ crouched down for a closer look. The soil around the sweet-smelling hedge was disturbed. There were dark stains on the stones of the walkway. "I bet it's blood. Could Robin have been killed here?"

"No idea," Craig said quickly. "I'll get the lab guys out here, but right now, we need to find Nelson. Let's keep moving," he ordered.

Not far away, the salt water of the Bay lapped at the long shoreline of the property protected with riprap stone. A wood dock jutted out over the water ending in a gray boat house and that's when I noticed it. I touched Craig's arm and pointed. Smoke was rising from the boat house.

As we headed toward the dock, gulls stopped squawking at our invasion of their domain, there was the howl of a boat engine. Stuck with our feet planted firmly on land, we watched a large cabin cruiser burst out of the boat house, headed toward the middle of the Bay.

Craig pulled his phone out of his pocket and started stabbing buttons. The uniformed commander spoke into the microphone attached to his shoulder in a way that commanded attention and obedience.

They all had something to do. I just stood there and watched, amazed at the arrogance of a man respected by many for his leadership in the community and all he had accomplished with his newspaper. That is why I saw what happened before we heard it.

A massive ball of fire blossomed from the stern of the boat. The flames of blinding yellow and deep sooty orange rose in the air and along the wooden decks until the entire boat was engulfed in a blazing inferno. Then, in a fraction of a moment, the whole scene blew itself apart. It was so intense, I felt the pressure of the blast slam against my body and overwhelm my ears. Heat came in a wave. Ash and debris rained down onto the tranquil waters of the Chesapeake and us.

"It must have been an old wood boat," TJ said. "Must have been a gasoline engine. Its tank must have been full. Short of a bomb, that's the only way it would go up like that."

Along with the truth of what happened to Robin. Nelson took it all with him.

Chapter Thirty-Nine

"Some of our greatest historical and artistic treasures we place with curators in museums; others we take for walks."

— *Roger A. Caras, American Wildlife*
Photographer and Writer

TJ and I watched the flames burning on the water. What was left of the boat sank quickly, taking one charred body and answers to the bottom of the Bay. Watching it all happen right in front of us and not being able to do anything left me with a hollow feeling inside. I don't think I'd ever felt so helpless, except in those few seconds in the accident before impact, but that was different. Of course, survival was utmost then, but now, saving a human being and getting answers to our questions surrounding Robin's murder were vital. We should have been able to do something instead of standing on the shore and just watching things go horribly wrong.

TJ's voice pulled me back to the present. "There's nothing more we can do here. Let's go home. I'm exhausted."

In reply, I took his arm, and we made our way back to his truck. I ignored the members of law enforcement scurrying around the property, looking for something to find or do. I focused on the strength of TJ's arm, its support and comfort, and the eager barking coming from his truck. TJ dropped my hand and took off running to see what was wrong with Ghost. By the time I had fast-walked to the truck, Ghost was busy washing TJ's face. His tail was wagging so fast, it was banging against everything. When I climbed into the truck, Ghost came at me with his slobbery wet tongue. It was amazing how the dog could rebalance our world in mere moments. On the short drive to the Cottage, our attention was focused on the happy dog in the back seat.

TJ dropped me off and I watched him head to Waterwood House. Once inside the Cottage, I mentally kicked myself when I saw Emma's painting leaning against a chair. It belonged in its proper place in the alcove. Sure, it could wait, but I wanted it out of the Cottage so I could get back to normal as soon as possible. There were too many uncomfortable moments of awful events associated with the painting, including Emma's unwillingness to tell me about the unmarked grave. Well, the only way for it to get back to where it belonged was for me to carry it up the road. I planned to slip into the house, rehang it, and slip back to the Cottage. I wouldn't bother TJ. He was so tired. He was probably already asleep upstairs. I picked up the painting with the black frame. How appropriate, I thought, as I headed outside.

As I walked along the edge of the gravel drive, the ground felt different. Spring had softened the sharp edges made by winter's cold temperatures. A sweetness on the breeze drew my attention to a little patch of wild flowers growing close to a line of pine trees. There was no order or arrangement. Mother Nature had created a lovely mess of color with early spring flowers. These early blooms were circles of small petals like tiny parasols. Did this area have a magical population? I was seeing a cluster of early spring flowers, but could that be the spring collection for a tiny umbrella/parasol shop? Joy from such an enchanted thought welled up from deep inside, banishing the effects of chaos and death I'd seen at Nelson's farm.

All was serene at Waterwood House, too. I imagined Ghost, the ever-faithful watchdog curled up on TJ's bed, watching over him while he slept. I let myself in through the front door. There would be less of a chance of waking anyone upstairs.

As I stepped quietly inside, I heard voices coming from the front parlor. Curious, I paused for a moment and listened.

"...for you to break into my home like this," TJ said in anger. "After everything that's happened—"

His words filled with rage and something else. Uncertainty? Fear? Who had broken into his home? Who was confronting TJ in his parlor? I was tempted to march into that room to see for myself, but something held me back. Instead, I put the painting on the floor and moved so I could slowly peer around the door jamb into the room. The angle was wrong, and I couldn't see anyone. I pulled back and tucked myself in the corner to listen.

"Now, now, TJ don't get so upset. Oh, this is a most uncomfortable seat. Be that as it may, this will all be over th-oon. Everything is going the way I planned with a few blips, but it is all going to be fine in the end."

I gasped when I heard that voice with the lisp and plastered my hands over my mouth, hoping the men had heard nothing. I knew who was talking to TJ. We had talked in the field at Witches Point while we watched the forensic teams at work, waiting for updates. I peeked into the room again and saw his wavy hair and his face in profile. But it wasn't possible. The man had been blown apart in the boat explosion. How could Nelson Jennings be sitting in the front parlor of Waterwood House, chatting with TJ?

I had missed part of what the man had been saying while I recovered from the shock of hearing his voice, but I needed to hear every word he uttered. I crawled closer to the doorway, settled on the floor with my back against the wall, and listened.

"...naïve, Ye-th, that is the best word to describe you. One would think at your age, you would know how the world worked. You shouldn't be shocked that politicians are often paid off or blackmailed. How else do you think they are *persuaded* to do the right thing?"

"This isn't about me," TJ shot back. I could imagine TJ's nostrils flaring like an angry bull. "This is about what you've done—"

Nelson interrupted him again. "Why, I've done my job as a good newspaper man, editor-in-chief, and media owner. I've kept the welfare of my readers in mind and offered guidance to the community."

"You're supposed to do that on the editorial page, not—"

"Oh, sth-op this drivel. Our little part of the world needs to follow the lead of those who are better informed, who under-stand the way things get done, and have the people's-th well-being at heart. That is truly my job."

It took all of my resolve to stay still and not yell out what a hypocrite he was. I drew up my knees and hugged them tightly to my chest, listening carefully.

"And I used the sth-ources I have available to me."

His tone was so nonchalant, I could imagine Nelson coolly inspecting his fingernails as he spoke, so confident, so self-assured.

"Blackmailing the politician was surprisingly easy. I just

had to know where to look. I have access to records and stories people don't even realize exist. I discovered some things from the man's youth to show what a phony he is. Here he is strutting his sth-upport for the environment and concern for the citizens, while unconcerned about a deep, dark sth-ecret he thought was long buried. He is no better than the rest of us.

There was a creak from a piece of furniture in the parlor followed by footsteps. Someone was walking around. Was he coming my way? I tensed every muscle in my body, ready to react in case I was discovered. But then I heard another creak.

"Ah, that's better. TJ, you really must get that settee repaired. There is a spring in the sth-eat that is ready to sth-prong." Nelson laughed at his feeble little joke.

"Yes, you took on a lot of responsibility when you took over Waterwood. You've done rather well with some things, but obviously, you've fallen down on others. You should think about the comfort and well-being of your guests the way I've kept the best in mind for my readers."

While he chuckled, I seethed. Who was he to berate TJ? Who was he to point out his shortcomings? Nelson, of all people. He—I calmed down so I could hear what he was saying next.

"Your eyes have always been too big for your abilities. I remember when you were a boy of about eight. You would come down to Waterwood to spend time with your family...*out in the grand and glorious fresh air*, as your mother used to say. Only it wasn't good enough for her. It only took her a day or two before she would hotfoot it back to the city and its parties and bright lights. She would leave you here the whole sth-ummer and any sth-chool vacation she could. Maybe that is what turned you into a spoiled brat."

"I wanted—" TJ began but was interrupted again.

Nelson Jennings was in control. "I know, I know. You

wanted to be here. You said you hated city life. Here, you could run free like a swamp rat and ride the tractor with your grandfather or some other worker. You tried, but you failed. You'll never fit in here." He made some grunting sounds that might have been laughter. "Do you remember what you used to do? You liked to stop at our property boundary and stare at my land. You'd tell anyone who would listen that sth-omeday, you were going to tractor those acres, too. My acres." Disgust dripped from each word. ""Everybody thought it was so cute."

In the moment of quiet that followed, he exploded. "It wasn't. It wasn't cute at all. You were threatening my family *again*. Your kind never changes. It's always about *you*." Then he sneered. "But not this time." Calmly, as if he was now having a friendly chat, he asked, "Don't you realize they lied to you?"

TJ chose to wait him out by not saying a word.

"I see by the expression on your face you have no clue. All those times, you were tractoring land that rightly belongs to me."

TJ couldn't keep quiet any longer. "What?"

Nelson let out a laugh that bounce off the walls. "Don't you realize that all those years ago, when your precious Emma married the neer-do-well son of the neighbor next door, your family lost Waterwood to mine?"

TJ barked, "What?"

"Look it up. When my relative married Emma, daughter of Benjamin and Elizabeth, Joshua, the bridegroom, took control of all Waterwood land-sth. You should know this. Don't you have the family bible? Their marriage would have been entered there."

"It was. I know more about her marriage to that awful man than you ever will."

Was TJ bragging about what we'd learned from the letters

from Daniel and Emma's diaries? Was he going to lose control and tell Nelson everything? Should I get in there and... The next words out of Nelson's mouth made me sit still. He didn't rise to the bait. Thank goodness.

"I don't have time to school you in your own family history. Oh, for appearance-th thake, Joshua kept the plantation name, Waterwood. It was much better than the name his no-good father gave his plantation. Land I own now. It was so sad when your uncle was land-rich, but cash-poor. He was thrilled when his trusted neighbor—me—swooped in and made an offer for acreage he couldn't refuse. He was thrilled his land would not be in the hands of some money-grubbing developer." Again, his laughter echoed through the rooms. "What he didn't realize was I was just buying back what was mine."

"Wait," It was TJ's turn to interrupt. "I know something about that time in our history. You're right. Joshua married Emma in an arrangement to join the two plantations..." An edge came into his voice. "To get your ancestor out of debt."

"Yes, that condition seemed to run in the family back then," Nelson said with a sigh. "The man experienced some financial reversal."

"But Joshua was an only child. I thought all his siblings died in infancy or something. No one else ever made it to adulthood."

"Sh-hows how much you know. According to *my* family bible, he had a younger sth-ister. Sth-ickly, frail. Good for nothing really, but she survived the measles outbreak. A shame when two brothers did not. Measles was a devastating disease. It sth-truck down a lot of little children." The more excited Nelson became, the more his lisp was evident.

"How do you know that?" TJ demanded.

Nelson sighed again, but with impatience this time. "I own a newspaper. I have access to the morgues of many papers.

You're a farmer. You don't know about journali-thm. The morgue is the storage place for past issues of a newspaper. It might also have reporters' notes and journals kept by editors. It's a lousy name, but a treasure trove of information. The local paper kept track of who was sth-ick, and which prominent families lost a child. Yours wasn't the only prominent family in the area."

"more like notorious," TJ mumbled.

Nelson went on the attack. "What did you say?" he growled.

TJ rallied quickly. "Noteworthy. This information is noteworthy."

"Yes, yes, it is." Nelson sounded satisfied. "It is noteworthy, because Alice is why I'm here, why I have an interest in Waterwood." He said the name as if he was spitting out something foul-tasting. "She survived the scourge, but she was at the mercy of her father. He had sold off his land to guarantee a good life for his son. After he paid his debts, he still had a stake to set himself up in a city. He wanted to get away from this place, from anything having to do with farming and slaves and abuse by the weather. But he still had Alice hanging on his coattails. Sthickly, whiny, that was the way he described her in his journal. She was a burden he didn't want. Quickly, he married her off to a small plantation owner down in Dorchester County who wanted a connection to a prominent Talbot County family. The wedding was held so fast, Alice had to wear some other woman's gown. It had to be before his family heard about his disgrace. Her father left the same day the vows were spoken."

"Nice."

I barely heard TJ's response and hoped Nelson would ignore it.

"We agree. He was a scoundrel, no question, but it was the

best thing he could have done from my perspective. Alice didn't last long. She died in childbirth, but the baby survived... and there was a baby after that. All of them on the family tree, right down to me.

I gasped, but the sound was covered by TJ's reaction.

"We're related..." TJ sputtered. "You ... you're part of the Ross family?"

Chapter Forty

"Climate change is happening, and humans are significant contributors, and that raises some really important policy questions."

— Mark Walport, English medical scientist, and Foreign Secretary of The Royal Society.

"Yup," he sneered, "I'm a Collins or Ross--- use whatever name you'd like. I am another child of Waterwood, just like you."

"We're related?" TJ couldn't believe it.

"Come on, you're repeating yourself."

"I'm in shock. We are related."

Nelson sighed. "Unfortunately... And that means I have a claim on Waterwood. Now, I want what belongs to me."

Nelson rambled on about how he'd planned to take over Waterwood lands for a long time. While he was lost in his own fantasy, I tried to figure out what I should do now. I should slip out the door, get away, and call Craig.

Nelson Jennings was a murderer. If TJ wanted to tell me about the family connection later, that was his choice.

While trying to figure out a way to get out of the house silently, I tuned in on Nelson's explanation in time to hear him say, "I figure I deserve at least half of what still exists of Waterwood since my many greats-grandmother was cheated out of her rightful inheritance."

TJ had had enough. Along with shuffling sounds, he said, "I don't have to listen to this."

"STH-IT DOWN!" Nelson barked.

"Oh, for heaven's sake, stop waving that gun around, Nelson. Somebody could get hurt."

Gun? If I contacted Craig, could he get here in time to help TJ? What if Nelson discovered I was in the house? No, I wasn't going anywhere. I couldn't leave TJ alone with this maniac.

The maniac wasn't done with his orders. "You're going to sit there and listen to the rest of my story."

"Okay, okay. Calm down. I listen and then what?"

"You'll see," Nelson cackled, "when I'm ready."

I didn't like the lilt in Nelson's voice. He sounded like a bully on the playground who had something no-good, very-bad planned. I took a deep breath and straightened my legs that were falling asleep. I had to be ready. I didn't know for what. I just had to be ready.

Nelson must have settled back in his chair, comfortable while holding a gun on TJ. "All these years, I couldn't figure out a way to take over Waterwood. I'm not getting any younger and I'm fed up with the newspaper business. I felt so cheated by life, then fate walked into my office one day. The man was a real estate developer, a smart one. He wanted to learn about the possibilities and political situation here in the county. Instead of going to real estate agents, surveyors, and such, he came to

297

the one person who has his finger on the pulse of the community. Me!"

Nelson's pride made me want to throw up.

"We realized we had a lot in common, goals that could help us both get what we wanted. We started negotiations and I figured if I couldn't have the old land, at least I could make life miserable for the family who stole what should have been mine. You!"

"Let me get this straight." There was an edge in TJ's voice. "You were negotiating to sell your farm to a developer?"

Nelson chuckled. "And people think a farmer is dumb. You got it in one." He laughed again. "And you'll appreciate this…The man doesn't want to build big homes on my land. He wants to create a village with postage-stamp lots. The houses won't be cookie-cutter, prefabricated homes. He plans to offer different layouts, perfect for second homes. They will have some style and flair… and there will be a lot of them. Won't that be nice?"

I almost choked. There was no way TJ would tolerate such a setup. It would be a nightmare for him… and for me, I realized. Windswept Farm wasn't far from the Cottage. And the traffic, not only on the roads, but boat traffic on the water. I cringed.

In the next room, Nelson let out a deep sigh. "We were just about to close the deal when Little Miss Robin stuck her nose in."

"What could she do to hurt you?"

Nelson sighed again. "You know all this talk about climate change? She was covering all different aspects of the story like those long lists of things farmers have to do and have to stop doing. Plus, environmentalists are proposing additional restrictions for property owners with land on the water. The developer started getting cold feet. He was making noises about pulling out of the deal. I couldn't have that."

"What could you do about the federal and state—"

"TJ, I take back what I said about you not being a dumb farmer. You are really ignorant of the way things work here in Maryland. I can tell you, because you won't have a chance to tell anyone else. The local governments, in our case, the commission council...sth-upid name, bureaucracy at work. Anyway, the commission council declares the sth-etbacks from the water, the boundaries with other properties, and so much more. The changes they're talking about would hamstring me. We're talking about my backyard. I figured out a way to sway the vote, at least long enough for my deal to close, and I could leave town. As you know, I'm not without some influence here. And I found a little weakness in the background of one of our esteemed elected representatives. When the vote comes up, the climate activists would be one vote short."

"How did Robin get involved?"

TJ was dragging things out, stalling. Was he coming up with a plan?

Nelson cleared his throat. "I'm getting to it. She overheard one of my conversations. What an interfering, eavesdropping minx."

"I thought those were standard skills for a good reporter?" TJ suggested.

"Hmmm, maybe they are but she should have known better than to eavesdrop on her boss. I tried to talk to her when I realized what had happened. She misunderstood what she heard."

"She overheard you blackmailing him?"

"No, not really." Nelson sighed. "I was just reminding the representative how he should *do the right thing*. Isn't that what the lobbyists say on Capitol Hill in Washington? She was confused, but very clear on one thing. She was going to expose me."

"But you own the local paper. You would never publish—"

"Of course not. I would never print the story. Then I found out she had an appointment with the editor-in-chief of an Annapolis paper." He laughed.

"What's so funny?" TJ asked. There was a growing tautness in his voice. He had little patience for theatrics.

"That's when *you,* dear TJ, saved the day."

"I did? How?"

I could hear confusion, impatience, and anger in his voice taking him to the brink of an explosion. Not a good thing when a gun was pointed at him.

"It was the day you walked into my newsroom demanding to see Robin, remember? You were hot about the story she wrote about the undiscovered treasure on Waterwood land."

TJ sagged. I could hear it in his voice. "How could I forget. I can't believe that would help you."

"Believe it." Nelson sounded gleeful. "It was the best thing you've ever done. I got in touch with Robin and told her how upset you were about her story. I suggested we all have a little sit-down and talk about it. Maybe smooth things over. I had the idea the paper could sponsor a concerted search of your property, keeping all the wannabes away. I told her I'd set up a convivial meeting at my house. She would have the exclusive. She balked. Said she had plans. But I knew her plans were to have a meeting with that editor on the other side of the bridge who has always hated me. I *persuaded* her to change her plans."

"How? Did you threaten to fire her?"

TJ was starting to go on the offensive. I held my breath.

"Sth-omething like that." Nelson sounded so proud of himself. "But I added a carrot. Talked about what a great story it would make, and it would be her byline on the front page day after day until we found the treasure. Her mouth was still saying no, but I saw the glint in her eye. The hunger. She was always hungry for the spotlight. Finally, Robin decided to take advantage of my offer if she could have some time off at the end of the week. That's when I knew she was going through with her plans to expose my efforts. So, she wanted time off? I agreed. Why not? It didn't matter. She only had hours to live."

"You killed her." It was a statement, not a question.

Nelson chuckled. "You would think that. I'm not a monster, TJ." Then the tone of his voice changed. He was all innocence. "True, she needed to be stopped. But I didn't do it."

Disbelieving, TJ asked, "Then who did?"

Did I sense a glow of satisfaction in Nelson's next words?

"You did."

Chapter Forty-One

"Nothing in a portrait is a matter of indifference. Gesture, grimace, clothing, decor even, they all must combine to realize a character."

— *Charles Baudelaire, French Poet & Art Critic*

"Me?" TJ shot back. "I didn't do a thing to the woman."

My body tensed. I recognized his tone. Nelson had just pushed TJ over the edge, something that almost never happened. TJ always considered situations carefully and gave his decisions a lot of thought before taking action. But TJ was human. If someone pushed his button hard enough, if something or someone he cared about was in danger, he could react, BAM! Just like that. I hoped he would calm down. After all, there was a gun pointed at him by a deranged person. But my fear was justified.

"Hey!" Nelson barked. "I told you to sit down!"

"You put the gun down!" TJ barked back. "You're going to hurt yourself."

"The only person who is getting hurt here is you. Now, sit down and listen. I want to finish my story. After all..." The self-satisfied tone was back. "I'm a professional story-teller. It's my name on the masthead of my paper. So, listen and learn."

The demand was followed by a creak. Of course, the furniture in the parlor dated back to Emma's time. I listened for another sound, any sound to indicate TJ was going after Nelson, but all was quiet. I wanted to do something, but I couldn't go into that room blind. A reckless act could get us both killed. So, I, too settled back to listen.

"Good," Nelson said. "Now, where was I? Ah yes, Robin agreed to the meeting with you and the plan to give her an ongoing story on the front page. She arrived at my place right on time. I led her out to the garden to see my amazing view of the Bay at sth-unset. She was impressed and so captivated by it, she never saw the shovel. It only took one sth-whack to cave in her pretty little head."

The image of his action made me shudder. My disgust at his cavalier description of ending Robin's life rose like bile in my throat.

"Now, I know you're lying. You called me asking if she had ever gotten back to me. You said you'd make sure she got in touch," TJ argued.

"Ah yes, I am ever the concerned neighbor and newspaper editor-in-chief serving his community."

"She sent me a text to meet her at the paper's office in Easton. It was after sunset." TJ's voice was climbing higher, fighting the realization of the horrible truth. "You couldn't have done what you said."

"Hmmm, you say *she* sent you a text?" Nelson was playing with TJ now. "No, you received a text from her phone. It was easy to guess her passcode. People are so predictable."

"But how did you erase the texts from my phone?" TJ demanded.

"Easy, remember when the police corralled us all into your kitchen to give statements? It was chaos. You put your phone down on the counter. I scooped it up. Tsk, Tsk, no password. You made it almost too easy, TJ. I opened your texts, two taps, deleted the conversation. Done!" Nelson chuckled again.

How I was beginning to hate that sound. I stayed quiet so I wouldn't disturb the story Nelson was spinning.

Nelson asked, "Remember, I asked you to let me know when she got in touch?"

"Yes," TJ replied slowly. "And I did, right before I left. It was dark."

"But we know she died before seven." Nelson encouraged TJ to continue. "That means..."

"She was already dead," he said with disbelief.

"And now, you're going to be charged with her murder."

"No, no. I was in my truck, driving to Easton."

"With nothing to prove it."

Frustration was adding strain to TJ's words. "I don't understand... I don't understand any of this!"

"It's really very sth-imple, brilliant in its sth-implicity. I needed to get you away from Waterwood House to sth-et the sth-cene. I collected some blood from her body before I put it in my truck along with a bottle of bleach and the shovel. I waited and watched while you came barreling down the drive. You really should drive more carefully at night."

"I almost hit a deer," TJ replied flatly, remembering.

"Yes, I sth-aw the whole thing. If you had damaged your truck, you would have upset my plan. Good thing you have quick reflexes. The only thing I was worried about was your dog. If you'd left him at the house...

"I didn't. He goes with me everywhere," TJ declared. He seemed to hold on to that simple truth in this tapestry of lies.

Gratified, Nelson went on. "Yes, you are so predictable. Another thing that worked in my favor. And being a true resident of the Eastern Shore, you left your house unlocked. It was easy to do what was needed. I came into this delightful room, spilled some blood on that lovely fireplace, swabbed some bleach to make it appear you had tried to clean up the murder scene. I was back in my truck and on Witches Point, as you call it, long before you got back."

"You went out there in the dark? How...? Why...?"

"It was the perfect place. My tire tracks wouldn't stand out. All those vehicles had churned up the land already, plus I had been out at the site several times during the excavations. It was perfect for burying another body. Like I said, the land was already torn up. I figured the chances of somebody noticing a little overturned earth were low. Nobody could see what I was doing. I used a shielded lantern. Besides, farmers are always out in their fields doing weird things at this time of year. Nobody could have seen me burying Robin. If it hadn't been for your dog..."

TJ must have read the man's growing anger. He needed to tamp it down in case... where was Ghost anyway, I wondered? I sent a silent thought to the absent dog: stay away.

TJ changed the focus. "You mean you dug the grave yourself?"

I almost giggled. My reaction was from nerves and my memory of Nelson's pudgy body perspiring in the field during the work at Gideon's unmarked grave.

"Of course! I always do what I have to do." The bite in his words revealed how much he resented TJ's comment.

"Okay, okay." TJ said, trying to placate Nelson. "I was just asking."

"It helped I was angry. It was a great release of all the pent-up emotion I was feeling."

"You were that mad at Robin? Why didn't you—"

"No, you idiot. I was mad at you and at myself for hiring such a nosy woman with great aspirations of being an investigative reporter. I think I was taken in by her cute looks—pixie haircut, fascinating platinum blonde hair, cute nose. I've always been a sucker for a fresh, young thing. In this case, I was grateful she was petite. I don't think I could have done it if she was any heavier. At least I did that right."

"And later, I did my part." TJ sounded disgusted. "I sent you a text from Easton that she never showed up."

"Yes, thank you for that. I knew I could sneak off the property and get home using a back road. Nobody the wiser."

"I'm such a fool." TJ sounded defeated by such elaborate deception.

I didn't like what I was hearing. TJ had to fight to save himself.

Nelson reinforced TJ's feeling of defeat. "Yes, I'd have to agree. You're an idiot." Pride shining through every word.

TJ let out a deep sigh. "So, what now?"

Had TJ given up? Was he going to let Nelson follow his plan?

There was that chuckle again. Hearing it made me want to grind my teeth.

"You should be upset, distraught even. An innocent man died today."

"Who?"

"ME, of course. The police got all distracted by Robin's phone and came to Windswept Farm like an invading army. I got scared, had no idea what was happening. I panicked. Needed to run. I didn't have time or the brain power to check the engine compartment." There was a shrug in his voice.

"BOOM! That's simple. You caused an unnecessary death because of what you'd done."

"Because I murdered Robin."

"Oh, you are quick when you want to be." Nelson sounded gleeful. "And now, you're filled with remorse. You can't live with yourself."

"Really?" Disbelief was evident.

My breath caught in my throat. My back straightened. Dread pulsed through me. I wanted to help, but I had no idea where they were in the parlor. Probably in front of the marble fireplace, but it was a large area with several chairs and a settee. If I made the wrong move, Nelson could hurt us both.

Nelson continued to describe the sad situation he had concocted for TJ. "You have to stop the pain. You're going to leave a note and put this gun to your head, and we'll close the book on everything." Nelson pronounced the death sentence matter-of-factly.

The gun! Just as I feared, Nelson was going to use the gun. I bit my knuckle to keep myself from crying out.

"And how will you benefit? You're dead, remember?" TJ sounded eerily calm. He must have a plan. Maybe he'd found a way to protect himself. I had to give him the chance to shut down Nelson.

"Oh, my lawyer has my will and information to contact my cousin, Joshua Jennings.

"*Joshua!*" TJ said what I was thinking.

"That's right. Yours isn't the only old family that keeps using the same names down through the generations. I'm Nelson Joshua Jennings."

Now, it was time for TJ to chuckle. "You have it all figured out."

"Yes, yes, I do. I've had to make some last-minute adjustments, but it has all come together well. There's nothing you can do to change things. Now, one last detail."

"And what is that?"

Nelson said one word with determined force. "YOU!"

It was time. I had to do something. I caught something moving out of the corner of my eye. Something white and large. Ghost!

He must have been outside, chasing squirrels or rabbits. No, his big yawn suggested he had been napping. And he had picked this moment to look for TJ. When there was a man in the house who hated him for digging up Robin's body. And that man had a gun!

I didn't move. Maybe Ghost would go back to the kitchen. When I saw his tail wag, I knew he'd seen me. He took a step toward me, toward the doorway to the front parlor. I waved my fingers at him, hoping to shoo him away and out of danger. Instead, he took a step closer. Then another. I waved an arm in the air a little, but he kept coming. Closer. Closer to the doorway. Maybe if I could get my arms around his neck, I could...

"Nelson, you're more of a fool than I thought you were," TJ said.

Ghost's ears perked up.

"You don't have a ghost of a chance of getting away with any of this."

That's all the dog needed to hear. Ghost trotted into the parlor. I had to get in there. But how?

"Well, look who decided to join the party," Nelson said, relishing the sight of TJ's dog.

"Leave him alone, Nelson," TJ warned. "He is just an innocent dog."

Nelson laughed. "Yeah, the dog that almost fouled up my carefully laid plans, but his natural instinct to dig made things ever better. Now the cops have a motive, opportunity, and a body, they can bring a tidy case against you. Too bad you've outlived your usefulness. Come here, boy."

I moved my head down close to the floor so I could peer into the room. I could barely see the top of TJ's head of light brown hair blocked by the high-backed antique settee on the far side of the marble fireplace. Nelson was sitting in a wing chair at an angle away from me but on the side closest to me. The gun was in Nelson's left hand braced by his elbow on the arm of the chair. The man's attention was on the dog. But if my sudden movement caught his eye, he could bring the gun around in my direction. But TJ could jump him. In time, I hoped.

"This is even better," Nelson hissed as he stroked the dog's head. "Poor TJ, overcome with guilt, couldn't leave his beloved dog behind."

That did it. Without taking a moment to second-guess myself, I untied the colorful scarf TJ had given me for my birthday, held two ends in my hands, and as quietly as I could, rushed up behind Nelson.

I threw the scarf over his face and pulled it tight, blinding him.

Startled, Nelson waved the gun toward the ceiling and fired. His free hand clawed at the scarf.

Not good enough. I dropped the scarf down around his neck and pulled with every ounce of strength I had.

TJ yelled at Ghost. Ghost barked.

I had to focus on cutting off this man's air. His arms flailed around. He reached over the top of the chair, grabbed a hunk of my hair, pulling me off balance. I hung on and screamed! Screaming gave me strength. I squeezed my eyes shut and pulled harder. I jerked my head. He released my hair.

Then the man pulled away from me. No. NO!

Hands covered my white-knuckled fists. Not grasping

hands. Not clawing hands. Gentle hands, a little rough, but with a tender touch. I opened my eyes and saw they were TJ's hands.

"You can let him go now. It's over." TJ said with a soothing tone.

It took me a moment to realize what he'd said, *It was over*. "But he—"

TJ squeezed my hands. "Let him go."

As I did, TJ jumped out of the way, grabbed the gun, and put it on the high mantle as Nelson's limp body crumpled to the floor. .

"Is he dead?" Part of me was horrified. "Did I do that?"

I noticed a smile playing on TJ's lips. "No and yes."

"Which is which? Don't tease me."

"No, he's not dead." TJ glanced at the body on the floor. "And yes, you did that. I just finished him off with my right hook. The guy's got a glass jaw."

"I don't know what that means, but I'm glad he does."

TJ let out a nervous laugh then took in a deep breath of air. He searched my face. "Emma, are you hurt?"

"No, no," I gasped, trying to catch my breath. "I'll be fine You?"

"I'm okay." He turned to check on Ghost who leapt forward to madly lick his face. With a little laugh, he said, "Easy there, boy. I'm fine. Everybody's good, except..." He reached over Nelson's body, untangled my scarf, and held up the stretched square of designer silk. "I don't think the designer will recommend it as a great defense against a killer, but it got the job done.

"Quick thinking, Emma. Don't worry, I'll buy you a new one."

I laughed. "Maybe in another color?"

"Any color you want."

"TJ," the serious way I said his name stopped our kidding around. I looked at Nelson's body then turned away. "TJ, I thought he was going to—"

"Emma, shhhh. It's over. We can talk later. Right now, we need the police to take this bag of bones out of my house!"

Thankful for something to do, I reached into my pocket and found my phone. I didn't dare text Craig earlier, in case the sound was on when the letters were tapped. "OH! I've got a signal on my phone."

"Must be that new tower. Call Craig. It's time for him to finish the job," TJ declared.

Chapter Forty-Two

"The portrait painter ... If he insults his sitters his occupation is gone. Whether he paints the should instead of the features, or the latter with all its natural blemishes, he is as presumptuous as if he shouted, 'What a face. Hide it.' which would never do."

— *Walter J. Phillips, Canadian Painter and Printmaker*

Fortunately, Craig had stopped in St. Michaels after the boat explosion to talk with the police chief. He arrived in short order with several marked police cars. I met them at the kitchen door when they drove up. When I told him we had captured Nelson in the front parlor, Craig gave me a look that clearly said, *You've lost your mind.* But he waited until he walked in and saw Nelson on the floor, moaning with TJ standing guard over him.

"I don't get it," Craig said in disbelief. "I thought he died on the boat."

"So did I,"TJ said. "But it was all part of an intricate plan. I think he'll be happy to tell you all about it—"

"Oh, my head..." Nelson mumbled.

"Maybe after you give him some aspirin," I added.

"Are you going to tell me what happened here?"

"We'll tell you everything *after* you get him out of my house," TJ commanded.

Several uniformed officers came into the room and gasped. It seemed everyone knew about the boat explosion that had killed the newspaper's editor-in-chief. The man who was very much alive, rolling around on the floor, holding his head.

"Gentlemen, please escort Mr. Jennings to the station and book him for ..." Craig looked to TJ for confirmation. When he nodded, Craig finished his sentence. "... for murder."

As we watched Nelson being taken away, Craig plopped down in a chair, looking like the crazy events of the day had drained away his energy. "Okay, tell me what happened. I can't wait any longer."

When we finished our report of the man's confession, threats against the lives of TJ and Ghost, Craig shook his head in disbelief. "It's almost too much to take in. I can understand craving more land. There's nothing new about that. It's been going on for centuries all over the world.

"But to kill an innocent woman," I said, the enormity of what Nelson had done was starting to overwhelm me.

"Don't forget, we have a politician, who has an important say in the laws and regulations covering development, succumbing to blackmail pressure," TJ said with disgust.

"But Robin was just doing her job," I countered.

Craig chimed in. "And it got her into trouble big time. Maybe she was a victim of her youth. A more experienced reporter might have known how to protect herself as well as her story. That part is almost too sad for words."

We all were silent for a time, each lost in their own thoughts.

Craig was the first to speak. "But what gets me is a family grudge that survived for so long. If he's feeling it this strongly now, I wonder what the other generations experienced."

"I'm not a psychologist," TJ declared, "but I think his hunger for Waterwood land was personal.

"His grudge was a convenient excuse for him to go after your land and justified in his mind his illegal actions like blackmailing a politician," I said with disgust. "He acted like a spoiled child."

Craig chuckled, "Reminds me of the feud between the Hatfields and McCoys."

"Only I didn't know we were feuding," TJ clarified.

"There's one thing I'm not looking forward to doing," Craig said with a sigh. "I'm not sure how Robin's brother Sam is going to reconcile all this when I tell him what happened."

"I'm not a psychologist either," I said, but I think he'll grow to accept it, process it, and go on with his life. He'll have a new baby to help him live in the present and look to the future."

TJ looked at me and smiled. "That's exactly what a farmer does. Looks like the Eastern Shore has taught the Big City Girl something after all."

Chapter Forty-Three

"Stop being a prisoner of your past. Become the architect of your future. You will never be the same."

> — *Robin Sharma, Author of* The Monk Who Sold His Ferrari: A Fable About Fulfilling Your Dreams and Reaching Your Destiny

S everal weeks later, TJ came to the Cottage carrying a package. It was from the highly-respected clockmaker with an amazing shop in Easton. He had agreed to clean and evaluate it for us, and he'd done the work in record time. I hoped the note inside the package would give us more information.

Thank you for the opportunity to work on this exquisite example of 19th century fine watch manufacture. It is a handcrafted antique 18K gold pocket watch dating back to early to mid-19th century. I would have to do some extensive research to date it properly, but my guess would be 1845-1855.

Considering where it was found, it is in remarkable condition. The cover is etched with a bouquet of flowers in the center. I am no expert on flowers, but I believe those in the center are all the same. There may be some significance associated with them. There is additional floral filigree around the edge and along the outer edge. The workman-ship is quite fine.

I think you will find the engraving inside the cover quite interesting. Also note, there is a cover over the back of the watch where the internal workings of the watch were accessed with a key to wind it. Do you have the key?

The key? The man had probably carried it in a pocket so he could wind the watch at any time. Dr. Bergstrom was right to take the time to look in the grave after the skeleton was removed. Only Ghost had found something more important, and we were all distracted. Now the key must be lost in the rich soil of Waterwood. With regret, I continued to read the note.

One more thing: The fob at the end of the watch chain had another use beyond that of an anchor to keep the watch secure. It is a seal that could imprint hot wax used on an important document or to close an envelope. It is a little worn, which is no surprise. The design appears to be a flower with the letter G in the center.

If you are ever able to trace the origin of either piece, I hope you will share it with me. I'm always fascinated by the history and background not only of the manufacturers, but the owners of such fine timepieces.

. . .

The letter G? It might stand for Gideon as Dr. Bergstrom said. Was the flower significant? Was it another clue that could lead to the man's identity, I wondered as I opened the box cradling the watch. I lifted it out, touched the button, and the cover snapped open to reveal the beauty of the gold watch face fashioned to give dimension and form. I didn't have the expertise to describe the impressive workmanship. Opposite the face of the time piece, the inside of the gold cover was engraved with this message:

G~ You saved us. Love always, M.

"TJ, this is beautiful!" I held it out so TJ could see, but he only glanced at it then turned away.

"What's wrong?" I asked.

"I'm tired. I'm tired of what it represents. I'm tired of all this upset."

Tired? Was he tired of me and my historical research? Cold fingers of panic crept up my arms making me shiver. Instead of asking for an explanation and reassurance, I opted for once to be quiet and listen.

"I hate what has been going on... finding the skull, Robin, Buck's abuse of the poor woman, and Nelson's arrogance and betrayal. All of it has taken a toll on me, on everybody and everything. There is so much to do in early spring, Not only me, every farmer, including my clients. If those things don't get done and on time, it affects the bottom line and the way of life for so many. I haven't been able to pay attention to what I should be doing. So frustrating!"

He looked at me with a weak smile. "Don't get me wrong. Looking into my family's history and everything has been great. Capturing all that history to pass on to future generations is great. But if I can't get my work done, there might not be a Waterwood to pass on to them."

He hung the reason for all this upset on my digging around in his family history. That meant I was to blame. His aunt had done some nosing around in the historical corners of Waterwood House. She had instilled in him the importance of capturing a family's history and not letting it disappear into the dust of time. He had humored her, but the real investigations had begun when I came to the Cottage. I was the one who decided to establish an ongoing correspondence with Daniel, the man who'd lived his whole life at Waterwood, played with young Emma, the daughter of the plantation owner, so long ago. More than 150 years had passed since they walked the halls of the main house and the fields of Waterwood Plantation. If I hadn't dug into Emma's history through her letters and diaries, I would never have found her secret room in the attic which led to our loving relationship again through correspondence. I bit my lip and steeled myself to admit what I had done and take the punishment.

"I get it and you're absolutely right. It's all my fault. All of it. If I hadn't insinuated myself into your family's history, your life would have been very different over these many months. Who knows what you would have accomplished if I hadn't moved the plantation desk into the Cottage, hadn't written to Daniel, and meddled in things."

I gave a weak laugh that had no joy in it. "When I found Daniel's first letter... if I had ignored it, none of this would have happened. Kid Billy, the Professor, even Robin might be alive today if—"

TJ rushed at me so suddenly I gasped.

He grabbed my arms and held fast. "Don't say that!" he thundered. "Don't even think that. People around here have heard about the treasure for years. Some believe those rumors.

paindidn't murder the professor. His obsession with history did. Do I need to go on?

"No," I said in a tiny voice. But, in that moment, I knew what I had to do. I had to move back to Philadelphia. I'd decide later what I would do with the Cottage. I couldn't, I couldn't...

"Emma!" He laced my name with desperation. His hands, so strong and capable, held on to my arms. He shook me a little. "Emma? Look at me, Emma!" It was a command.

I couldn't meet his gaze. I knew I would get lost in those hazel eyes I'd learn to read as they reflected his moods and feelings. I couldn't take the chance of seeing his disappointment in me. His regret.

He shook me again. And said in a voice as smooth and comforting as rich velvet, "Dearest Emma, You didn't make any of those things happen. Repeat after me, it wasn't my fault."

I dropped my eyes. I couldn't. I truly believed it was all my fault. He waited, but I couldn't do what he asked, not any of it.

Finally, he released my arms and took a few steps away. "Fine. You're right." He began to pace in tight circles. "I'll admit it. It's your fault."

He got close to my face and repeated, "It's your fault Emma and Daniel are together." He held up his right hand and tapped his index finger. "It's all your fault you were stubborn and found Emma's diaries. What she had written brought her alive and filled in gaps of Waterwood history. You unmasked the scoundrel she was forced to marry." He crossed his arms. "It's your fault Cookie had the wedding of her dreams right here at Waterwood House." He thought for a moment and added, "And that little Rosie is flourishing now."

"Yes," I insisted as I got to my feet. "But those things don't balance out the lives... I can't---" I turned to rush away, rush to the Cottage where I could close the door and lock out the world. Where I wasn't responsible...

TJ wrapped his arms around me and pulled me back against his chest. "Wait." He leaned down to whisper in my ear. "There is one more thing you've done, probably the greatest thing of all. You've touched my heart and opened it."

I stopped pulling against him and breathed.

"You've shown me it is time to put the past away. After all, it was a long time ago. You've made me think it might be safe to dare to trust again. To trust...you." He turned me around to face him. "The sad part is that you haven't felt the same way."

I started to object, but he put his index finger on my lips to still them.

"You've been hurt deeply, time and time again. I think the accident almost did you in.

Even when you were recovering and everything that came after—the pain, the fear, the hours of rehab—all of it almost broke your spirit. But you survived."

I stared at his lips as he spoke. The sounds, the words rang true. And it was terrifying. I didn't want to lose myself, again.

TJ brushed strands of hair off my face to behind my ear. His touch was light like an angel's wing. "I know these things. And I also know there were times you thought it would have been better if you'd died on that day."

I stiffened. I had never voiced those thoughts, those awful thoughts of—

"Don't worry," he said quickly. "I'm sure it was a normal reaction to all you've experienced especially on the heels of what that man you loved did to you. It was logical for you to run to the Cottage. When you were a little girl and had an owie, you would have cried to your Uncle Jack and he would have kissed it and sent you on your way, back to life. He had done it many times before, right?"

I could only look down and nod.

"I'm here now. It's time to reignite that light I saw in your eyes when you were with Rosie. I saw how you helped the little girl who saw her mother murdered. I saw you revitalize her spirit, the same way Uncle Jack used to do for you. That tells me we need to fan your creativity and excitement about life and that means, we have to get you back with children.

I took a breath to speak, but he continued.

"Don't worry. I know there are some hurdles to get over, but I'm going to help you, the same way I made the Cottage secure and safe for you on your first morning here. Safe enough to engage with Daniel to take us on these hare-brained adventures. I want to see the roses in your cheeks and the sparkle in your eyes. Above all, I want us to trust and love again, together. Shall we try?"

I hoped he could read the answer in my eyes.

He did. His lips tenderly touched mine.

I knew we had struck a deal... maybe for life.

Chapter Forty-Four

"The past can't hurt you anymore, not unless you let it."

*— Alan Moore, recognized as one of the best
comic book writers in the English language,
English author of* Watchmen, V for Vendetta,
Batman, *and more*

Days later, I walked up the path from the cabin to the Cottage. My slow pace was not because I couldn't walk faster or my steps were painful. It was a strange feeling, but I felt like I was learning to breathe again. I didn't want to rush this feeling. I was still trying to figure out what it was. I wasn't feeling like my old self. I was a new and improved version.

The thought made me smile.

TJ and I had not talked about what had passed between us, not yet. Neither one of us liked to talk holes in something so special, so precious. With an unspoken agreement, we were living forward and would see what happened.

It was a beautiful day with a clear blue sky and air scented with spring flowers. Mother Nature had finally made good on her promise of warm temperatures. With a light step, I hurried along. TJ was coming.

The night before, TJ had decided we should take a little time to celebrate. The tragedy of Robin Hunter was over with the confession given by Nelson. According to Craig, Nelson delivered a pompous and detailed interpretation of what happened and his justifications. At one point, they had to take a break because Nelson's lawyer thought he was having a heart attack. There was no way the editor was going to talk his way out of the charges. It was rumored the newspaper would be put up for sale to pay legal fees and outstanding debt. That wasn't all.

Maureen and I had visited Fred at the Pub. I was a little relieved that she was going to wait awhile before choosing another roommate. Her face showed a little strain and sadness whenever someone mentioned Robin's murder and the after-math of Nelson's actions.

The other rumor was Windswept Farm was going to go up for sale. If true, TJ would have a decision to make: Should he buy back the land that was once part of Waterwood? It was a huge decision, but he'd decided it could wait until next week or the week after.

Robin's brother had gone home and was eagerly awaiting the arrival of his daughter who he planned to name Robin. Buck wasn't headed home just yet. Craig's report had triggered some connections in the police system, and he was wanted for illegal hunting, poaching, and all kinds of violations in three states.

In a St. Michaels shop, I had found a light shawl of deli-cate coral for Maria. Then we headed to the Cove for our celebratory milkshakes. While we waited, my phone dinged with an incoming email, then another and another. I pulled out my phone, opened my email app, and read the subject line.

"Oh, somebody responded to my inquiry about a possible DNA connection..." I said, excited.

TJ just looked at me. No expression. Maybe he didn't understand.

"The DNA service has identified some possible matches to the man-in-the-field and..."

But he did understand and gently put his hand over my phone, covering the screen. "Emma, history can wait for a little while."

I had a feeling history didn't like being ignored, but I agreed. With the notifications turned off, I put my phone away. The world could wait. This was our time. The weather was too nice to stay inside so we took our treats in To Go cups along with a cup of vanilla ice cream for the dog patiently waiting for us in TJ's truck. We planned to sit with Ghost on a bench in Muskrat Park overlooking the harbor with its sailboats, power boats, and noisy ducks demanding food.

We didn't make it to the park.

It was Thursday and many tourists had descended on the village already. As we maneuvered our way along the crowded sidewalks, we heard a woman cry out.

"Thomas Jefferson Dorset! As I live and breathe." She was wearing a gracefully-elegant sundress that showed off her figure and a broad-brimmed straw hat to protect her delicate complexion. She whipped off her large, tortoise-shell sunglasses. She walked up to the man, threw her arms around his neck, and breathed his name, TJ. Then she delivered a deep sensuous kiss on his lips.

I had to fight down my urge to rip her away from him... then a yearning to fade away. Surely, I wasn't the only woman who found him attractive, and he'd lived on the Shore for a long time. Maybe he would want one of his old girlfriends…

After what seemed like forever, she ended the kiss, leaving behind a swath of red lipstick on his face. She turned to me and cooed, "Oh, TJ and I are old friends. In fact, we were serious college sweethearts." She returned her gaze to TJ. "Has he told you about me?" Her smile spread wide as if she was staking her claim. "My name is Rita."

Rita! The woman who had broken his heart in college!

I remembered when he had told me the story. It was easy to see the scars she'd left long ago. Under her withering stare, I wanted to hide my face in my hands, run away, anything but stand there.

"I hope you don't mind."

In my mind, I could hear her add that it wouldn't matter if I did. She was staking her claim.

TJ reached up, pulled one of her arms from around his neck, and said, "I don't know about her, but I mind." He stepped away from her, put his arm around my waist, and guided us away to Ghost and Waterwood.

"The past cannot be changed.
The future is yet in your power."
— *Unknown*

Author's Notes

Once again, special thanks to Keith and Beth Shortall of Shortall Farm. You inspire me to bring your love of farming to the page and keep me from making mistakes.

Also, the MPT television show Maryland Farm & Harvest helps me understand some of the details and challenges faced by today's farmer. Thank you for your segment about sunflowers at the Millers Farm, Maryland.

Special note to my daughter-in-law Maggie. The sunflowers are for you with love.

It's been fun to honor Cousin Bobby's number one passion, after family: Cars!

As you can tell from this series, I am fascinated by desks. Years ago, I discovered the Davenport desk in a little antique shop on Lake Winnipesaukee, New Hampshire. Then weeks later, I saw nine desks offered for sale in Chatham, Massachusetts. I wanted to bring one home, but the prices were prohibitive. Then two weeks later, I wandered into a shop down the road from St. Michaels in Royal Oak. It is a treasure trove of gems and junk for the antique and quirky-decorating collector. And there, holding a display of vintage Coke glasses was a

Davenport desk. I searched for the price tag and gasped! Affordable. The owner must not have known what he had. Then I flipped over the tag that labelled it a Davenport. My little desk still requires a bit more restoration, but it's all original and lovely as it sits in my living room. It is easy to imagine Emma writing letters there.

Since Ghost plays a bigger role in this book, I must thank Leo, my yellow Lab, for modeling Ghost's behaviors. I didn't make up anything, except the part about digging up a dead body! So far, Leo has only dug up a rose bush in the flowerbed outside my study's window. No idea why. It's been replanted twice... so far.

This book somehow focused on family, the one you're born to and the one you make. Some people call it Family by Blood and Family by Choice. I am blessed to have both! To each and every one of you, I send love and hope!

Susan Reiss
St. Michaels, Maryland
July 2023

About the Author

Susan Reiss trained as a concert pianist then worked as a television writer/producer for many years. Finally, as the head of her own production company, she produced national specials for networks including PBS and ESPN.

Her work received a New York International Film Festival Silver Medal, the Cine Golden Eagle, three Tellys, and a national Emmy nomination.

In 2011, she began writing mysteries and historical fiction set in St. Michaels, MD.

In 2016, she was named a Scribe of the Eastern Shore.

Check out her website at www.SusanReiss.com

Click to Sign Up for the Behind the Scenes Newsletter

Made in the USA
Middletown, DE
29 October 2023

41463794R00203